PRAISE FOR

THE VANISHING THIEF

"An engaging heroine . . . and a story that will keep you turning pages until you reach the end."

—Emily Brightwell, national bestselling
author of the Mrs. Jeffries Mysteries

"A delightful adventure in Victorian England with the motley crew that is the Archivist Society—a group dedicated to obtaining justice when all else fails."

—Victoria Thompson, national bestselling
author of the Gaslight Mysteries

Berkley Prime Crime titles by Kate Parker

THE VANISHING THIEF
THE COUNTERFEIT LADY

THE
COUNTERFEIT
LADY

KATE PARKER

BERKLEY PRIME CRIME, NEW YORK

THE BERKLEY PUBLISHING GROUP
Published by the Penguin Group
Penguin Group (USA) LLC
375 Hudson Street, New York, New York 10014

USA • Canada • UK • Ireland • Australia • New Zealand • India • South Africa • China

penguin.com

A Penguin Random House Company

Berkley Prime Crime Books are published by The Berkley Publishing Group.
BERKLEY® PRIME CRIME and the PRIME CRIME logo
are trademarks of Penguin Group (USA) LLC.

Library of Congress Cataloging-in-Publication Data

Parker, Kate, 1949–
The counterfeit lady / Kate Parker.—Berkley Prime Crime trade paperback edition.
pages cm
ISBN 978-0-425-26661-8 (paperback)
1. Women booksellers—Fiction.   2. Booksellers and bookselling—Fiction.
3. Women private investigators—Fiction.   4. Cold cases (Criminal investigation)—Fiction.
5. London (England)—Fiction.   6. Great Britain—History—Victoria, 1837–1901—Fiction.   I. Title.
PS3616.A74525C68   2014
813'6—dc23
2014005613

PUBLISHING HISTORY
Berkley Prime Crime trade paperback edition / August 2014

PRINTED IN THE UNITED STATES OF AMERICA

10 9 8 7 6 5 4 3 2 1

Cover illustration by Teresa Fasolino.
Cover design by George Long.
Interior design by Kristin del Rosario.

To John,
because you've always been there.

ACKNOWLEDGMENTS

A special thanks to my brother, William Henck, whose timely comments about the naval arms race of the 1890s provided the background to this story. Thanks also to my daughter, Jennifer, who doesn't mind revisiting historic spots in London or making a quick trip on BritRail to do research as long as there's time for the theater.

I'd be remiss if I didn't thank the people who helped me polish both this book and my craft. Hannah Meredith, the Ruby Slippered Sisterhood, the Pixie Chicks, and the HCRW all deserve a big thanks. My agent, Jill Marsal of Marsal Lyons Literary Agency, had important suggestions to improve this work, as did my editor, Faith Black. The cover artists and copyeditors at Berkley Prime Crime brought their special skills to the book and made it the best it can be.

And a thank-you to Ken Gates, who handed me a newspaper article on the RWA National Conference and told me to join them if I wanted to learn to write. That was many years ago, but the conversation ultimately led to the Victorian Bookshop Mysteries. The thought and the advice were appreciated.

While this story is based on the current events of the time period, I've reimagined those events as if they were acted out by my characters. Any errors not in the service of the story are mine.

CHAPTER ONE

"I need you."

I looked across the width of the shop counter at the Duke of Blackford and all the blood left my head. Pressing my fingers into the wood, I gaped at him as his words echoed in my brain.

I never expected to hear him say anything like that to me, Georgia Fenchurch, a middle-class bookshop owner. Never mind the fevered dreams I had about the duke. Broad shoulders, the fragrance of pristine linen and smoke, and a smile reminiscent of his pirate-raider ancestors haunted my nights. Left speechless, I gazed into his mesmerizing dark eyes. I hadn't seen him since spring, but I'd thought of him often.

Then he added, "Miss Fenchurch, Queen Victoria and our country need you," and my lovely daydream of sitting across the breakfast table from those dark eyes rose into the steam that encircled London thanks to a merciless heat wave.

"Perhaps we should go into my office." I nodded to my assistant, Emma Keyes, who was helping a customer, and walked out from behind the counter.

We entered my small office in the back of the shop, stuffy now with the unbearable weather, and the duke immediately headed for the window overlooking the alley. Before I could tell him the window was stuck, he had it open several inches and had turned to face me. "Is it safe to speak here?"

"I assure you, no one ever lurks in that alley. The jeweler next door suffers from paranoia." None of the papers stacked by the window were ruffled by the stagnant air. I shifted the books piled on both chairs over to the desk and then sat.

"We'll keep our voices down, if you don't mind." Blackford pulled his chair close to mine and lowered himself so our knees collided. "I do beg your pardon."

"Unavoidable if we're going to keep our voices down." The contact was sending little trembles of excitement through my body.

"There's been a murder and theft that has repercussions on the security of the realm. Georgia, we need your help and the help of the Archivist Society." He looked straight into my eyes with unflappable seriousness. Banging into my knees obviously hadn't flustered him.

At least he chose to call me by my first name. Did he remember our first investigation together as fondly as I did?

"Why didn't you go straight to Sir Broderick? He leads the Archivist Society."

"Because ultimately it's your help, and that of your lodger, that we need."

My lodger? What in the—? "I don't have a lodger."

"Lady Phyllida Monthalf."

"Aunt Phyllida? She's not my lodger." She was an integral part of my life. We were closer than many families.

"Aunt? That's even better. Then you're a relative, too."

"You're not making any sense." That wasn't unusual for the duke, at least on the few occasions we'd met, but I'd never known him to make a mistake on facts. "I have no relatives."

"You're not making any sense, Georgia."

" 'Aunt' is an honorary title. Lady Monthalf saved my life on one of my first investigations. Her brother had kept her in appalling circumstances for years. When he was arrested for murder and the ghouls on Fleet Street began to circle, I brought her home to live with me."

"I was acquainted with the gossip at the time." The duke could sound appallingly stuffy about the misdeeds of the aristocracy.

"The truth was worse than the rumors. I know. I was there." It was one of the Archivist Society's first cases. I wasn't yet twenty at the time, but I'd carry visions of that day to my deathbed. In my mind, Lord Monthalf again stood blocking the kitchen door through which I'd planned to escape with his latest victim, a battered prostitute named Annie. Only Phyllida's strike with a cast-iron skillet saved us from death by Lord Monthalf's knife.

I shook away the image and wondered what new investigation Blackford wanted our help with. And timid Phyllida's help, who'd never aided in Archivist Society cases.

"Tragedy has struck the family again. Lady Monthalf's cousin Clara Gattenger has been murdered."

Despite his bloodless announcement, I realized my jaw had dropped. I snapped it shut before I expressed my dismay. "This is terrible. When? What happened? Does Phyllida know?"

"Last evening. And no, no one has been in touch with Lady Monthalf."

"Then we must tell her immediately."

I started to rise, but he waved me back into my chair. "Georgia, wait. Hear me out."

Settling myself in my chair, I stared at him. "Go on."

"Yesterday evening, raised voices and crashes were heard coming from the locked study by the Gattenger servants. Finally, after a minute or two of silence, Kenneth Gattenger came out and shouted for someone to fetch a doctor and the police. The police found Clara Gattenger dead in the study. There were no signs of a break-in. Her husband's been arrested and is currently in Newgate Prison."

"A sad tale, but not one requiring the help of the Archivist Society." I waited for the rest of the story. Knowing Blackford, there had to be more.

"Do you know the name Gattenger?"

"It's Clara Gattenger's surname, and her husband Kenneth's. Other than that, it means nothing to me."

"Kenneth Gattenger is single-handedly keeping Britain in the position of the world's premier sea power. The man is the most brilliant naval architect of our times. His designs are visionary. He—"

I shook my head slightly. This wasn't telling me anything useful.

"Perhaps this will make the situation clear. He's designed a new warship. This new ship will ensure our naval superiority for years. Every other seafaring nation wants to know the design's secrets." He leaned forward, pinning me in my chair with his intense stare. "The plans disappeared from his study last evening."

"Surely they weren't the only copy." I still didn't understand what this had to do with poor Clara's murder.

"No, but they represent a radical new concept, and if a set fell into the wrong hands . . ."

"Germany." Our rivalry with Germany was in all the papers. I understood this much.

He nodded. "The race would be on. Whoever builds the design first wins. The balance of power could be irrevocably changed."

"So if someone stole the design, why is Kenneth Gattenger in prison for killing Clara?"

"There was a fire in the fireplace while this argument took place and no sign of forced entry. There were only two people behind that locked study door. Gattenger could have burned a set of plans in the minutes between the end of the sounds of the scuffle and when he unlocked the door."

"You want the Archivist Society to discover his guilt or innocence." Blackford should have taken the case to Sir Broderick. However, I was glad he was here. I'd forgotten how commanding his voice could be, even when pitched to a murmur.

"We need to find out what happened to the plans in Gattenger's study. The entire fate of England rests on recovering them if Gattenger is innocent." He leaned back in his chair and made a sweeping gesture. "If he didn't kill his wife and burn them himself."

I didn't believe the fate of England hung in the balance. The Admiralty and Whitehall could make a crisis out of misplacing a shopping list. "How are you involved, Your Grace?"

"I have"—he studied my face for a moment—"contacts in many countries. They have proved useful to Her Majesty on occasion, and so I've been called in again."

"Do they know you're involving the Archivist Society?"

"Not yet. It all depends on your aunt, Phyllida."

"Why?"

"Let's talk to her, and all will become clear."

I doubted that very much. The duke always held something back.

Nevertheless, I rose from my chair, being careful not to rub knees with him, and walked back into the bookshop. It was nearly one, and the shop was empty. "Put up the Closed sign, Emma. We need to go to the flat. His Grace has some bad news for Aunt Phyllida."

Emma looked from me to the duke and bit back whatever remark she was on the verge of making. She put up the sign, we put on our hats and gloves, and I locked up the shop as we left.

The sun blistered the sidewalk and put everyone who dared go out in a foul mood. In the short time it took to reach our building, my back was drenched and I needed a cooling drink. We went up to our flat and let ourselves in. Phyllida called out from the kitchen, "Are you here already? Luncheon's not quite finished."

"Please come here, Aunt Phyllida. We have some news," I replied.

She came out into the hall, her sleeves rolled up to her elbows, her hair wildly escaping its knot, and an apron protecting her frock.

"Lady Phyllida Monthalf, may I present—" I began.

Aunt Phyllida was already in a deep curtsy. "Georgia, I know who this is. He favors his father. Please come in, Duke. This is a great pleasure."

The duke bowed and kissed her hand. "The pleasure is mine, Lady Monthalf. I wish I didn't have to come bearing bad news."

Phyllida paled. "What has happened?"

I put an arm around her and led her forward. "Perhaps we'd better take this conversation into the parlor."

We all sat down on ruffled, floral-print-covered chairs. Phyllida unrolled her sleeves, her eyes never leaving Blackford's face. Emma glanced at me, looking for signs of what I knew about the bad news.

The duke cleared his throat and said, "I bring bad news concerning your cousin Clara Gattenger."

Phyllida twisted her fingers. "My cousin Isabel's daughter? She's been so happy since she married Kenny." She looked from one face to another as she bit her lip. "What has happened?"

"Mrs. Gattenger was murdered in her home last night."

Phyllida half rose and then sank back down. "No. Not Clara. Not poor, dear Clara. Have they caught her killer?"

"Her husband is in Newgate Prison for her murder," Blackford said.

"No. That's wrong. They were very happy." She reached over and grabbed my arm. "Georgia, can't you do something? Kenny would never have murdered Clara."

"Are you sure, Phyllida?" I asked.

"Yes. Quite certain." She rose and walked over to the open window overlooking the street. The lace curtains hung limply across the space without a breeze to stir them. "Do something, I beg of you. She was Isabel's only child. Her killer must be punished. And that isn't Kenny."

"How far will you go to see her killer apprehended, Lady Monthalf?" Blackford asked. He rose and walked over to her.

She stared up into his face, her jaw set. "As far as necessary."

"Are you willing to face aristocratic society again, to answer their questions, to put up with their gossip?" When his sharp voice silenced, his mouth slid into a cruel smile.

Phyllida stared into his eyes and for a moment I thought she would burst into tears. Slowly, she steadied herself and finally replied, "Whatever it takes to find Clara's killer and free Kenny."

His smile grew joyful. "I knew I could count on you, Lady Monthalf. On behalf of the queen, thank you."

I could see only one way to proceed. "Then I think we need to send a message to Sir Broderick to set up a meeting of the Archivist Society tonight. You'll attend, Your Grace?"

He nodded. "I'll speak to Sir Broderick now, if you ladies will excuse me."

Emma and I stood. He bowed to Phyllida and Emma, who curtsied, and then he took my arm to escort him to the door. "I didn't think I'd see you again so soon. In one regard, I'm glad this has happened."

He was glad! In response, my heart whistled a merry tune and my soul kicked up its heels. We stared, facing each other by the door, no longer touching but with an intimacy that had me leaning forward on the balls of my feet. His dark eyes smiled before he picked up his top hat and cane from the table by the door.

As he moved into the hallway, I said, "I'm glad you came to us. Aunt Phyllida seems set on seeing justice for her cousin, and apparently the police have the wrong man. Emma and I want to help her." Knowing the duke could open many doors the rest of us couldn't, I asked, "May I see the study where the attack took place? The servants wouldn't have been allowed to clean it up yet, surely."

"I'll arrange it for this afternoon. I'll pick you up at the book-shop." He nodded to me and strode off.

I went back into the flat to find Emma and Phyllida putting luncheon on the table. "I'm afraid it's just"—Phyllida stopped to see what she'd set on the platter she carried—"cold poultry and salad."

The platter landed on the table with a thump. "Oh, Georgia, Emma. I'm so upset I don't even know what I'm serving." Her breath caught on a shudder. "Poor Clara."

"I'm so sorry, Phyllida." I gave her a hug and then stepped back so Emma could do the same. After we sat at the table and said grace, I said, "I've heard you speak of Clara many times, but not her mother."

Phyllida sighed and moved her food around on her plate with her fork. "Clara's mother, Isabel, and I were close as children. She married an Admiralty man, Lord Watson. Once my brother, William, gained control of my money and my life, he never let me see her again. Not even when she was dying."

She put her napkin over her mouth and shut her eyes. I studied my plate until she said, "There. I won't be silly. It's all in the past. But you must find out what really happened to Clara. For Isabel's sake. It's the only thing I can do for her now."

I wanted to distract Phyllida from remembering her evil brother as much as I wanted some background on the victim whose death I knew I'd soon be investigating. "I only saw Clara a few times a year when she visited us on a Sunday. I thought she was sweet, but I know nothing of her background. Tell me about her."

"She was an only child. Her parents both doted on her. After Isabel's death, she and her father were very close, and her father's interests were in shipbuilding. That's how she met Kenny Gattenger. They were in love from the first time they met, but he wouldn't marry until he had enough money to support her properly, and she wouldn't leave her father on his own. They broke off their engagement twice, but they finally married a year ago.

That was after her father's death, when his title and property had gone to some cousin."

"Ken Gattenger wasn't from money?"

"No. His parents ran a small shop. He was apprenticed to a draftsman. The man realized Kenny was brilliant and made sure he received a good education. As Kenny gained more experience, he found powerful patrons. Naval architecture became his specialty. He was a hard worker and a strict saver. All those years of saving made him a little mean with money. Clara said he didn't pay the servants well, so she was always having to hire new as soon as one found a better-paying post."

"What kind of couple were they?" Emma asked.

"A happy one," Phyllida snapped.

"No, I mean, were they always fighting and making up? Did they entertain a great deal, did they share interests, did they like to travel, things like that." Emma gave her a smile.

"Oh." Phyllida turned pink. "They were quiet. They both liked to read, to stay home together in the evening in the study. They went out to the theater or to a dinner party on occasion, but that was all. Clara was content to visit friends during the day and wait for Kenny to come home to her in the evenings."

"Did you see her often?" I asked. "Besides those Sunday visits when she brought her husband along, did you see her alone?"

"We'd have tea once every few weeks after I came to live here, during the day while you were in the shop. She's the only relative I wanted to see after my brother"—she shuddered—"died."

Her brother had been hanged at Newgate Prison, where Gattenger was now. However, her brother had murdered a string of East End prostitutes and was captured by the Archivist Society.

We'd find a lack of evidence in Gattenger's case, I feared, and that would present problems proving his innocence.

"She was very happy in her new life as a married woman," Phyllida said.

"Did you see much of Mr. Gattenger besides on their Sunday visits?"

"No. During the week, Clara always came by herself for tea. But I saw them together several times over the years of their long engagement, and they were very happy. Happy in their own quiet little circle, even when there were other people present. Do you understand what I mean?"

"They were happy with just each other for company," Emma said.

"It's more than that, there's a whole world two people can share that no one else can enter. My parents were like that," I said. Sometimes frustrating for me as a child, but beautiful to think back on.

"Yes. That's how they were," Phyllida said.

"Last night, the servants heard shouting in the study. When the door was unlocked, Clara Gattenger was dead." I looked at Phyllida. "Are you sure everything was all right between them?"

"Yes. I know evil. I lived with my brother long enough. Evil had never entered their home. They were in love."

Glancing at my plate, I found I'd finished my luncheon. I never tasted a bite.

THE DUKE OF Blackford returned to the shop in the middle of the afternoon to tell us what time to be at Sir Broderick's and to escort me to the Gattenger house. Even with a hand up, I still had to struggle to get into the tall, ancient carriage given to the duke's family by Wellington. Glancing out the window, I saw Emma in the bookshop doorway, grinning at my lack of grace.

I looked forward to seeing the scene of the crime, but I would rather the duke had used one of his normal-sized carriages.

The Gattenger home was one of a row of similar houses in a fairly new, middle-class section of South Kensington. Once the duke caught me around the waist as I half tumbled from the carriage and set me safely on the sidewalk, he walked up the steps and rang the front doorbell. I straightened my skirt to give myself a moment to recover from the ridiculous flutter in my chest from his touch. I glanced down the steep concrete steps behind the black wrought-iron railing and caught a glimpse of a young woman's face looking at me before she drew back from the trades-men's entrance.

The front door opened and I saw Inspector Grantham stand-ing in the hallway. I hurried up the steps as the men exchanged bows and followed the duke inside.

"Inspector Grantham, is this your case?" I asked.

"Yes, Miss Fenchurch. I suppose I'll be working with the Archivist Society again?" He sounded weary. I hoped it wasn't due to working with us.

"Yes. Phyllida Monthalf, my friend, is the murdered woman's cousin. She says the husband couldn't have killed his wife."

"It gave me no joy charging him. The navy has already in-volved itself in this case because of his importance to British ship design." He looked at Blackford. "I suppose that's why you're interested. But there's no evidence supporting his story." The inspector spread his hands in the air.

"May we look at the room where the death occurred?" I gave Grantham a hopeful smile.

The inspector held my gaze for a moment before shrugging. "If you think you can find something we missed, go right ahead."

Detective Inspector Grantham had worked several cases over the years for Scotland Yard that the Archivist Society was interested in, including the one last spring where I had first met the Duke of Blackford. I knew he trusted our abilities. Whether he liked working with us was another story.

The duke led the way down the wide hallway, past the staircase going up and a narrower one going down. I followed until we reached a door near the back of the house. The duke stopped and let the inspector open it. I was the last to enter the small study, making it a little crowded as we moved around. None of us stepped near the fireplace with the bloodied hearth rug.

The duke strolled to the triple bay window facing the garden. With the heat, only the lace curtains were across the open windows, while the heavy dark blue drapes were pushed back to the ends of their rods. "Were these windows open when you arrived?"

"Yes. With the dryness of the weather, there were no footprints outside, and the climb wouldn't have been difficult for an agile man. The cook says she was in the kitchen, which is by the tradesmen's entrance in the front under the dining room. The maids were clearing away dinner. You saw where the stairs are, and the first door we passed in the hallway leads to the dining room. There was no reason for the servants to come this far toward the back of the house," Inspector Grantham said.

"There're no back stairs?" the duke asked.

The inspector and I stared at each other in surprise for an instant before we must have had the same thought. *He's a duke*. "Not enough room in a house this size," I said. "There're only the three servants? The cook and two maids?"

"Yes," Grantham answered. "One of the maids heard the argument and stopped to listen. Her excuse was the master and

missus rarely argued. The other came to find her after a minute
and heard the end of the argument and the crashes. There were
two loud noises."

"Could the servants make out what was said?" Blackford
asked.

"They said no."

"Did they try to open the door or knock?"

"It was locked."

"How long before the door—" I began.

"A full minute at the very least," Grantham said as if the
words hurt his mouth.

I took in the room without moving. There were two comfortable chairs with ottomans, one on each side of the fireplace. Gaslights were set to shine down on those two spots, and a small table
by each chair held a stack of books. Shelves across the room from
the fireplace held a large collection of volumes. A desk was set by
the window to catch the best light. A jumble of papers, pens, ink
pots, books, a diary, and a paperweight were scattered across the
floor from the desk toward the fireplace, and the desk chair was
knocked over in that direction. The fireplace held a pile of ash.

"Where were the plans kept?" the duke asked.

"In there." Inspector Grantham pointed to a low chest with
three drawers across the room from the windows and close by
the door.

"I was told there was a burned fragment of a drawing found
in this room. Where is it?" The duke stood facing the inspector
with his arms crossed.

Grantham stared back, his jaw jutting aggressively. "Locked
up by Scotland Yard until the trial."

If they continued to act like schoolboys, I'd never learn anything. "What fragment?"

"A small singed piece of the last page of the missing blueprints was found at the edge of the fireplace."

I needed to know more. "How many pages are there in one set of plans?"

"In this case, seven. It's the master from which working drawings are made for the manufacturing process."

"Are they large?"

Grantham held his arms wide. "When unfolded, each is this big."

"Is this the only master set of drawings in existence?"

"No, but the other sets are locked up in the Admiralty."

"Why wasn't this one?"

"Gattenger said he had an idea that he needed to work on. He sometimes worked from home."

"In this room? At night?"

I had both men's attention now. "Yes," the inspector said.

"This was also the room where he and his wife frequently read in the evening."

"Yes."

"So from the outside, last night wouldn't have looked any different from any other night. But the thief chose last night to strike." I looked from one man to the other. "If the Germans stole the drawings, there would have to be a leak in the office where the drawings are kept. Someone would have had to tell the burglar that Gattenger took a set of ship plans home last night. The only way that could happen is if there's a traitor in the Admiralty."

CHAPTER TWO

MY conclusion made me even less popular than I expected. The Duke of Blackford looked as if he'd like to throw me out the window as he muttered, "Bloody hell."

Inspector Grantham glared at me. "There's no sign of a burglary. The Gattengers argued, he killed her, accidentally most likely, and then burned the plans he was working on to cover his guilt and blamed everything on a housebreaker. There's no traitor."

"That's the answer you and I and Whitehall want," Blackford said. "If we're wrong, we have a bigger problem than anyone had dared mention before now. Thank you, Miss Fenchurch, for ruining my day."

His dark eyes bored through me, making it hard to breathe. I reached out a white-gloved hand and grabbed his sleeve. "You think I'm right, don't you? That Gattenger's story is true."

His answer meant more to me than I wanted to admit, even to myself. He continued to glare at me without speaking.

"How was Clara killed?" I needed details if I was going to help Ken Gattenger.

"A blow to the back of the head. Probably from striking that side table. She fell there, where the blood is on the hearth rug," the inspector told me.

"Pushed in a struggle with a burglar over the plans?" I certainly hoped so. The other answer, pushed by Gattenger, would break Phyllida's heart.

The duke finally gave one sharp nod. "We'll have to investigate this until proven wrong."

We. The duke had described himself and me as *we.* I prayed the investigation would take a very long time. The stuff of my dreams only happened in the light of day when I was conducting an Archivist Society investigation. Under no other circumstances would a duke spend time with a bookshop owner.

"Scotland Yard is proceeding from the assumption Kenneth Gattenger killed his wife. If you find proof of his innocence, we need to know." The inspector glared as he looked from Blackford to me.

I nodded as I walked over to look out the open windows. Paving stones made paths through the small dry patch of grass. Anyone could have walked through the back garden without leaving tracks. "Did the Gattengers entertain last night?"

"No. They ate alone. The dining room is the front room on this floor. Immediately after, they came in here."

I turned and faced into the room. It was small and cozy. I could picture the Gattengers sitting in their matching chairs, reading in front of the fire. I imagined this was a room no outsider was ever invited into. "Did they frequently lock the study door from the inside?"

The inspector shook his head. "The maids said they'd never known that to happen before."

The duke asked, "Have you searched the house for the ship plans?"

"Of course. They're not here, and the Admiralty records office swears Gattenger took a set with him yesterday just after midday."

"Did he take a set home with him frequently?" If he did, my thoughts of treason in the Admiralty disintegrated like the ashes in the fireplace.

"No." The inspector strode to the door and held it open as he tapped his foot, letting his impatience show. He had work to do. I understood. I did, too.

From where I stood, I could see a foot or more of space between the back of the door and a bookcase. Could someone have hidden there when the Gattengers came in? Beyond the inspector, I saw a young woman in a black maid's dress with white cuffs and collar. Dressed in her good uniform, she was ready to answer the door if there were any afternoon callers. I couldn't imagine anyone but the ghoulish calling here.

I brushed past the inspector and stopped in front of the woman. When I looked at her closely, I discovered she wasn't a woman but a girl younger than Emma. "I'm Georgia Fenchurch, a relative of Mrs. Gattenger's cousin." Better not to get too specific with the kinship. "What's your name?"

"Elsie, miss."

"May I ask you some questions, Elsie?"

"Do you think Mr. Gattenger killed his wife?" she asked, twisting her apron.

"No."

"Good." She gave one jerky nod with her head. "What do you want to know?"

"Tell me about yesterday."

"All day?"

"Yes." Behind me, I heard two male sighs.

"The day was the same as any other. I brought up the breakfast tray. Then Mary helped Mrs. Gattenger dress. Mr. Gattenger did for himself, being brought up that way."

"Did Mr. Gattenger leave after breakfast and stay away for the whole day?"

She nodded. "Just as usual."

"And Mrs. Gattenger?"

"She went out calling in the afternoon with Lady Bennett, then came home and dressed for dinner."

"Did she always dress for dinner, even when it was just the two of them?"

"Yes. She was raised that way, her being the daughter of a lord."

"Was she good friends with Lady Bennett? Did they make calls together often?"

"No. The lady had never called here before. The missus looked surprised to see her, but she went off in the carriage with Lady Bennett after they spoke in the front hall for a few moments."

What had made Lady Bennett call on Clara that particular afternoon? "Did you hear what they said?"

"No. The missus looked furious at first, but then she put on a false smile when she spoke to me."

"What did she say?"

"She said, 'Lady Bennett and I are going out. I don't expect this to take long.'"

Where had they gone? It didn't sound like Clara had wanted to go. "Did she return before the master came home?"

"Yes, she was only gone an hour or two."

"How did she look?"

"Ready to do murder."

I glanced up to catch the eye of Blackford, who now stood behind the maid. He gave one slight nod, his face a ducal mask. "Elsie, where did the Gattengers first meet at the end of the day?"

"In the study. He'd wait in there until the mistress came down dressed for dinner. Last night, she was in there waiting for him. He went in and shut the door. I was busy in the dining room and didn't hear anything."

"Would you have heard if there was shouting?"

"Yes, and there wasn't. There never was, well, not until after dinner last night."

"What happened next?" What had changed their routine so dramatically?

"We served dinner."

"No shouting?"

"They hardly said a word to each other."

"Was that usual?"

"No. They usually talked about their day, people they saw, things they read. Last night, they were both upset and quiet."

"You're sure about that?" Inspector Grantham said from behind me.

The maid nodded.

"How were their appetites?" I asked.

"Neither one ate hardly a bite. Cook was furious, but Mary and I looked at the leftovers and danced around the kitchen. We get the leftovers. Well, some of them."

"They don't feed you very well?" Elsie was thin and pale. I wondered how she'd look if she were fed like a lady.

The girl shrugged. "Better'n some."

"But they sat through all the courses?"

"There were only four when they were alone. Soup, fish, roast, and pudding. Master would have done without the soup and the fish, said they didn't eat enough to make it worthwhile, but the mistress insisted on it. Sometimes they had fowl, too, but not last night. The mistress didn't touch her pudding, and the master only had one spoonful. Then she said, 'Let's get this over with,' and he put his spoon down and they went into the study."

"And locked the door." I was getting a picture of what had been an unusual night, even if no one had died.

"Yes, that was strange. They never locked the door. I couldn't bring the coffee in, for one thing."

"They always had their coffee in the study after dinner?"

She nodded. "Always."

"With them not talking, and not eating, how long was dinner?"

The maid grinned. "Fastest ever. Mary and I were kept running."

"How long was it after they locked the door before you heard shouting?"

"The shouting must've come first. I never heard the key in the lock for them yelling."

That was different from what Inspector Grantham had told us. "Then how did you know the door was locked?"

"I brought up the coffee, like I was supposed to, and when I tried the handle, I couldn't get in."

"What did you do with the coffee?"

"Put it in the dining room. I thought they'd stop after a minute and let me in. They'd never behaved like this before."

"How long did the shouting continue?"

"Long enough for Mary to clear away the pudding dishes and come back up. I couldn't decide whether to knock on the door or not when there was a big crash. There was more noise, a shriek, and a second crash. Then it was quiet. We both banged on the door and called in." The maid's eyes widened as she recalled the drama.

"And then?"

"It was silent in there for the longest time. Then we heard sobbing and a moment later the master opened the door. He was crying." Her eyes and mouth were round with amazement.

"How long was the silence? A minute? An hour?"

"A minute, at least."

"And you didn't go for another key?" I studied her face carefully.

Her shoulders slumped. "I tried looking in. The key was still in the lock on the inside."

"What did Mr. Gattenger say when he came out?"

" 'Get a doctor and the police. I can't wake Clara.' "

If Phyllida was right, Ken Gattenger must have been devastated. "What happened then?"

"I ran for Dr. Harrison, two blocks away. Mary ran for the bobby. Mary got back before me."

"The inspector has mentioned a burned fragment of paper in this room when the police arrived. Do you know anything about that?"

She shook her head. "The master or mistress probably burned it in the fireplace."

"Why did you have a fire last night?" I'd seen the ashes, but I was so used to seeing ashes in fireplaces they hadn't made an impression. With the current heat wave, living in London was like living on the sun. Why would anyone need a fire?

"The mistress asked for it as soon as she returned from her carriage ride with Lady Bennett. I thought it strange, but I laid it and lit it while she dressed for dinner."

"Did she give you any reason? It was an odd request."

"I didn't get a chance to say anything. She just ordered me to do it right then. She looked like she might cry, so I just went ahead and did what she asked."

"Did Lady Bennett come in the house with your mistress?"

"No, the mistress returned alone."

I was as suspicious of Lady Bennett as I was of the unknown burglar. "What happened once you lit the fire?"

"I got back to my regular duties. I helped Cook while Mary dressed the mistress and did her hair."

I patted the girl's arm. "Thank you, Elsie."

She pressed her lips together and then said, "Excuse me, ma'am, but what's going to happen to us? The master's in prison and the mistress is dead. Will we be chucked out without our pay or a reference?"

I looked at the duke, who shook his head. I kept staring. I wouldn't allow him to leave a scrawny young girl like Elsie to starve. Finally, he pulled a calling card out of his card case and said, "When the inspector is finished with you and the house is closed up, go to this address and see the housekeeper. She'll see about finding you and the others a place to stay and employment, at least until we know the fate of your master."

The maid dropped a curtsy and said, "Thank you, sir. I'll tell the others."

She hurried downstairs as Grantham stepped toward Blackford. "Why are you being so considerate of the help?"

"We'll know where they are. Did you learn anything new, Inspector?"

"Yes. And none of it looks good for Gattenger." He frowned. "Although the business with the fire seems odd in this heat. Are you two finished here?"

"For the moment," the duke said. "You did well, Miss Fenchurch."

"Questioning people is what I do." Nevertheless, as I walked toward the front door, I couldn't hide the lightness in my step caused by his praise.

Once we were back in Blackford's carriage, he asked, "What do you know of Lady Bennett?"

"Nothing."

The edges of his mouth curved upward. "She's the widow of an impoverished lord, yet she lives in great style. She's rumored to be the paramour of a German diplomat, Baron von Steubfeld."

"A kept woman?" I asked, raising an eyebrow.

"Or a spy." There was no hint of a smile on his face now. "The baron's accredited as a diplomat, but in reality he's the kaiser's spymaster in Britain."

"Whatever Lady Bennett is, she caused discord in the Gattenger home. What did Clara burn, or what was she planning to burn, in that fire? And what do I tell Phyllida?"

He looked out the window of the carriage and watched the traffic for a moment. "To come to the Archivist Society meeting tonight."

"Could you arrange something for me, Your Grace?"

"What is it?"

"I'd like to go to Newgate Prison and speak to Ken Gattenger."

"Difficult, but not impossible. You'll find the prison unpleasant."

"I need to speak to him. It's important if we're to understand what happened."

He studied me for a moment. "I'd forgotten how determinedly you approach whatever needs to be done. It does you credit. I'll arrange for you to speak with Gattenger. And I'll accompany you."

He was the most helpful aristocrat I'd ever met. Only one of the reasons I appreciated the duke.

PHYLLIDA AGREED TO come to the meeting with us, but she seemed hesitant. She took much longer over her toilette than I'd seen before. She seemed unable to decide what to wear and told Emma to redo her hairstyle twice. She backed away from the hired carriage before we finally talked her into the vehicle.

But once she entered Sir Broderick's home, her attitude changed. Her chin lifted, and she led us in a stately procession up the stairs to the study.

"Lady Monthalf," Sir Broderick said, wheeling himself away from the fire to come forward and kiss the glove on the back of her outstretched hand. "I'm so glad to finally meet you. Georgia speaks very highly of you."

"Thank you for inviting me, Sir Broderick." She favored him with a sweet smile.

"The pleasure is mine. Please, sit anywhere. You'll find we're very informal in our customs within the Archivist Society. It comes from needing to trust each other as much as family."

I winced as the smile slipped from Phyllida's lips. "More than family," she said, taking a half step back.

"In many cases, yes. Let me present everyone to you." Sir Broderick gestured to each member who was present at this meeting as he introduced them to "Lady Monthalf."

Jacob, Sir Broderick's assistant, gave her a deep bow. An East End urchin when he first asked for help from the Archivist Society, he was still deferential to anyone with a title. Frances

Atterby, the widow of a hotel owner, greeted her with the genuine warmth she had shown thousands. Adam Fogarty's bow was stiff, a telltale sign that the injury that had ended his career in the police ached. Then we all stood around, waiting uncomfortably for someone to say something.

"Sit down. I'm tired of twisting my neck," Sir Broderick growled as he wheeled his way back to his customary spot in front of the fire. I didn't know how he could abide sitting so close to the heat. The evening was warm, the fire was hot, and sweat poured down my back.

As I took my seat on the sofa next to Phyllida, the Duke of Blackford entered the room. "Good evening," he said as we all rose and bowed or curtsied. He in turn gave Sir Broderick and Phyllida each a bow. "Has Miss Fenchurch brought you up to speed on this investigation?"

"Not yet. We've just arrived," I said. "Why don't you tell them?" We all settled in for a long meeting.

The duke nodded, sat in a wing chair facing Sir Broderick, and leaned back. "Kenneth Gattenger is a naval architect who's designed the newest type of warship, one that will ensure Britain's dominance on the high seas for years to come. He's also a newly-wed, married only a year. Last night, his wife was murdered while the two of them were alone in a locked room. There was no sign of a break-in. A set of plans to Gattenger's new battleship design disappeared from the room at the time of the murder, a room where a fire burned on the hearth."

"You make it sound like he murdered my cousin," Phyllida said in a quiet voice. She sat completely still, looking totally composed.

"Those are the facts, and based on those facts, Gattenger has been arrested for his wife's murder. Scotland Yard is certain he's guilty." The duke stared at her as if daring her to disagree.

"They are wrong."

"How do you know?"

"I've seen Kenny and Clara together. They fitted each other like a hand in a glove." Phyllida spoke with aristocratic certainty as she waved her hand.

The duke looked around the room. "I was called in as soon as Scotland Yard informed Whitehall and the Admiralty. There is another possibility, which our government both fears and refuses to acknowledge. A possibility I want the Archivist Society to investigate."

He gave his words a moment to sink in, and then continued. "There is a chance that a burglar entered the room, killed Clara Gattenger, and removed the drawings. Our hot, dry weather meant their windows were open and the ground around the windows was hard. There are paving stones stretching across the back garden to the gate in the fence leading to an alley. A burglar could have conceivably entered and left without leaving a trace."

The duke waited for a response. When no one spoke, he said, "We believe the intended recipient of the ship plans, the employer of the burglar, is the German master spy in Britain, Baron von Steubfeld. He's a member of the kaiser's embassy staff here in London. Von Steubfeld was already under watch by our Naval Intelligence Department. Furthermore, he knows it. So far we don't believe he's received the drawings, but we'd like more eyes on him. Eyes he doesn't know."

"We can help with that," Sir Broderick said.

"Good. The drawings are on seven sheets of very large paper, about a yard in each direction, either rolled in a tube or folded into a package. The last sheet was found partially burned by the fireplace and may not be with the others."

"Are we to believe von Steubfeld will be upset to receive less than the entire package?" Sir Broderick asked.

"Yes. The last sheet is key if the Germans want to build a ship to these specifications. The baron will not be pleased if he receives less than what he paid for." The duke gave us a smile that made my blood chill.

"Why would the Germans want our designs? They have their own naval architects. I don't understand why they'd bother to steal our plans." Despite the kaiser's affection for our queen, I knew the German government didn't think highly of Britain.

The duke gave me a disapproving look. "If they know what our ships are capable of, they can build their ships and create their battle plans to defeat us."

"Battle plans?" I bristled at his disparagement. What a ridiculous point of view. Our navy was the greatest the world had ever seen. "Why would the Germans want to fight us? They'd lose."

He leaned toward me, a determined glow in his eyes. "They will fight us. And they'll do anything they can to ensure they'll win. That's why they're speeding up their shipbuilding schedule. That's why they have spies in our country. We're in a naval arms race with the Germans, whether or not we like it, and we need to protect our superiority."

I didn't like to be lectured to. I pressed my lips together in irritation even as fear slid down my skin, mixed with my sweat in the overheated room. I liked what he told us even less, especially since Blackford was uncanny in his ability to see complications before anyone else was aware there was a problem. In a tone barely above a whisper, I asked, "Are you certain?"

He sprawled back in his chair, the glow gone from his eyes. In a quiet voice, he said, "I don't like it, either."

Sir Broderick broke in. "I know you came here for more than to lecture us on European conflicts."

"I did." The duke looked around the room. "The baron goes

out in society a great deal with Lady Bennett. She could be used to pass on the drawings."

The duke's gaze fell on me. "We need to dog their heels night and day if we're to recover those drawings. The plan I've devised is tricky. I want to place a member of the Archivist Society in a position to mingle with him in aristocratic society. A position that no one will associate with counterespionage."

Sir Broderick pressed the tips of his fingers together and looked over them at Blackford. "When you came by this afternoon, you told me you had something in mind."

"I want to set up Georgia Fenchurch as a cousin of Lady Monthalf, recently arrived from some part of the empire. I want the two of them residing in a household in fashionable London. I want them to go to the opera, to the theater, to balls and parties. And I want them to befriend Lady Bennett."

Visions of waltzing and attending the opera warred in my brain with thoughts of my bookshop in ruin. "What about Fenchurch's Books? I can't just leave it shuttered for weeks."

"Oh, Georgia, don't sound so middle-class," Blackford said in an annoyed tone. "Our nation's security is at stake."

I couldn't leave my bookshop for that long. Both my business and my reputation would be destroyed. "I am middle-class. My shop is my life. I'll attend social events with you, but my days will be spent as they always are. In my bookshop."

The duke shook his head. "No. You'll have afternoon teas and visits. You'll have to dedicate your life to this role for some time."

I glared at the duke. The devil I would.

CHAPTER THREE

"GEORGIA, we wouldn't expect you to close your shop. Frances Atterby and some of the other Archivist Society members can run the shop for you. Frances has certainly helped you out enough that she knows how the shop should be managed," Sir Broderick said. "And you'll be there part of the time. Frances can handle a few hours without you."

"Frances? What about Emma? She's always in charge when I have to be out." I caught the look between Sir Broderick and the duke. Had they discussed this before our meeting?

Of course they had, which only made me angrier. I pushed my hands down against the atmosphere building in the room as I said, "No. As much as I trust you, Frances, running a bookshop for days is a big responsibility."

"Emma will be working closely with you on this investigation. You'll both be away days. Weeks. As long as it takes," Blackford said.

Frances's eyes widened at his words. Sir Broderick cleared his throat when he saw the look on my face.

How dare the duke make that determination? I was steaming from the heat in the room and from my temper. "As long as it takes? No. There's more than just looking at the price and selling off the shelves. There's ordering, bookkeeping, unpacking stock, paying bills. Frances has never done any of that, and she's never handled antiquarian stock. No, I won't—"

"But I have." Sir Broderick's voice cut through my argument. "You can do the ordering, the bookkeeping, the paying, and what you don't have time for, I can do from here. I do know a crown-octavo edition from a red-cloth-cover edition, and I'm aware of the discounts the publishers should give you. I'm no novice to the business."

All that was true, but there was something he couldn't do. I took a deep breath before I said, "And the antiquarian business? Excuse me, Sir Broderick, but you can't pop down to the store every time we have a customer for an old book."

He smacked the armrests of his wheelchair and looked away. The only sound in the room was the crackle from the fireplace. I could have cried in shame for bringing up his affliction, especially since he'd sustained his injury in helping me attempt to rescue my parents.

He'd been in partnership with my father in the bookshop, viewing it as an investment where he could indulge his passion for antiquarian books. I ran to him when I escaped the madman who had held my parents hostage over the matter of a Gutenberg Bible we didn't possess.

Arriving ahead of the police, we saw the cottage where my parents had been taken burst into flame. We entered, trying to save them from the inferno. A roof beam collapsed on Sir Broderick.

My lengthy struggle to drag Sir Broderick to safety meant the house collapsed before I could reenter and release my parents. My failure as a seventeen-year-old girl left Sir Broderick crippled and my parents dead. As angry as I was at myself, I was angrier at the duke for forcing me to point out Sir Broderick's life-altering injury.

"I could pop over and bring the book to Sir Broderick, and he could send me back with instructions." Jacob, Sir Broderick's assistant, glanced from Sir Broderick to me.

"How would you know to 'pop over'? Sir Broderick can't do without you all day." Only Blackford could create such a disaster and then sit listening to us with an expressionless face.

"Use the telephone." Jacob pointed to the shiny black object now sitting on Sir Broderick's specially designed desk.

"I don't have one in the shop."

"I'll put in the order in the morning," the duke said.

"It takes weeks—"

"I'm a director of the company. It won't take weeks." Blackford permitted me to see a brief smile. Smug cad. He appeared to be enjoying the trouble he'd started.

"This is going to cost a lot of money. Where are Phyllida and I going to stay while we're playing our roles? We'll need new clothes. And servants. We don't have time to set this up properly." Even as I gave the reasons why this plan of the duke's wouldn't work, I felt defeat looming above me.

"Lady Phyllida and I will set up the house and begin ordering the clothes. My housekeeper will arrange for your servants. Miss Keyes"—the duke turned to Emma—"it would help us immensely if you'd play lady's maid to Lady Phyllida and Lady Georgina.

That way you'll be present to run messages and can question servants without arousing suspicion."

"Do lady's maids carry knives?" Emma asked.

"This one will," Blackford assured her.

"Shouldn't Emma play the aristocrat and I play the lady's maid?" Despite her childhood in the East End, Emma was a beautiful blonde who had every man she met groveling at her feet. My looks let me fade into the background, like a good maid should.

"Only a scullery maid would have your unruly mass of auburn hair," Emma said with a grin, and I immediately reached up to see how much my hairdo had slipped in the humidity despite a fistful of pins.

"Won't the aristocracy we've dealt with in previous cases recognize me?" Not too long before, I had acted the part of Lady Westover's country cousin and met the duke. Besides my curly reddish hair, I had freckles, violet eyes, and a long, graceful neck. The combination made my looks stand out in London society.

"Lady Westover is in the country with the Dutton-Cox family trying to nurse Lady Dutton-Cox back to health. Lord Waxpool is failing, and his family is staying close by his side, also in the country. Daisy Hancock is in France with her mother's family. Lord Naylard is on the racing circuit, and his sister never goes out in society. The Mervilles are at their country estate. Most of society has left London. You have nothing to fear," Blackford assured me.

I glanced at Sir Broderick. "You can't think of anyone I'd meet in the course of this investigation who would know my association with the Archivist Society?"

Sir Broderick shook his head.

"There's no one." Blackford looked at me in satisfaction. "I plan to immediately and publicly take the widowed Georgina as my paramour, ensuring her inclusion in all invitations, and smooth the way for Lady Phyllida to also receive invitations from biddies who want to press her for gossip."

I jumped off the sofa. "And I suppose this widowed Georgina is my role?"

"I don't want to use your real name. Georgina is close enough we won't make a mistake, and it sounds more regal." The duke looked up at me, and I could see laughter in his eyes. Eyes I could have cheerfully scratched out.

"Paramour? Publicly?" I remained standing, glaring down at him. The philistine remained seated in the presence of a lady. Well, me, but he should have stood. He was showing bad manners, and Blackford never showed bad manners.

"Miss Emma is a young lady. You, on the other hand, are a mature woman. Easily passed off as a widow. One more likely to tempt a duke. And the 'publicly' part just calls for a bit of flirtation, some hand holding, a few glances where you don't look like you're measuring me for a coffin."

Mature woman? "You might stand when you address me." My words sizzled when they passed my lips.

The duke rose, lifted one ungloved hand, and trapped my chin on top of his forefinger. "Ah, Georgia. Now you begin to sound like an aristocrat. You're the one best suited to play this role. Britain's mastery of the seas and our safety as a nation are at stake. We can recapture those plans and keep your bookshop running, but only if you trust me."

I thought about jerking my head back so I could bite his forefinger. "Mature woman?"

"A youngster fresh out of the schoolroom is hardly going to tempt me. A woman with some substance is much more alluring." His eyes glowed with lust.

"Paramour?" I raised an eyebrow. I wasn't buying his act.

He took a deep breath. The glow left his eyes and his tone became businesslike again. "Easily faked. People see what they expect to see, if you can refrain from looking daggers at me."

"I hope I'm that good an actress."

Someone in the room snorted.

"Are you on board with this plan, Georgia?" Sir Broderick asked.

"I don't seem to have a choice." I sat down and glared at Blackford. Only then did the duke resume sitting, his legs crossed at the knee, a faint smirk on his lips.

"Wise girl. Get everything in order in the bookshop. Bring me any paperwork or bookkeeping that you need me to help with after work tomorrow. As soon as possible during the day, you and Emma need to take off at different times for fittings for new wardrobes. Madame Leclerc can be speedy and discreet with the right amount of incentive." Sir Broderick nodded as he ticked off his instructions.

"Cash being her incentive?" I asked and glanced at the duke.

"Of course. Lady Phyllida, if you would assist me in selecting the most appropriate property, I'll escort you to your fitting." Blackford nodded to her in a sort of seated bow.

"You realize I'm doing this not for Britain but for justice for Clara," Phyllida said, staring at the duke.

"I am, too," I told her, taking her hand. Not precisely for Clara but for Phyllida and those few in her family who treated her decently.

"Your nation and your sovereign appreciate it, no matter what reason you have for helping us," Blackford said to Phyllida.

"You speak for all of Britain and the queen now, Your Grace?" My feelings were hurt by how the duke used Sir Broderick to force me into playing my part in his plan. A part that would keep me out of my bookshop far too much.

"Yes."

And they'd been so busy pushing me into my role that they'd overlooked Ken Gattenger's part. "I think we're missing a part of this investigation."

"What are we missing?"

"If we're right about the plans being stolen from the Gattengers' house on the only night they'd have been available, the baron has bought the loyalty of someone in the Admiralty office where the drawings are kept. We need someone in that office to find out which clerk told the burglar, or the Germans, when to break into the Gattengers' house."

Emma said, "It has to be a young male. The best choice would be Jacob, but he'll be running messages between us and Sir Broderick concerning this investigation, and antiquarian books between Sir Broderick and the bookshop."

"Sumner can take on that function. Unless you have a better answer, Your Grace," I said. John Sumner served as the duke's bodyguard, but I'd never figured out if the former soldier had other duties. I only knew how much the duke trusted and relied on him.

Blackford scowled for a moment before he nodded. "I don't. I'll see about making the arrangements to add Jacob to the Admiralty records office staff in the morning."

I gave him a satisfied smile. Now I wasn't the only one whose life would be turned upside down by this investigation.

"I recently had a woman who'd nursed her invalid husband approach me for a position. We'll investigate her and then I may take her on," Sir Broderick said, "depending on how long Jacob will need to be absent."

Sir Broderick eyed Jacob and shook his head. "You need to understand the burglar already killed once when he was cornered. You should only identify the clerk who's in the payroll of the Germans and pass the information on to Inspector Grantham at Scotland Yard. Let them get the clerk to name the person who received the information."

Jacob gave him a cocky grin. "I grew up in the East End, just like Emma. No one warns her not to follow a lead. Don't worry about me."

Sir Broderick slumped in his wheelchair. "Oh, but my dear boy, I do."

MY ANNOYANCE AT the duke's interference had barely lessened by the next afternoon when Blackford escorted Phyllida into the bookshop. I glanced out the windows, surprised not to see the tall, ancient Wellington coach Blackford normally used. "Where's your usual carriage?"

"I assured His Grace I couldn't manage the coach he brought to Sir Broderick's last night, so he kindly brought this one today," Phyllida said. She appeared more assured than I'd seen her before. She held her chin at that disdainful angle the aristocracy employed and she spoke up immediately, not waiting to see if anyone else spoke first.

If the duke could help Phyllida recover some confidence, I could forgive him almost anything. But if Sir Broderick and Frances damaged my business while I was involved in this investigation, everyone, including Blackford, would have to pay merry hell.

"How did your morning go?" I asked.

"Oh, Georgia, the duke has the cutest little house in Mayfair.

It's a good size for the two of us and a small staff. There's a room in the back on the second floor for Emma as our lady's maid that connects to the dressing room and then into a room for you, Georgia. It'll make it easier for you two to sneak around planning and investigating without alerting the servants."

"Mayfair." Emma said the name of the area with a tone of wonder. "I never thought I'd be living there. Even as a lady's maid."

I looked around my shop in the neighborhood of Leicester Square, my middle-class shop on my middle-class street, and wrapped my arms around my waist. "Don't get too used to living there. This investigation will be as short as I can possibly make it."

Phyllida patted my shoulder. "Sir Broderick and Frances will take good care in assisting you with the shop."

"I inherited the bookshop from my parents. It's all I have left of them, and it's the only thing that keeps me from living on the street. I've worked hard to keep it going. Sir Broderick and Frances know bookselling, but they don't know my shop and my customers like I do. They don't care like I do." I could feel my insides twisting in anxiety.

Phyllida's answer was to give me a hug.

"It's kept me from returning to a life of crime in the East End. That thought should increase Sir Broderick's commitment," Emma said with a grin.

Emma had been a cherub-faced child who gained access to wealthy houses through upper windows for an East End burglary ring. When the group struck a house during a murder, the entire group, including Emma, was arrested for the killing and thrown in jail. The Archivist Society identified the true killer at the request of the victim's son. Sir Broderick then used up a great number of favors to convince the judge to have Emma placed in my custody. Emma's sass gave Phyllida a reason to smile, and the two had formed an unshakable bond.

Emma joined in the hug. "It'll turn out all right, Georgia."

Perhaps it was a never-ending, three-way bond. With the two of them beside me, I felt my confidence returning.

"Later this afternoon, Miss Fenchurch, you need to go to Madame Leclerc for your fitting. When you return, Miss Keyes can visit her." Blackford's voice punctured my fragile calm.

"I'm getting new clothes, too?" The duke had Emma's full attention.

"Smart but out of date. A lady's maid gets her mistress's cast-offs," Blackford said.

"How do you know about ladies and their maids?" I asked, my eyes narrowing. I thought the duke only knew about ducal things and investing.

"Knowledge imparted to me at a very young age by my mother." Despite his formal tone, his eyes laughed at me. He must have guessed his words sparked jealousy.

Between the rent on the furnished house we'd use and the money for our outfits, this was costing Blackford more money than I saw in a year. "You're going to great expense for this investigation, Your Grace. Why?"

"The safety of our nation is at stake."

"Stuff and nonsense. I repeat. Why?"

"If the Germans obtain this ship design, it will alter the balance of world power. That in turn will affect my pocketbook. That's the answer you're looking for, isn't it, Miss Fenchurch? As true as it is, I am also a patriot. My great-grandfather received that coach from Wellington for valuable and heroic service. I have the family honor to maintain and a country to protect. It is my duty." His dark eyes shot fire at me. His always-straight posture became as rigid as his jaw.

For once, I believed him.

"I've arranged for you to meet Ken Gattenger, Georgia. Shall we go?"

I nodded and set aside the books I'd been shelving. "Emma, you'll be fine on your own? Phyllida, do you have any message you want me to take to him?"

Emma shrugged her answer as she looked around our empty shop.

Phyllida considered for a moment. "Tell him I know he couldn't have killed Clara. Tell him I believe his story about the burglar. And tell him everything will be all right, since you are helping him."

NEWGATE PRISON, NOW used for prisoners awaiting trial or execution, sat next to the Central Criminal Court, or the Old Bailey, as everyone in London called it. The building was a stone fortress with nothing to recommend it but its forbidding, unbreakable nature. The facade had absorbed decades of smog and now appeared as grim as its reputation.

I climbed out of the duke's carriage and followed him through the first of many gates manned by many guards. We trailed our guide down corridors still cool with stale air left from the previous winter. A faint odor of mildew and rot seemed to come out of the stones themselves, along with eerie echoes of disembodied voices and metallic clanks.

Finally we arrived in a small room with stone floors and walls. Iron bars made up the fourth wall and covered the window high in the opposite wall. Inside was a wooden table and two chairs.

A third was brought in by our guide while another guard stood by silently. An oil lantern gave off a kerosene smell along with adequate light.

Kenneth Gattenger sat slumped in the chair on the opposite side of the table, fair stubble on his cheeks matching the blond hair that fell lankly over his brow. He'd always looked boyishly handsome when I saw him with Clara. Now, instead of slender, he was thin. His most prominent feature was his red, swollen eyes.

He began to rise when I entered the room, but a barked command from the tall, burly guard standing like a pillar to one side made him drop back into his seat like a deadweight.

I glared at the guard, but he stared straight ahead, saving him from viewing my wrathful stare. Changing to a pleasant expression, I turned to Gattenger and sat down across the scarred table from him. "Lady Phyllida Monthalf sends her greetings and her assurances that as an innocent man, you can be certain everything will turn out for the best."

He turned the saddest blue eyes that I have ever seen toward me and said, "How can it be all right? Clara is dead."

The Duke of Blackford sat down next to me and said, "Tell us what happened that night."

"I've told my story over and over, and no one believes me. What good will it do?" He buried his head in his arms on the tabletop and sobbed.

The duke shared an annoyed expression with me and then glared at the top of Gattenger's head. "Pull yourself together, man. We're trying to help you. We don't believe you killed your wife."

"It doesn't matter. Clara's still dead," he mumbled from beneath his arms, but at least the sobbing seemed to have stopped.

I smacked my hand on the table. "It matters to your wife that we find the man responsible and have him face justice. What do you think she'd say if she saw you like this?"

Gattenger sat up and wiped his eyes on his sleeve. "You're right. Clara deserves to have her killer punished. But I don't know who the man is."

I spoke quietly, not wanting to upset him again. "Just tell us what you do know of that night."

"We went into the study as we always did after dinner. Someone, a man, was hiding behind the door. Once we stepped into the room, he shut and locked the door. He had the drawings to my newest ship design in his hand."

He stared at his fisted hands. "I told him to give me the drawings. Clara asked him how he got in, why he was there. He said nothing; he just moved cautiously across the room toward the windows. Furious at his silence, I raised my voice. To my surprise, Clara did the same. The man just kept facing us as he edged his way toward the window. He never said a word. I decided to be a hero. What a fool I was." With a moan, he shoved his fists into his eyes.

"And then?" If he'd keep talking, we might learn something.

"And then? I tried to stop him. I struck out at him. I grabbed hold of the blueprints in his hands. I tore one sheet. He gasped as if in fright and swung at me. I ducked and swung back. Clara shouted at both of us to stop, and then I shouted at him. His answer was to punch me in the side of the head." He shrugged. "I don't remember any more. The next thing I knew, I was leaning over Clara's body, begging her not to be dead, but I knew she was."

"Were you standing? Sitting?" the duke asked.

"Lying on the floor next to her, half sitting, holding her. Her head was bloody and her eyes stared at me. Accusing me. I failed her."

A clank reverberated along the stone-lined hallways, making us all jump. "And then?" I pressed.

"I pulled myself to my feet, went to the door, and unlocked it. I told the maids to get a doctor and the police, but I knew it was too late."

"Did you see the burglar or the drawings when you came around?"

"No. I thought he'd taken them until the police found part of one in the fire. I guess he burned them."

"Why would he burn them?" the duke asked. Actually, he demanded to be told, but Gattenger didn't appear to notice Blackford's overbearing tone of voice.

He shook his head. "I don't know."

"You must be able to think of a reason. Those drawings are valuable, but they're not the only copy." The duke leaned across the table. "Why would anyone destroy them?"

Gattenger slammed his fists on the table. "I. Don't. Know." He rose halfway from his seat, glanced at the guard, and sat back down. "I'm sorry. I know you're trying to help, but I don't know why someone broke into my house, killed my wife, and burned my drawings."

"What did the man look like?" I asked.

He stared at the table and spoke in a monotone. It was as if all the air, all the life, had left him. "Thin, in his twenties, a little shorter than me."

"Did he have any scars? Did he have a receding hairline? Did he limp when he walked toward the window?"

"No limp. No scars. I didn't see his hairline. He wore a cap."

"What kind of cap?"

"Just a regular workingman's cap."

I glanced at Blackford. He nodded slightly and I continued. "What color was his shirt?"

"Faded. Brown or gray or something."

"Did he wear a collar?"

"With that shirt? No."

"His trousers?"

"The same. Faded. He looked and dressed like a workman."

I pulled a sheet of notepaper and a pencil from my bag and passed them over to Gattenger. From the corner of my eye, I was aware the guard moved. He didn't demand the paper and pencil, so I guessed Blackford stopped him; I suspect with a ducal glare. "Can you sketch his face?"

He began immediately and in a matter of moments had drawn the outline of the man's features.

"Why did you bring a set of plans for your new warship home with you that night?" Next to me, I felt Blackford stiffen. I kept my eyes on Gattenger, who kept working on his drawing.

"I wanted to check something."

"What?"

"Someone had questioned one of the calculations that day, and I wanted to verify my figures." He looked up at me. "The calculation affects several different facets of the ship, so I needed a full set of plans to check all the possibilities."

"Was your calculation correct?"

"I don't know. I hadn't had time to study it once I got home."

"And why was that?" Blackford asked. "Because you and Mrs. Gattenger had an argument?"

"We didn't have an argument."

"We know you did. Your wife was very upset before you two went into the study that night."

"We didn't have an argument. She wasn't upset." Gattenger didn't look up from his drawing at either of us as he spoke. He was lying.

I decided to ask what had puzzled me the most. "Why did you have a fire burning in that room on the hottest night of the year?"

"There was no fire."

Leaning forward, I said, "I saw the ashes myself."

He stared at me as he banged his fist on the table hard enough to make it jump. "There was no fire."

For the first time, I doubted Phyllida. This liar sounded like a murderer.

CHAPTER FOUR

THE sound of Ken Gattenger banging his fist on the table echoed in the small stone room. Blackford and I looked at each other, and he gave me a tiny nod. I was to make the first attempt to get the man I now saw as a possible murderer to tell us the truth.

"We know there was a fire. We know you and Clara had a fight. Tell us what happened. It's the only way to find her killer."

The air seemed to escape his body. "We didn't—it wasn't an argument. Clara was told—oh, why bother with this now? She was told I had cheated the navy. That my design was basically flawed and I'd be the laughingstock of England, if I wasn't thrown in jail for treason. Just as she told me what she'd heard, dinner was ready. We didn't want to discuss it in front of the servants. I told her someone had questioned an equation, and I would verify it after dinner. There was nothing to worry about. Someone had blown the story out of proportion."

"Did she stop worrying?" I asked.

He shook his head.

I pressed on. "Could there have been another problem?"

"No." He snapped his answer.

A woman comes back upset after talking to another woman, and the only problem was business? I was certain something else was wrong.

"Here." He slid the drawing of his attacker across the table to me.

"This is very good. I didn't realize you're an artist."

"Comes from learning drafting at a young age. You start to see everything on a grid. Even faces."

As I put the drawing of the killer in my bag, Blackford said, "Who raised the question about the calculation?"

"Sir Henry Stanford."

"The shipbuilder?"

Gattenger's look at the duke said there couldn't possibly be two Sir Henry Stanfords. "Yes."

"Did you and Stanford discuss the problem at the Admiralty the day of the break-in?"

"Yes."

"You and Sir Henry Stanford were together in the Admiralty records room that particular day discussing your calculations in tones that could be overheard?"

Gattenger and I gave each other a puzzled look. "I suppose," he said.

The duke rose from his chair so quickly he nearly knocked it over. He strode to the door but stopped before the guard reached the iron-barred gate to let him out. Then he marched back and sat down again.

"Who else was in the records office?" I asked.

"The clerks who work there. No one else."

"Did any of them comment on your discussion of this problem with the calculation, or on your removing a drawing from their files?"

"No. They were all busy. Too busy to do more than fulfill my request." Then Gattenger leaned toward me. "You don't think Sir Henry Stanford was behind the theft, do you? He and Clara got on well. Clara got on well with everyone." He loosed one sob and then fought to regain control.

"How would Sir Henry know anything about your calculations? The people at the Admiralty aren't that far along in having your battleship built, are they?" the duke asked.

"Yes, they are. The drawings have been shown to three ship-builders with instructions to bid on the work without taking the drawings outside of the records room. That's where Stanford saw them."

"Who are the other two?"

The names Ken Gattenger provided, Lord Porthollow and Mr. Fogburn, must have meant something to Blackford. I had never heard them before.

"Nothing is missing from the Admiralty and no one outside the records office has made any copies," the duke murmured. "Thank you, Gattenger. That's all we need for now." He stood and waited for the guard to unlock the door.

"Wait!" I said as I sprang to my feet. "What about the fire?"

"What about it?" Gattenger asked.

"Who asked for the fire to be lit in the study?"

He huffed out a breath as he stared at me. Then he lowered his eyes. "Clara. She'd not been feeling well, and she was cold."

I didn't believe that any more than I believed his story about Clara's worries concerning ship design flaws. And I hated being lied to by someone I wanted to help.

Blackford snorted and walked out of the sarcophagus-like space. Afraid I'd be trapped in this impenetrable fortress, I said good-bye to the prisoner.

He grabbed my hands and said, "This is all my fault. I'm to blame."

I saw the anguish in his eyes, but I also heard Blackford's footsteps marching away from me. "Why?" came out as a demand as I pulled my hands free.

Kenny Gattenger covered his face with his hands, shook his head, and sobbed.

"Why?" I asked again, torn between the fear of missing something important and the fear of being lost in those twisting, unforgiving corridors. When he didn't speak, I left the room and rushed down the stone-paneled hallways, trying to catch up with Blackford and anxious to be out of this prison. I was out of breath when I reached the duke and then had to struggle to keep up with his long strides. As we crossed the last gate and exchanged the prison gloom for London's sunny, humid streets, I grabbed Blackford by the sleeve. "What's wrong?"

He didn't answer until we were both in the carriage and riding away from Newgate Prison. The smell of mildew and rot stuck to my clothes and remained in my nose. The duke didn't appear to notice anything amiss. "Stanford is in financial trouble. I didn't think he'd turn to treason to buy his way out."

"You think he's the link to the German spy?"

"I know he is. And I can't question him. You, as Georgina Monthalf, will have to learn his secrets and retrieve the plans alone."

"Why can't you?"

"We aren't on speaking terms. Haven't been for years."

He wanted me to accomplish all this while inhabiting another woman's skin. I'd played this type of role before, but never for so long a time as this promised to be or in such a complicated investigation. If it weren't for Phyllida, I'd have quit that instant.

THE NEXT FEW days passed in a blur. When I wasn't in the bookshop, I was constantly at Sir Broderick's, ensuring I'd planned for every possibility. We seemed to have more customers than ever, but Frances acted as if she were born to be a shopkeeper. Our elderly patrons thought she was a joy. Our other regulars loved her. I'd have been jealous if I weren't so busy.

The telephone was installed on the shop counter only three days after the meeting at Sir Broderick's, setting a record in our part of town. Emma immediately called Sir Broderick's and got Jacob. She and Frances had great fun practicing with the instrument. I knew I'd be able to measure their squeals of delight in shillings when the bill arrived.

The next afternoon, Adam Fogarty came in the shop, nodded to me, and walked toward the back. I signaled Emma to watch the shop and followed him into our office.

"We have a problem." Fogarty paced the narrow space like a caged animal. He'd been a Metropolitan Police sergeant before an injury shortened the career he loved. Most of that career was spent outside on his feet. We'd worked together on Archivist Society investigations for nearly a dozen years, and I knew better than to even think of offering him a chair.

"Only one?" We were trying to help a man in prison who didn't appear to want help.

"One of my sources, a desk sergeant, told me the highest levels of Scotland Yard have decided Gattenger is guilty of murder and treason and they aren't looking any further. No one knows what kind of evidence they have, but it must be conclusive. They're going to keep holding Gattenger, but Whitehall and the Admiralty are in charge of the investigation now, not our guys."

"Murder and treason?" Good heavens. This was worse. Much worse, since they were adding treason.

"Yes. The whole case has landed in the steamy pits." Fogarty picked up a book and set it down again.

"Thanks, Adam. We need to learn what the evidence is." When the duke and I were at Newgate Prison, Gattenger had said everything was his fault. Was he guilty? Being blackmailed? Or a heartbroken and wronged man?

Fogarty stuck his head out the window and looked up and down the alley. When he pulled his head and shoulders back into the room, he said, "I met up with Inspector Grantham. He told me the case had been taken off his hands and placed with someone senior. He doesn't know what the evidence is, but he believes it's enough to hang Gattenger."

He marched to the doorway and back. "I'll see what I can find out from my sources in the police force, but they're all too low level to know anything if Grantham doesn't. I think we'll need the duke to talk to Whitehall. Ask him, Georgia."

"I will. Whether he decides to share that information is another question."

"He needs to understand he isn't the only one working on finding those warship plans." Fogarty limped out of the office and waved good-bye to Emma, jingling the bell over the door as he left.

I walked to the counter and looked at the new contraption that had invaded my shop. "Emma, could you show me how to call the duke on this thing?"

"Gladly." She walked over, gave me a superior smile, and

picked up the narrow black tube. Lifting the earpiece off its cradle, she waited, then said, "Operator, I'd like to speak to the Duke of Blackford's residence."

A moment later, she handed me the instrument, and I found myself listening to the ghostly voice of Stevens, Blackford's butler. I nearly dropped the telephone before I was able to reply.

Shortly after I asked Blackford to find out what evidence Scotland Yard and Whitehall had found against Gattenger, the afternoon post arrived. On top was a letter with South African stamps. I grabbed the letter opener and dispatched the envelope with one savage stroke.

The letter inside bore more information than I'd expected. "Emma, how do I call Sir Broderick?"

By the time he came on the line, I was clutching the black candlestick device with a stranglehold. "I heard from Mr. Shaw, the antiquarian dealer in Cape Town you recommended, Sir Broderick. A man who fits the description of my parents' killer has recently been in Cape Town searching for a copy of the Gutenberg Bible. He apparently didn't find what he wanted and has returned to Europe by ship."

"You don't need to shout, Georgia. The telephone works well. Does Shaw have a name for this man?"

I lowered my voice. "He called himself Mr. Wolf, but Mr. Shaw thinks it was a false name."

"What else did Shaw say?"

"The story seems a bit confused, but this Mr. Wolf apparently decided an antiquarian collector named Vanderhoff had Wolf's stolen Gutenberg Bible. Wolf clubbed Vanderhoff over the head and tore the man's house apart, but didn't find the book. By the time the police arrived, Wolf was gone. In fact, he sailed that night for Europe with some of Vanderhoff's correspondence."

There was a long pause over the line. Then Sir Broderick's voice came back loudly and I pulled the small black speaker away from my ear. "Did these letters mention the Gutenberg Bible?"

"Shaw writes that he thinks they must have. Wolf called on Shaw once asking whether he'd seen Vanderhoff with the Gutenberg. At that time, Wolf told Shaw he intends to find his stolen Bible and reclaim it, and no one should stand in his way."

"Tearing the house apart and attacking Vanderhoff sounds like the violence used by your parents' killer. But Vanderhoff wasn't killed?"

"No. He was knocked senseless and still hadn't regained consciousness two days later when Mr. Shaw wrote."

"At least this time he didn't kill his victim, although it sounds like he may yet succeed. And you now have a name for the murderer."

"I have more than that." I could barely contain my excitement. "The only passenger ship leaving Cape Town that night sailed for Southampton. There's a good chance this Mr. Wolf is here in England. I need to drop out of our current investigation and search for him."

"No." Sir Broderick's voice boomed down the wire. "You will not let everyone, including Lady Phyllida, down." Softening his tone, he said, "We'll pick up his trail once this is over. I'll help you, and I have contacts that can help you."

"But—"

"No buts, young lady. Your parents wouldn't approve of you letting your friends down. You've waited a dozen years. You can wait a little longer."

The line went dead.

I set the telephone down with a crash. I didn't want to wait any longer. The investigation to find and capture my parents' murderer had hit too many brick walls over time. This was our first lucky break since I'd seen him a few months before.

Unfortunately, Sir Broderick was right. I couldn't let Phyllida or the Archivist Society down. And I was looking forward to working with Blackford again.

THE NEXT MORNING, a neatly dressed man with silver cuff links to match his silver-headed cane walked into the bookshop and peered around nearsightedly. "Miss Fenchurch?"

I stepped forward to wait on him. "Yes. May I help you?"

"Georgia Fenchurch?"

"Yes."

"I'm Sir Jonah Denby. My office in Whitehall is investigating the stolen warship blueprints, and I understand you're helping uncover the circumstances of their disappearance."

"Where did you hear that?"

His green eyes bore into mine. "There's no reason to be alarmed. The Duke of Blackford mentioned it. Do you have any information for us yet?"

I drew him back to my office in case anyone should come into the shop. "Gattenger caught a thief stealing the blueprints from his study. He drew a picture of the man, which we're showing to Scotland Yard. Do you have any information you can share with us?"

"Regrettably, not yet."

"But Scotland Yard says Whitehall has proof of Gattenger's guilt. What proof?" I didn't attempt to hide the demand in my tone.

When he smiled, the wrinkles on his weathered face deepened. "I can't tell you at this time. I'm sure I'll be speaking to you soon. Good day, Miss Fenchurch."

Setting his top hat on his silver hair, he walked out of the shop with a jaunty step.

A LITTLE MORE than a week after our Archivist Society meeting in Sir Broderick's study, Phyllida came into the shop with a message from the Duke of Blackford. Emma and Frances were both helping customers look for ordinary books, and I was assisting an antiquarian collector. I excused myself and read the note while my customer examined the volume.

The duke wrote that some of our clothes from Madame Leclerc's had arrived at the house in Mayfair. We would need to go there immediately. Phyllida and I had an invitation to attend Lord Francis's musical evening that night. I muttered, "Tonight? And he wants us to leave immediately? He doesn't give us much notice, does he?"

"You've known this day was coming for the past week. How much more time do you need?" Phyllida asked.

"Are you closing up shop and leaving?" the antiquarian customer asked.

"No. I'm going to be in and out of the shop for the next several days on—family business. I didn't realize I'd be called to a meeting tonight."

"Will Sir Broderick be handling your antiquarian business in your absence?" I saw a gleam in the man's eye.

"Yes." And it gave me no pleasure to admit that. Sir Broderick's sympathies lay with the buyer. He had a vast, well-known book collection. I hoped this time he'd remember he was acting for the seller.

"Perhaps I'll just finish my negotiations with him." The man shut the book and turned to leave, still clutching the volume.

"No. I have time to finish our business." I held out my white-cotton-gloved hand.

Blushing at his lapse in trying to leave with unpaid-for goods, he handed the book over while Phyllida said, "Georgia, he said immediately."

"You go ahead, Aunt. Emma and I will catch up."

She planted herself across the counter from me. "I'm the only one who knows where we're meeting."

"Then you'll have to wait. Have you closed up the flat?"

"No."

"Collect everything you think we might need tonight and then come back for us. That should give us enough time to negotiate." I gave my customer a smile.

He reached inside his coat pocket for his wallet, his jaw raised pugnaciously. "Twenty-four, ten, and sixpence. That's my final offer."

Since that was ten and sixpence more than I expected, I began to wrap his purchase. At that moment, Sumner came into the shop. After a nod to me, he walked over to wait until Emma was available.

Emma and I finished with our customers at the same time, and I crossed the shop to talk to Sumner. "What's happened?" I whispered.

"I met with Jacob at a pie shop this morning before starting time in the records room. He's been in the Admiralty records room three days, and already he can eliminate most of his coworkers. There's one who's been teased about his sudden financial improvement, but he won't say where the money came from. Makes a joke about it. Jacob is trying to pin him down, but so far he's been cagey.

"Sir Broderick sent me over to fill you in and to ask if you need any help. I'm not to meet with Jacob again until the day after tomorrow."

"You'll have to come to our house in Mayfair. We've been summoned to begin that part of the investigation this afternoon," I told him.

"What reason do I give for calling at a house in Mayfair?" Sumner asked.

"Play the role of my gentleman caller," Emma said. "I think Phyllida and Georgina will be lenient employers, as long as I get my work done."

I nodded. "Good idea."

Emma and Sumner grinned like a couple of kids given a holiday. Even the scarred side of Sumner's face showed a hint of a smile.

The bell over the shop door rang and, seeing Frances was busy, I went to greet our new customer. When I glanced over a few minutes later, Sumner and Emma were carrying on a hushed conversation, using hand gestures for emphasis. I couldn't tell what they were discussing, but Emma did not look pleased.

We'd finished with our customers by the time Phyllida reappeared with a holdall. Frances wished us well and told me she could handle the rest of the day in the shop by herself. Emma took Phyllida's bag and they walked outside. After hurried last-minute instructions to Frances, I followed them and flagged down a hire carriage that looked reputable. The inside had been swept recently and the seats weren't torn, so we wouldn't look out of place when we arrived in Mayfair.

The house the duke and Phyllida had chosen was on a quiet side street, its brick front measuring four windows wide on the floors above the entrance. We walked up the three front steps rising over the kitchen entrance, Emma taking the holdall. The front door was opened by a young man in livery. "Welcome, your ladyship."

Phyllida smiled at him. "Thomas, our cousin Mrs. Monthalf has arrived. Georgina, this is our footman, Thomas. You'll meet the rest of the staff shortly. Emma, if you'll take the case upstairs to Mrs. Monthalf's room. Second door on the left. I hope you'll like it, Georgina."

"I'm sure I will. Everything's been a bit overwhelming since I arrived."

"Prepare to be even more overwhelmed. We're attending Lady Francis's musical evening tonight, and her entertainments are always inspiring."

All this conversation in front of the staff was a trial if you weren't born to that world, and I wasn't. At home, I never had to deal with cleaners and tradesmen, because Phyllida handled all that for me while I was in the bookshop. Now we'd have servants around all the time. What did the wealthy do during the day if they weren't working, while their servants kept busy around them? "May I see the house?"

"Of course." Phyllida took me on a guided tour of the ground floor (dining room and morning room) and the first floor (main parlor and back parlor/study), and then we climbed to the second floor. Her bedroom was next door to mine, also facing the street, but smaller. Mine had the dressing room that led to the back room where Emma would sleep. This high up, with all the bedroom doors and windows open, we were blessed with a little breeze.

"Both our rooms have sea chests," Emma whispered, "where our clothes from Madame Leclerc's are packed. Give me a hand in unpacking."

We did, while Phyllida kept a watch out for any servants. One of the toughest things I'd face was hiding my lifelong habit of jumping in and helping at whatever task needed to be done.

I couldn't resist running my fingers over the dresses Madame Leclerc had made. The fabrics, silk and satin, taffeta and thin cotton, cashmere and lace, whispered against my skin. Emma and I held them to ourselves and swung around, the colors flashing in the sunlight, before we hung them in the wardrobe.

One part of this investigation would be a pleasure. I'd had neither the money nor the reason to dress in finery before.

Before we were half finished, carters arrived with two more sea chests, one carried up to Phyllida's room and one to mine. I tipped the two men, and a maid showed them out. We opened them to find more silks, more colors, and new shifts and petticoats and nightgowns in soft, cool cotton. My hands slid over everything, reveling in the freshness while the rest of London felt stale.

We'd almost finished when we heard a jangle like my shop doorbell. A moment later, we heard male voices and then footsteps on the stairs. A maid stood in the doorway to my room, a silver tray in her hands.

Phyllida reached out and picked up the calling card on its shiny surface. "Well, well. The Duke of Blackford has come to call."

CHAPTER FIVE

PHYLLIDA and I walked downstairs to find Blackford waiting for us in the parlor. He rose when we walked into the room decorated in dark purple and light blue. I curtsied and then walked over to the first window and shoved the draperies back as far as possible to get more light into the room. Then I opened the window.

"You don't like the house?" Blackford asked.

"It's by far the nicest leased house I've ever seen. Right now, I hope to get a breeze through the room." I opened the draperies in the second window and tugged until the sash rose a few inches.

"What have you learned so far?"

"I have customers who will cheat me if they deal with Sir Broderick in my absence." I shoved the third window drapes back and tugged on the wooden frame. It was stuck. "I also learned this afternoon I'm going to Lord and Lady Francis's musical evening tonight."

"You sound upset."

"I wish you would tell me things before the last moment." I yanked on the window. Still stuck. "Is Phyllida also invited?"

"Yes. But you're the one who needs to flirt with me so we can begin our affair in record time."

Affair? Record time? I jerked on the window and it flew up. I set the lace curtains to rights and turned to face the duke. "Aren't you supposed to flirt with me?"

"I will, Mrs. Monthalf, but you have to flirt back. From the look on your face, I'd say that won't happen."

"What kind of a woman do you think I am?" I didn't think wealthy Mrs. Monthalf would fall for a duke so quickly.

Phyllida looked from one to the other of us and slipped from the room.

The duke walked over to me and cupped my face in his hand. He didn't squeeze my cheeks or hurt me in any way, but I couldn't have moved if I tried. And I didn't want to try. Standing so close to him I could smell old leather and older whiskey. "I think you're a woman who was in love with me when we were younger, but I failed to ask for your hand and Mr. Monthalf did. You left and I never saw you again. You're back in my life now, and I won't make the same mistake twice."

He held my gaze with his dark, mesmerizing eyes, and I felt the power of his declaration. For an instant, I thought he was talking to me. My heart soared. Then I remembered I was middle-class, he was a duke, and he was talking about the woman I was pretending to be. The duke's primary interest was the fate of an empire, which rested on finding the plans for a warship.

Blast.

After I recovered from my deflating realization, I asked, "Where did we meet, Your Grace? Here in London?"

"Too many people would wonder why they couldn't remember

you. I spent time in India. You could have been living with your British army officer father. Then you married Monthalf and moved to another colony, and I came home."

"Where were you? Calcutta? In how much danger are we of meeting someone who would have known my father or me?"

"Yes, Calcutta will do nicely. I don't know of anyone involved in this who's been to India. And where did you and Phyllida decide you moved after your wedding?"

"Singapore. She had a Monthalf cousin, Edgar, who was in business there. He never married and died a few years ago. Are we in any danger of being discovered from that choice?"

"Not that I know of."

The duke still held my face in his bare hand, skin touching skin. I didn't move, not wanting the moment to end.

His expression turned grim. "You've been against playing the role of a widow since we began planning this investigation. Is this because you were a mistress who never took your wedding vows?"

I jerked backward, the mood between us broken. "No. As a single woman, I'm against leaving my shop, my source of income, in the hands of others while we search for Clara Gattenger's killer."

"And the blueprints to the greatest warship ever designed."

Crossing my arms over my chest, I took a full step backward and blinked away my tears. "Are you worried I can't play my role convincingly because he died before we reached the altar?"

"No. I'm worried you won't be able to play your part convincingly because it will hurt too much."

I was surprised at the kindness I heard in his voice. "This role has nothing to do with my real life."

"Nevertheless, you'd be less than human if it didn't bother you."

I looked into his eyes, letting him see into my deepest being.

His genuine concern demanded complete honesty. "Your Grace, if there were any man today I'd let into my bed, it would be you."

He took my hand and raised it to his lips. The skin of his lips was slightly rough against my flesh. Would they feel as rough if I kissed him? "I'm honored." He lowered my hand. "What happened to your lover?"

"We had had a long, cold winter. Just as we entered spring and began to plan our wedding day, he came down with a fever. It quickly grew worse and traveled to his brain. He died the day before they read the banns the second time."

"I'm sorry. And I'm flattered you're letting me follow him, if only as a pretend lover."

I held his gaze for a long time as I wrapped his startling consideration around me. Then I shook my head and said, "How do we want to begin our affair tonight?"

"Before the musical performance begins at the Francises', we'll meet and exclaim over how long it's been. That will give me an opening to sit with you and we can begin our flirtation." He strode away from me, running a hand through his hair.

A breeze fluttered through the window, cooling my heated skin. I closed my eyes and drank in the refreshing air, nearly missing his next words.

"Baron von Steubfeld will be in attendance tonight. We need to keep him aware that his every move is being scrutinized."

I opened my eyes and stared at him. "Why do you think the drawings haven't already been passed to him and then sent by diplomatic pouch to Berlin?"

With perfect timing, Phyllida reentered the room. I suspected she had eavesdropped. My cheeks grew warm despite my suspicion that Phyllida already knew my fiancé had been my lover.

"We know the baron hasn't received them yet," Blackford said.

"How?"

The duke waved me closer and lowered his voice as he stood between Phyllida and me. "We've been reading privileged diplomatic messages between von Steubfeld and Berlin. The baron complained in a telegram this morning that he's been watched too closely to take possession of the plans yet."

I was shocked. Such things were not done. I didn't even think they were possible. "You can't do that," I said, my voice rising. "That was a private message from an embassy to its government."

His dark look made me clamp my mouth shut. "That it was in code made our task even more difficult. We aren't supposed to read other nations' messages. Neither is Germany or any other country. However, on those few occasions when we gain access to dispatches, we do. So does everyone else."

"It would start a war if anyone found out," I whispered.

"That's why I must trust you and Lady Phyllida with complete discretion."

We both nodded. Then I had to ask, "Why are you trusting us with this? You didn't have to tell us anything."

"You are risking not only social embarrassment but physical danger by taking part in our efforts to stop the transfer of those plans. Someone has already killed to obtain them. They won't shy away from another murder."

He looked at Phyllida. "I shouldn't be asking you to do this."

"Clara died trying to prevent those warship plans from falling into the wrong hands. The least I can do is see that her death is avenged." Phyllida crossed her arms over her chest and looked from the duke to me as if she thought someone would try to stop her.

My mind was working furiously. "If Baron von Steubfeld hasn't been able to get the drawings because he's too closely watched, he'll have to change his situation so his movements aren't so easily observed. Or use someone else to handle them."

"We know. We have our ears open for word on how he plans to change the circumstances."

"Was that the royal 'we,' Your Grace?"

The tiniest hint of a smirk crossed his mouth. "You didn't think it was only the Archivist Society working on a problem of national importance, did you?"

Once again, his attitude annoyed me. "Is there anything else we need to know today? We won't be able to speak freely tonight. Not if we're going to deliberately draw an audience."

"I suspect Sir Henry Stanford. He's been watched closely, but he's not been to the embassy. He did dine with Baron von Steubfeld two nights ago in a restaurant, but no packages passed between them."

There was danger in focusing too closely on only a few people. "What about someone else in the German embassy?"

"Most of the staff at the embassy went home for the summer before the theft. No one has left the country since the burglary, and Scotland Yard has been watching all those still here."

"There are three shipbuilders who've seen the design to bid on it. Why are you only focusing on Stanford?"

"The other two weren't in the Admiralty when Gattenger took out a copy of the plans. They've never met von Steubfeld and they aren't mired in debt. They're being observed, but there's no sign either of them is involved."

I moved closer to the duke and looked him in the eye. "What has caused this bitterness between yourself and Stanford?"

"Stanford owes a great deal of money from the expansion of

his shipyard. One of the people he owes is me. He's in arrears in his payments and he and I have had nasty words in public."

That might be the only public reason anyone knew of for their argument, but such animosity over a business loan seemed out of character for the duke. "I don't believe you."

"Sorry, Georgina, but sometimes men fall out over investments. It's really that simple."

I didn't believe him. No, that wasn't entirely true. I'd put my faith in Blackford before and been rewarded. I trusted him to deliver on his promises. I'd also learned that not everything he said was the truth. "I need to know more about Stanford before I can approach him."

Blackford shrugged. "He's a widower with a full head of dark hair heavily mixed with gray, although he's only in his early forties. He knows how to attract the attention of women, but he doesn't have any long-standing relationships, if you get my drift."

He meant lovers or mistresses. That helped if I were to attract his attention and find out his connection to the Germans. I gave Phyllida a smile and said, "We'd better not take anything at face value with these people. Espionage isn't the usual line of work for the Archivist Society."

Phyllida took my hand. "I hope they take us at face value, Georgina. Otherwise, everything we've done is for naught, and poor Kenny will hang."

KNOWING I NEEDED to make a good impression on everyone at Lord Francis's that night while flirting with the duke, Emma set to work to make me look attractive.

Emma was breathtakingly beautiful. She should have been

playing this role, but I would have been jealous knowing she was flirting with the duke.

Someday Blackford would have to marry to provide an heir and I'd envy the woman. In the meantime, I was determined to play my role to perfection. I wanted him to love me. Or at least admire me.

"I think—hold still—just one more pin. No, we need another one here. This would be easier, Georgia, if your hair wasn't so thick," Emma mumbled around a hairpin.

"Georgina," I muttered back.

"Yes. Georgina. Or rather, ma'am. There. That's got it. Now for some jewels. Something understated, I think."

"I don't have anything understated."

Emma was looking through the jewel box we'd been lent for my role, ignoring me. There was a knock on the door before Phyllida came in and joined her. I sat at my dressing table, looking in the mirror at their reflections as they looked at various pieces, looked at me, and shook their heads.

"It can't be that bad," I finally told them.

"You have to look like you belong there, but not fade into just another society matron. We want all the old cats to see more in the duke's interest in you than simply a matter of a former acquaintance." Phyllida came up behind me and lifted my chin. Then she forced my shoulders back. "You must move like a lady."

Hard to do when I was accustomed to moving stacks of books around. "I'm not supposed to know the duke will be there."

"All the more reason for you to look your best. You're stepping out in London society for the first time, and you know you'll be judged by everyone there. You've lived in the colonies for years. Now you're in a foreign land among strangers and you want to make friends. If you want to get more invitations, you need to look like one of them, but a little bit more. Not too much more. Understand?" Phyllida pulled a pair of diamond earrings from the jewelry box. "These will do."

Emma hooked the long strands of tiny diamonds in my ears. "They emphasize your long neck."

They did. They also must have cost a fortune. I was immediately worried about losing one.

"A necklace, do you think?" Emma asked.

"No. She's a widow. She doesn't want to look like she's advertising for another husband. That would set everyone against her. She's trying to fit in. I think she's perfect the way she is." Phyllida smiled at my reflection in the mirror.

I rose from my chair and slowly twirled for their inspection.

"Perfect. The lilac in the dress brings out the color of your eyes," Phyllida said.

"I think you're ready, ma'am," Emma said.

I thought I was, too, until we set foot inside Lord Francis's stately London home. In our furnished rental, we could seat twelve for dinner and perhaps as many in the parlor if we squeezed them in, and I was amazed at all the space and servants we had.

When we reached his lordship's first-floor parlor—really two rooms opened into each other and reaching the entire depth of the house—there was seating for at least fifty plus a piano and space for the soprano to stand. Sparkling chandeliers hung overhead. Velvet draperies were pulled far back, allowing fresh air to enter the open windows and ruffle the lace curtains. The draperies matched the flowers in the wallpaper and in the thick rug that covered most of the gleaming wooden floor.

A formally dressed footman announced us, we thanked our hosts for inviting us, and then we moved past them into the room. Guests wandered from group to group of dazzling women and black-evening-coated men, all laughing and chatting amiably. I didn't know a soul and felt like an interloper.

And I didn't see the duke.

"Anyone you know?" I asked Phyllida. My heart was beating out *You're a fraud. You're a fraud. You're a fraud.*

"Not a soul," she whispered back.

A moment later, a masculine voice behind me said, "We haven't been properly introduced, but I can have our hostess remedy that when she finishes with her duties in the front hall if you'd prefer."

I turned around and found myself staring into the blue eyes of a man who appeared too young to have that much gray hair. Could this be Sir Henry Stanford? "Your presence here is introduction enough. I'm Mrs. Georgina Monthalf, and this is my late husband's cousin, Lady Phyllida Monthalf," I said with a small curtsy. Lady Phyllida inclined her head with an aristocratic nod that had to have been learned in her girlhood. I wondered if she could teach me how to move so I appeared to own the universe.

"Sir Henry Stanford, at your service."

"I'm pleased to meet you, Sir Henry. Have you lived in London long?"

"All my adult life. And you, Mrs. Monthalf?"

"Oh, no. Never. I lived in the Far East with my husband, and after his death I sold out and moved here."

"Your husband was in trade?" Sir Henry asked. Phyllida was being ignored in this exchange, but she seemed perfectly happy to be on the fringe.

"Yes. I understand that it isn't to be spoken of in this society, but he didn't inherit a title and a man must have an occupation. Don't you agree, Sir Henry?" I knew the answer; I wanted to hear what Sir Henry would tell me.

"I agree. I myself have invested time and money in shipyards. An important field in an island nation."

"And important for anyone engaged in trade. Or traveling. I just arrived from Singapore. A very, very long ocean voyage. I wonder if I was on one of your ships." I tried to put an expression on my face that signified interest.

"I'm afraid I'm only involved in building warships and freighters." His eyes didn't scan the room, so I seemed to be holding his attention.

Just how much attention was pointed out a moment later when Sir Henry said, "We won't have much time to talk tonight. May I call on you ladies later?" He bowed to Phyllida but I knew his intentions were aimed at me.

"Of course." I gave him our address.

Around us, the buzz of conversation grew louder and the room grew stuffy with too many bodies enclosed in a small space in the heat.

Over my shoulder, I heard, "Georgina Monthalf? It's been a few years, but I never forget a beautiful face."

I schooled my face to look surprised. I recognized the voice, and I knew it was time to begin the flirtation that was to be my cover. What I really wanted was to ask the Duke of Blackford why he was always late.

Putting on a confused expression, I said, "Have we met before, sir?"

"We have indeed, Miss Georgina. Ranleigh? Remember now?"

"My goodness, yes. It's been a lifetime, Mr. Ranleigh. How are you? Are you residing in England now?"

He put on a falsely deprecating smile. "I've become the Duke of Blackford."

"Oh! Your Grace." I gave him a deep curtsy.

"I'm afraid so," he murmured.

"My condolences on the death of your father." We were attracting an audience of aristocrats who realized there was a new subject to gossip about. I hoped I could keep up the pretense.

"Thank you. He died not long after you left. Is Monthalf here tonight?"

"No. I'm afraid I lost him last year." I needed a reason not to be in mourning.

"My condolences. Monthalf was the luckiest of men."

I inclined my head regally at the compliment and said, "Have you married, Your Grace? Is the favored woman here tonight?"

"I'm still a bachelor, pining over the one who got away."

I raised my eyebrows. The duke was going overboard, and I was sure our audience would recognize his insincerity.

"Too much?" he asked.

"As flattery, or as fact?" I replied.

"Either."

"Both." I heard a few feminine chuckles around us.

"How long have you been in London?" The duke moved his body slightly to block Sir Henry from slipping closer to my side.

"I just arrived. Lady Phyllida, this is an old friend from India, Mr. Ranleigh, now the Duke of Blackford. Your Grace, this is Lady Phyllida Monthalf, my late husband's cousin. Lady Phyllida has been kind enough to take me under her wing to introduce me around London. And do you know Sir Henry Stanford?"

"Yes," both men growled in unison.

"Ladies, why don't we take a seat? The musicians are tuning up." Blackford tucked my arm in his.

I swung around ungracefully to face the shipbuilder. "Sir Henry, I'm very glad to make your acquaintance. I hope we meet again soon."

"So do I, Mrs. Monthalf." He bowed to me and then shot a look at Blackford's back that should have drawn blood. Nearby, I noticed two old biddies, dripping with lace and jewels, whispering as they looked in our direction.

The duke escorted us to a small, delicate sofa and then sat on a sturdy chair on my side of the sofa. "You look delectable." I must have appeared surprised, because before I could revel in his words he added, "You could attempt to look enamored of whatever I'm saying."

"Where's Baron von Steubfeld?" I whispered and smiled up at him before scanning the room. Every seat was taken and latecomers were squeezing in wherever they could. With all these bodies, the room was becoming sweltering despite the relief of a small breeze.

"Directly across the room from us. In the fancy Prussian uniform. Fair haired, sitting very straight, talking to the woman on our side of him."

I could see his face clearly as he talked to the gray-haired woman in mourning next to him. It was a lean, cruel face, thin lipped, sharply beaked, with a wide mustache like his kaiser's.

Past him, I saw Sir Jonah Denby coming in the doorway. "There's your friend."

The duke looked in the direction I indicated. "Who?"

"Sir Jonah Denby."

"Who?"

"Sir Jonah Denby. Works in Whitehall. You told him I was involved in—this." No one seemed to be listening in, but I wanted to be cautious.

Blackford leaned over and murmured in my ear, "I don't know anyone by that name, and I'd never tell anyone about your role."

I swallowed, my nerves making my hands tremble. "Who is he?" When I looked around again, Sir Jonah had vanished.

Blackford shook his head slightly. "Don't worry. We'll find him."

"He knows who I really am. He could ruin everything," I whispered in his ear.

He moved his head to nuzzle my cheek. "We won't let him." Then a man slid past us and Blackford shifted away from me.

I looked around the room, trying to spot Sir Jonah. Here was a danger we hadn't planned on; someone who knew the duke, someone who knew me by my real name, and someone we knew nothing about. He could ruin our plan. He could be the man who'd hired the thief.

I studied the baron, wondering if he was truly behind this plot. At that moment, he looked past the woman he was talking to and directly at me. I was shocked for a second at being caught staring, but then I remembered my role and smiled and nodded in acknowledgment. He glared for an instant before he nodded in response and then turned to the lady on his other side.

I glanced up at the duke and he gave me a reassuring smile. "We're in this together," he murmured.

That night I saw the baron's glare in my dreams just before I heard Blackford tell me we were together.

EMMA AND I rose earlier than usual the next morning to eat, dress, and travel to the bookshop to begin our usual day. I immediately checked the cash box and the ledger from the previous afternoon while Emma dusted and straightened a few shelves. Within minutes, both Frances Atterby and Grace Yates came in and set to work.

Grace, one of our younger Archivist Society members, began dusting shelves with Emma while Frances talked to the day's first customer. I glanced over to see the middle-aged woman selecting the *English Illustrated Magazine* and the *Illustrated London News*. Apparently she was a fan of short stories and serialized novels, and I was happy to see her spend her money with us.

I joined Grace and said, "What are you doing here? You have a full-time job as secretary and librarian to Lord Barnwood."

"With this heat, he's closed up his London home for a few weeks. Gone fishing in Scotland 'til the heat ends. I told him I needed to stay in London, so I have some time off. I just need to check at the house once or twice a day for messages and to take care of any correspondence."

"I'm sure Frances is glad of the help."

"She is. And we can call Sir Broderick anytime we need reinforcements." She reached out and patted my arm. "Relax, Georgia. Everything is fine."

I covered a wide yawn. "Thank you, Grace, for the help."

She smiled at me. "What are you doing here? You have an investigation to conduct. Aren't you worried someone will come in here and see you?"

"Not in the morning. I've learned aristocrats don't show their faces before luncheon, and that's held at a late hour."

"Because they're sleeping all morning, as you should be."

In answer, I yawned again. "I returned late last night, but I'm sure most evenings will be much quieter. Now, on this investigation. Could you please have Sir Broderick learn anything he can about a Sir Jonah Denby?"

Despite my absence on the previous afternoon, the bookshop had run smoothly. None of our customers remarked on my disappearance. Maybe I shouldn't have worried so much.

I looked over to see Charles Dickens, a brown-striped cat with a notch in one ear from a fight, stroll through our open doorway and hop up in the front window. After rearranging the stock on display to suit him, he curled up on the ledge and went to sleep. He must have temporarily run out of mice on our block to murder.

A few minutes later, while waiting on a woman interested in the newest novels, I spotted Emma picking up Dickens and holding him against her shoulder. The cat never let me do that. But then, Dickens had a stare that reminded me of Blackford's. They were both first-class hunters.

CHAPTER SIX

IN the early afternoon, Emma and I took the sweltering omnibus most of the way to our borrowed home and then walked in the glaring sunshine to our doorstep in time for luncheon. As soon as I gobbled down a light meal, Emma had to dress me for afternoon calls.

Before I'd finished dressing, a maid brought up a card from Sir Henry Stanford. "Tell him I'll be down in a minute, and let Lady Monthalf know he's here. Emma, help me get ready, please."

As soon as the last pin was in my hair, I rushed downstairs. Phyllida was already in the parlor discussing the weather.

Sir Henry rose to his feet and said, "Mrs. Monthalf. How nice to see you again."

"And you, Sir Henry. Did you enjoy the musical evening last night?"

"I would have enjoyed it more if you had been sitting with me."

"I'm sorry. Ranleigh has always been a bit arrogant." It felt disloyal, but I needed Sir Henry on my side if I were to discover his secrets.

"Unless he's already claimed tonight, I'd like to take you ladies to dinner and then to the theater. The Lyceum is showing the last Shakespearean play of the season."

"I'd enjoy that. And you, Phyllida?"

"Oh, absolutely."

"Then I'll pick you up by carriage at a quarter to seven."

"Are we having dinner at your home, Sir Henry?"

"Yes. I'm throwing a small dinner party and then we'll go on to the theater."

"Wonderful." I'd received a heaven-sent opportunity to search his study during dinner. If the thief had passed the plans to Sir Henry, this might be my best chance of recovering them.

Once Sir Henry left, Phyllida and I were to travel by hired carriage to the homes of several women. We'd drop off our calling cards to announce my arrival, as Georgina Monthalf, widow of Mr. Edgar Monthalf, newly arrived from the colonies. Hopefully, the interest that both the Duke of Blackford and Sir Henry Stanford had shown in Mrs. Monthalf would already be making the rounds of afternoon gossip.

"We've been invited to stop by Lady Ormond's this afternoon," Phyllida said as she settled herself on the scorching black leather seat in the carriage.

"Was she at the musical evening at Lord Francis's?" The lowered windows let in more heat than they allowed to escape.

"Yes. She was the most awful gossip thirty-five years ago when she was Lady Mildred Fessent. From the way she was studying you and the duke before she invited us to stop by today, I'd guess she'll be hunting for more details to pass around London."

Phyllida gave me the address and I passed it on to the driver. Traffic was slow moving in the heat and it took us five minutes to arrive at the Ormonds' unremarkable town house in the middle of a block near our new home.

We climbed out of the carriage and walked our calling cards up to the door. A young footman answered, held out a silver tray for us to put our cards on, and had us wait in the hall. He climbed a flight of stairs with the tray to the main parlor. As soon as he was out of sight, Phyllida said, "He's barely out of the nursery."

"Perhaps he's just begun his training," I suggested, looking around the empty hallway, where old framed silhouettes decorated otherwise bare walls.

"Mildred always fought a battle between having everything perfect and being miserly. At his age, his wages would be minimal. I guess miserly won out." Phyllida shook her head.

I didn't get a chance to warn her to keep quiet before the rapid steps on the stairs proclaimed the boy's arrival. "Her ladyship is this way."

We followed at a sedate pace and walked into a parlor full of statues. Busts covered every table. A full-sized Greek maiden stood between two windows. A piece of a frieze stood in a corner. After we finished our round of curtsies, I asked, "Are you a collector?"

"Not me. My late husband. He shipped them back from Italy and Greece when he was a young man. Aren't they lovely?"

"They are," Phyllida said. "Thank you for inviting us today, Lady Mildred. I'm so happy to have dear Georgina here so I can introduce her to all my friends."

"It's lovely for you to have family around you again, after—" Lady Ormond gave a sniff as if something smelled bad.

"And I'm so happy to finally get to see London," I added with a big smile.

"You weren't presented at court?" Lady Ormond asked, the beginnings of horror etched on her voice.

"No. I went overseas to join my father before I would have been presented. I married overseas and lived there until my husband died." Phyllida and I had never completely organized my story, and I was starting to worry.

"What did he die of?" Lady Ormond asked as she handed me a cup of tea.

"A fever."

"So common in the colonies, I've heard." There was that sniff of distaste again.

"Unfortunately, yes."

"How did you get back in touch again?" Lady Ormond was a born inquisitor.

"Who said we were ever out of touch?" Phyllida asked in a haughty tone I'd seldom heard, reminding both Lady Ormond and myself that she was the daughter of an earl.

Lady Ormond gave her a brief smile and turned her beady-eyed attention on me. "Tell me about the Duke of Blackford when he was in India. It's a period of time he doesn't discuss often."

"Then perhaps I need to honor what appear to be his wishes and not say anything," I replied with a smile. "Do you live in London year-round, or do you spend part of the year at the Ormond family estate?"

"The current Lord Ormond and I find time spent apart suits us both. As he rarely leaves the countryside, I find the London home quite satisfactory. Have you found living halfway around the world a solution to any troubles you have with whoever inherited your late husband's estate?"

"I inherited." I smiled and took a sip of tea.

"One of the perks of marrying a businessman," Phyllida said with a hint of a smirk. "No entailments."

Lady Ormond gave a smile as weak as her tea. "Are you planning to spend much time in the Duke of Blackford's company?"

"That rather depends on the duke, don't you think?"

"Is he planning a country house party to celebrate your renewed acquaintance?"

Dear heavens, the woman was nosy. Fortunately, there was a ritual about these visits that required us to leave after a short time. Otherwise, I would have struggled not to run screaming out of Lady Ormond's parlor during this inquisition. I tried a neutral "I have no idea."

Then, when it was time to leave, Lady Ormond said, "What a shame your cousin Clara didn't survive to see you arrive in London."

"You knew my husband's cousin Clara Gattenger?" I asked, hoping I didn't sound as eager as I felt. As a gossip, I couldn't trust Lady Ormond's remarks, but there might be a nugget in there.

"Not well. She didn't go out much in society, burdened as she was with a husband who was neither titled nor wealthy."

"I heard his ship designs were brilliant."

"That may well be, but how often can you design a ship? They only need one design to build many ships. The Gattengers were short of money, and Clara was getting tired of doing without."

I could hardly wait to get out of Lady Ormond's house to ask Phyllida if the Gattengers were in financial trouble.

Her response to my question in the cab was a mulish "Kenny would never have killed Clara. Not for all the money in the world."

I kept my doubts to myself and said, "I didn't say he would, but could he have been involved in something that led to another person coming into the study and killing Clara? Were they short of money?"

Phyllida gave a sniff and said, "They were the happiest of

couples." Her stiff-necked gaze out the opposite window told me I'd get nothing more from her.

Mercifully, we only left our cards at our second stop, since the lady was not at home. Whether she was truly out visiting or lying down to escape the heat, I couldn't guess. I did feel certain I hadn't offended anyone yet and so wasn't being snubbed.

As luck would have it, at our third stop, Lady Bennett was receiving callers in her drawing room. Since Clara Gattenger had spent the last afternoon of her life with Lady Bennett and came back "ready to do murder," in the words of her maid, I looked forward to this encounter.

Years of training hadn't deserted Phyllida, and I took my hints from her. She waited in the doorway for the footman to announce us, and then she strolled across the room to our hostess. I followed, staring at our hostess.

The closer I moved to Lady Bennett, the better looking she appeared. Perhaps over forty, she had been gifted with creamy skin, fair hair, wide blue eyes, and the money to dress in a style that best suited her taste and her figure. I have freckles, unruly reddish hair, and seldom any money to waste on clothes. In short, she was a woman I instinctively disliked.

"Lady Bennett, I'm Lady Phyllida Monthalf. I'm glad we called on your at-home day. I'm introducing my cousin's widow, Mrs. Edgar Monthalf, to London society. Mrs. Monthalf has just returned from the colonies." We both curtsied.

"How are you enjoying London, Mrs. Monthalf?" I could tell by the appraising look and fake smile that Lady Bennett had looked me over and decided she could afford to dismiss me even as she returned the curtsy.

"It makes quite a change from life aboard ship or living in the Far East. This room is lovely."

"Thank you. I made all the decorating decisions myself."

"How fortunate you are to have such an agreeable husband," I said, wanting to learn as much as I could about this woman.

"I'm a widow, too. I was fortunate that my husband left me this house and the wherewithal to enjoy life." She looked me over again. "Few women are so lucky." Her expression said she didn't include me in that number.

The pink sleeves of her dress were large enough from shoulder to elbow for her waist to fit through. Mauve material peeked between the pink in every pleat set into her sleeves and skirt. Her dress had elaborate dark blue and mauve trim on the wrists, waist, and hem. No doubt next year the style would be different, and she'd have new dresses made.

While I liked my yellow linen shirtwaist dress, with its pretty tucks and wide sleeves, I'd remake mine as I had time. My dress was plain, due in part to a lack of time for Madame Leclerc to work her magic and in part to my sensible tastes.

I really didn't like Lady Bennett's overdone gown and didn't want to lie and say I admired her taste. Falling back on convention, I said, "I'm very sorry for your loss. Was this a recent event?"

She withdrew slightly, showing her contempt for an ignorant provincial. "Over two years ago. Otherwise, I'd be forced to wear black."

"Imagine. Being forced to abandon colors for two years. That would be so dreary. And they say the colonials are backward." Before, we'd just been mildly catty. Now I'd let my claws out a little.

Phyllida gave me a sharp look while Lady Bennett was faced away and said, "I can't wait for this ghastly weather to end. I like sunny days, but not ones where I feel as if I'll melt into my shoes."

Lady Bennett turned to gaze at her. "Yes, hasn't it been frightful." Motioning us to sit down, she took a wing chair and continued, "Lady Phyllida, I don't remember seeing you out in society in London in recent years. Where have you been?"

"Oh . . ." Phyllida blushed and stammered, "Abroad for a while. In the country for a while." Then she took a breath, raised her chin to look down on Lady Bennett, and said with complete assurance, "I felt a need to be away from the bustle of London after the horror my brother inflicted on us all."

Lady Bennett mustn't have expected Phyllida to be so forthright, because she blushed and quickly said to me, "Are you planning on remaining in London?"

"I hope to. I was a child the last time I had a chance to explore all London has to offer. If that's all right with Lady Phyllida."

"But will it be cosmopolitan enough for you, having lived in the—Far East, you said?"

Either she didn't believe me or she was testing me for something. I wondered which it was. "Yes, a very hot and humid Singapore, so I don't find this weather so shocking. And I believe London is cosmopolitan enough for anyone."

"Singapore? How lovely. My sister and her husband will be arriving very soon from Singapore. Perhaps you know them? The Viscount and Viscountess Chattelsfield."

My mind froze for an instant. I hadn't planned on this at all. "I didn't know anyone titled. My social contacts were among the businessmen and traders of the city and their families."

"What a pity. I thought everyone knew them."

Into the uncomfortable silence that fell, I said, "Tell me, did you redo your entire house after your husband died? I ask because we've taken rented quarters while we try to decide what to do."

She smiled as if I made very easy prey. "I'd lived here with my husband for several years before his death. I'd redecorated most of the house before his passing, so there was little left for me to do to put my imprint on all the rooms."

"This room is very light and feminine. And the wallpaper is quite striking." The oversized blue flowers in the wallpaper were the same color as Lady Bennett's eyes. I'd have disliked it less in any other house, where it didn't proclaim *Compliment my mistress*.

She must have missed my dislike because she gave me a genuine smile and said, "When I saw it, I just knew I had to have it."

I'll bet she did. Phyllida frowned at me before I could say what I was thinking, so I changed the subject. "How do you keep cool in this weather? We went to a higher elevation in the East, but that's impossible in London."

"Anyone who is anyone is leaving London for country house parties. Parliament has adjourned until the weather improves. The queen and the court left for the seaside at Osborne House."

"So the government just shuts down in midsummer?"

"This frightful heat wave has been of surprisingly long duration. And while not at a higher elevation, country estates are far from London's traffic and the heat isn't trapped between street after street of houses."

I gave her a vacuous smile. "I feel cooler just thinking about it. Country houses. The seaside. It all sounds wonderful."

She gave me a pitying look. "Oh, but you have to have friends with country houses to invite you. Otherwise, every year London becomes so stuffy and dreary at the end of the season. That's not until mid-August," she added as if to the socially deficient.

I really didn't like this woman.

There was one more subject I needed to cover before Phyllida and I finished our standard quarter-hour visit with Lady Bennett. I needed to mention the real reason I was there that day. "I believe you knew my husband's cousin, Mrs. Kenneth Gattenger. Clara Gattenger."

Lady Bennett paled. She tapped her lips with one well-manicured finger. "Mrs. Gattenger. I know we were introduced, but we were barely acquaintances. I don't think I've seen her in six months."

Clara's maid had said this woman had called on Clara only the week before. "When Mrs. Gattenger knew I was coming to London, she mentioned she would introduce us, as you and she were friendly."

"We had been, but since her marriage, she only seemed to have time for her husband."

"Well, we widows don't have that problem, do we?" I said and smiled.

"Yes. How lovely," Lady Bennett said, but whether she meant the freedom widows have, or the arrival of more visitors, which effectively blocked my questions about Clara, was hard to tell.

As we went through curtsies and introductions, I wondered why Lady Bennett wouldn't admit she'd visited with Clara the day of her death.

Her guests were introduced as the Dowager Duchess of Bad Ramshed and her youngest daughter, Lady Magda. Magda was a quiet blonde who stayed out of reach of her mother. The duchess heard my name as Mrs. Monthalf and asked, "What does your husband do?" as if I'd announced I carried bubonic plague.

"Nothing now. He died. He was a businessman in the Far East."

"He was a shopkeeper?" Her tone rose as if I'd stepped into the parlor in my shift.

I smiled and said, "A little wealthier than that."

Lady Bennett maneuvered us toward the door and quietly said in our ears, "My condolences on the loss of your cousin."

"What has happened?" the dowager duchess demanded. She had excellent hearing and dreadful manners.

We all turned and stared at her in silence. Lady Bennett blushed and looked down. "She was murdered. Her husband is in prison for the murder."

"Not the ship designer, Gattenger?" the dowager grumbled, her accent thickening with harsh syllables.

"Yes," Lady Bennett said, looking more uncomfortable by the moment.

I took a step toward the older woman. What would a visiting female German aristocrat know about British engineers? "Do you have connections to the Royal Navy and the Admiralty?"

"No. I just know this wouldn't happen in Germany. Their work is too important to allow them to be involved in tawdry scandals."

Phyllida made a small choking sound.

I turned to Lady Bennett and said our good-byes before taking Phyllida by the arm and leading her out of the parlor.

"Why do they let people like that into the country?" Phyllida growled.

I wasn't certain whether the ladies heard us. I certainly didn't care.

After leaving our calling cards at a few more houses, we returned to discover the duke sitting in the most comfortable chair in our parlor. He rose when we walked in and bowed to Lady Phyllida. "I hope you ladies will attend the theater with me tonight. It is the final performance of Shakespeare for the season at the Lyceum. Everyone will be there." He put a slight emphasis on everyone.

"I'm afraid Phyllida and I already have an escort to that play," I answered.

"What?" Even his questions could sound like commands.

I lowered my voice as I stepped close to the duke, ensuring the servants couldn't eavesdrop. "You wanted me to question Sir Henry. Not only will I be able to do that, I will get a chance to search his study. We're having dinner at his house."

"That's not safe."

"You think he's involved with the theft and you want me to question him. We need to find out if the plans are in his study."

"How are we supposed to begin our affair if you're seen with Sir Henry?"

I grinned. "You'll have to work harder. Now, if you'll excuse us, Your Grace, we need to dress for dinner and the theater."

"Georgia, be careful. One lovely, courageous woman was killed over those blueprints. We don't want to lose another."

My smile widened. It was nice to see Blackford discomfited. "It won't be the first time I've done something like this. Just in nicer surroundings this time."

He reached out and grabbed my wrist. "Georgia, I'm serious. This man has a dangerous reputation."

"So do you, Your Grace."

"Georgia." He stared into my eyes, and I glimpsed a flash of fear.

I slid my hand around to hold his wrist. I could feel his pulse speed. "It'll be all right, Ranleigh."

Blackford drew in a deep breath, his face taking on the expression of his pirate-raider ancestors before a massacre, and strode out of our parlor.

"Oh, dear," Phyllida said.

CHAPTER SEVEN

OH, dear, indeed. The dinner party turned out to be just four of us: Sir Henry, his brother Robert, Phyllida, and me. The two men shared a town house laid out like the Gattengers', with the dining room in front on the ground floor.

The study—every gentleman had a study—would be the room behind the dining room or one floor up behind the parlor. I hoped I'd find it on the ground floor, which would make my job easier. But I had no idea how Phyllida would be able to keep both men occupied while I searched Sir Henry's desk.

The clear soup course was good. The next, an ordinary fish, was fair. We discussed the weather, gossip about the royal family, and, on Robert Stanford's part, the dearth of interesting people in London during this heat wave. It turned out he was leaving the next day for a holiday at a hotel in Torquay, where he claimed the fashionable were staying.

"Are you in the shipbuilding business with your brother, Mr. Stanford?" I asked.

He shuddered. "No, I'm a barrister in Gray's Inn."

"I hope I never have need of your services," Phyllida said.

Sir Henry smiled weakly and said, "I suppose, Mrs. Monthalf, you had quite an experience with solicitors while sorting out your late husband's business affairs. Especially since it was a large fortune."

"I don't know that I'd call it a large fortune, but Edgar made certain I'd be more than comfortable." Phyllida and I had never considered how much money my fictitious husband left me. I didn't think the question would come up. Discussion of money was never allowed in proper society.

"I hope you have it invested wisely," Sir Henry said.

At that moment, the maids served the fowl course, some rather dry chicken, and conversation stopped. As the maids were leaving with the fish plates, I decided to turn the conversation away from money. "Mr. Stanford, as a barrister, have you heard of the case of Mr. Kenneth Gattenger, accused of murdering his wife? He's innocent, of course."

"Yes. Interesting case."

"His wife was my husband's cousin."

"Oh? Who's Gattenger's solicitor?"

"Do you know, I've never thought to ask. We must remember that the next time we visit him, Phyllida."

Phyllida gave me a faint smile.

"The newspaper reporters have already started circling the Inns of Court about the Gattenger murder. It will be a sensation. Do you know why Whitehall is holding back the prosecution?" With the scandalous gossip he'd already shared and the eagerness in his voice, Robert was leaving a bad taste in my mouth. He was not someone I'd want to see on a regular basis.

Phyllida looked like she might be ill.

Sir Henry must have seen the looks on his guests' faces, because he said, "That's enough, Robert."

"I'm sorry. I let my enthusiasm for the law run away with my good manners."

We both nodded to him, and Phyllida asked if he ever had time with his busy profession to read literature.

The mutton course, the salad course, and the iced fruit course passed without me finding a way to check out the study. As the coffee and cheese course arrived, Robert stood, wished us enjoyment of the play, and said he had a previous engagement.

We said how nice it was to meet him without displaying a trace of irony. Listening to his footsteps, I could tell he went out the front door immediately after leaving us.

After waiting a moment to make sure he didn't return, I asked if there was somewhere where I could freshen up. Sir Henry reddened and gave me directions to the back of the house on the landing between this floor and the next.

I gestured toward Sir Henry with my eyes as I looked at Phyllida, hoping she read my meaning. Then I rose and excused myself.

Phyllida started a stream of talk aimed at diverting Sir Henry before he had time to resume his seat or I had left the room. There were no servants in sight as I hurried to the door toward the back of the ground floor.

It was still daylight out and the draperies were open when I looked inside to see I'd found the study. Now if I could search it thoroughly without anyone finding me, the evening would be a success.

I started with the drawers in the desk. Knowing the blueprints would be bulky, it wasn't hard to eliminate possibilities quickly. Most of the books on the shelves were too thin, even hollowed out, to hold the plans. The few that were thick enough were intact. None of them were law books. Robert must have his study upstairs while Sir Henry used this room.

The only place left to check was a handsome file cabinet. Locked.

I pulled out a hairpin and began to poke around in the lock. I heard a click and slid the first drawer open. Blueprints.

Dozens of blueprints. I'd have to look at them all to make sure Gattenger's warship plans weren't there.

I checked the other drawers. More blueprints. I pulled out one page. I could tell it was for a ship, but I couldn't tell which one. It was dated from three years before and numbered. Sliding the paper back into place, I checked another, and then one from a different drawer. Different pages, different dates, probably different ships.

This would be the perfect place to hide Gattenger's stolen blueprints. The trouble was, I'd need a long time to check each page to know whether it belonged to the stolen plans, and there were hundreds of sheets.

Phyllida's voice came loudly through the closed door. "I'm sure she'll be back in a moment. Let's wait in the dining room, and you can tell me the family story behind the cutlery."

"Of course." Sir Henry sounded both puzzled and resigned.

I quickly refolded the sheet I had opened, hoping no one heard the paper rustling, and shut and locked the drawer. I shoved my hairpin in my coiffure and listened at the door for their receding footsteps. Then I opened the door enough to peek into the hall. A maid was coming up the stairs. I hurried toward her to make it appear I had just come downstairs and then walked into the dining room. "I hope you haven't been waiting long."

The maid came in the room behind me and gave me a funny look. There was no way to know if she'd tell her employer her suspicions. At least she wouldn't have an opportunity to tell him until after the play.

On the carriage ride to the theater, Sir Henry asked, "Are you getting good advice from your bankers on where to invest your money?"

"It sounds reasonable. Why?"

"I'd hate to see you taken advantage of with your unfamiliarity with British businesses."

"They've been very conservative."

"Not always the best policy," he said, nodding sagely.

I suspected I knew where this was headed. "Why not?"

"The only way to get a decent return on your money is by investing in new fields, new manufacturing processes. Old methods will just slowly drain away your money. And bankers prefer the tried-and-true methods of the past."

"What would you advise?"

He smiled. "I'm not advising you. As a friend, I'm just pointing out a fact of business that you should consider." Then he turned the conversation to Shakespearean plays he'd seen.

If he were planting a seed, hoping I'd invest in his shipyard, he did it very carefully. Sir Henry was shrewder than I'd thought.

We arrived at the Lyceum to find the usual bustle and noise of a theater crowd. The sun sat low on the horizon behind the buildings, but it was no cooler in the long shadows. It wouldn't be fully dark, bringing the hope of a breeze, until after the performance.

Two couples who'd chosen to stop and talk in the middle of the sidewalk trapped Phyllida outside the theater, while a cluster of dandies jostled me as I attempted to enter the main doors. Sir Henry kept busy moving us forward with a polite word to the two couples and a quelling look at the dandies.

Once inside, the lobby was jammed with heated, perfumed

bodies, and I couldn't draw a breath until Sir Henry created a path through the crowd and we slipped through the door leading to the inside of the theater.

Baron von Steubfeld was already seated along the aisle with Lady Bennett. As they stood so we could get past them to our seats, the temperature dropped ten degrees.

Of course, there was no choice but for a round of introductions and pleasantries, especially since Lady Phyllida said before she sat down, "Why, Lady Bennett, I didn't expect to see you again tonight. Your house is so lovely."

She inclined her head. "Thank you."

Sir Henry did the introductions while the baron glowered at us, but he did a perfunctory job of kissing Lady Phyllida's hand and then mine.

Seen close up, even on the sloping floor of the theater, the baron was tall. He appeared to have the lean musculature of a horseman or a fencer beneath his high-collared Prussian military uniform. His eyes, a bright blue, were cold with dismissal.

He returned to his seat and pointedly addressed a comment to Lady Bennett, ignoring the rest of us.

"I beg your pardon, von Steubfeld, but we need to get to our seats." Hearing Blackford's rich baritone, I turned quickly to find him standing in the aisle by our row with an attractive brunette in her early to mid thirties.

The baron rose and he and the duke exchanged the stiffest of bows. When Blackford squeezed past us, he introduced us to the brunette as Lady Peters. She greeted Phyllida and me formally and then Sir Henry with greater warmth.

Wanting to push forward with the investigation, I turned to Blackford and his companion. "How nice to see you again, and to meet you, Lady Peters. Do you reside in London year-round?"

"Most of the year. I have family who have a château in France and I try to spend the winter with them. The weather is milder there." She had pretty brown hair that her maid must have spent hours putting curls into, and soft brown eyes. She looked kind, gently bred, ordinary. Would she be the successful candidate for Duchess of Blackford?

I went for the blandest reply. "Is London weather truly so awful?"

Sir Henry tapped my arm to get my attention and said, "Lady Bennett said you lived in Singapore and didn't know who the Viscount Chattelsfield is. Surely you know he's a member of the executive council for the governor of the Straits Settlements."

I gave him a smile as I made a quick decision. "I knew who he was. We weren't important enough to socialize with people like that, and I stayed away from politics. I was never introduced to him, and so didn't know him."

Turning back to Lady Peters, I glanced at Blackford's face. He looked worried.

"Lady Peters—" I began.

She gave the stage a quick glance. "Would it be forward of me to ask you and Lady Phyllida to call tomorrow? I'd so like to talk to you, and I'm afraid the play is about to start."

She was right. The houselights were being lowered. "We'd enjoy calling on you."

After exchanging smiles with me, she turned her attention to the stage. I gave Sir Henry, who'd been watching me, a flirty grin and then gazed at the rising curtain.

At intermission, we all rose and joined the throng in the lobby. I glanced around and made sure I didn't know anyone in the audience who might endanger my role in our real-life drama. The men went off to battle the crowd for chilled wine while we ladies looked at each other, smiled, and hoped someone else would start the conversation.

"How are you handling the heat, Lady Peters?" Phyllida asked.

"This is the worst summer I've seen in London. I don't know how the residents of the East End can survive, poor creatures."

"That's their problem. They are poor creatures," Lady Bennett said.

"Let us pray for a break in this weather," I said. "For everyone's sakes."

"I'm grateful to be leaving London in a few days," Lady Bennett said, a smug smile on her face.

"Where are you going?" Phyllida asked.

"Lord Harwin is having a country house party at his estate in Gloucestershire. The rural air must be cooler than London, all hemmed in as we are here."

"Does he have a large house?" I asked, unable to ask the question I wanted the answer for. Is Baron von Steubfeld leaving London?

"One of those massive Georgian palaces, with gardens stretching in all directions," Lady Bennett replied.

"I went to a house party there years ago. Chaperones behind every fern," Phyllida said. "Of course, the old countess is long dead, and I'm sure no such protection is needed for widows."

Her neat insinuation made Lady Peters's eyes widen and I had to bite my lip. Lady Bennett flared. "If you're asking if the baron will be there, he will be. I can assure you our behavior is above reproach. The current countess is as protective of her household's good name as some long-ago lady."

Which only meant they had to be discreet. All of us knew that, but no one dared mention the obvious.

"What are your plans, Lady Peters?" I asked into the silence that had fallen between us.

"I don't know. I hope to leave town soon, but my plans aren't finalized. And you, Mrs. Monthalf?"

"I've only just arrived in England. I've put myself completely in Lady Phyllida's hands, and so far, she's been full of surprises." Oh, my, yes. She seemed to be recalling all the skills she hadn't needed in nearly twenty years. I doubted that after this investigation was over she would be satisfied to live with a mere bookshop owner. Especially if that bookshop owner found Ken Gattenger was involved in the death of her beloved cousin. The possibility dropped a boulder onto my heart.

Lady Bennett gave me a vicious smile. "My sister and her husband are due to arrive in just a few days, probably before we leave for Lord Harwin's. I look forward to introducing you to them, since you never had the opportunity to meet them in Singapore."

I gave her a wide-eyed innocent gaze in return. "That's very kind of you, but they might not approve. Neither Edgar nor I were important enough to know the colony's rulers."

Then I sent up a prayer this investigation would be over before the Chattelsfields arrived.

SIR HENRY SAW us into our rented dwelling and then drove off as soon as we went inside. We'd no sooner shut the door when the footman answered a knock. It was Blackford. "Was the evening instructive?" he asked.

My insides sank with fatigue. I was going to have to learn to get by on very little sleep if I planned to spend any time in my bookshop. "You might as well come upstairs. Sir Henry has file drawers full of ship blueprints. It would take longer than I had to go through them all to see if the stolen plans were mixed in with drawings he has legally."

Phyllida reached the parlor first and collapsed into a chair. "When will this heat wave end?"

I stood by an open window and fanned myself with my hand. "How did you manage to sit in the same row as us? We didn't know we were going until this afternoon."

"After I spoke to you, I found out where you would be seated and exchanged the seats next to you for other tickets. Winky Cavendish was most happy to oblige."

I resisted the urge to ask who Winky Cavendish was and what Blackford had paid to get him to "oblige." I was more interested in who Lady Peters was and whether she and the duke were an item. "Have you known Lady Peters long?"

"Actually, I'd known her late husband much longer. He died four years ago, leaving her in a delicate condition. Fortunately for her, the child was male, so she gave birth to the current Lord Peters. She's a lovely woman. You'll like her. And she's frequently squired about by Sir Henry Stanford."

"So you and she aren't—"

"Good grief, no, Georgia. You are not coming between me and a lady friend." He paused for a moment, shook his head, and said, "But that's not your concern. Worry about catching the burglar and finding the plans for the warship before they end up in German hands."

I set aside my surprise and relief at his words and said, "I've been thinking. The drawings would be easy to pass in the privacy of a carriage before or after a dinner or a theater performance. Then it wouldn't matter how bulky they are. And have you considered the drawings might come into the embassy wrapped around fish or greens from a nearby shop?" There were too many ways to get those warship plans into the embassy. This was a hopeless enterprise.

"I hope, Georgia, the Germans aren't as clever as you. We're watching every time they go to the shops and markets. Their mail is being examined—"

"That's illegal."

The duke was in front of me in an instant, leaning forward and glaring into my eyes with a frightening intensity. "The Germans must be stopped from getting their hands on those plans. I don't exaggerate when I say Britain's future depends on it. Everything else is secondary."

I put my hands up, palms out, to stop him, but I immediately bumped up against the front of his coat. The wool was smooth and fine, like thick satin under my fingers. I was close enough to smell smoke and old dust on his fresh linen. And close enough to see in his eyes that arguing would be pointless. "All right. We will stop them. What have you been doing besides bartering theater tickets and reading other people's mail?"

"Seeing to my interests, and my country's interests." Our gazes remained locked.

There was one point Fogarty couldn't get the answer to and the duke hadn't told us. "Why is Scotland Yard holding Ken Gattenger for the murder of his wife if they believe the Germans are trying to get their hands on the warship blueprints? That has to argue for a third party."

"They believe Gattenger was a willing participant in the theft, and Clara's death was due to her objection to his treason."

"Kenny wouldn't have killed Clara," Phyllida said quietly, staring straight ahead.

Blackford softened his tone. "Perhaps it was an accident. One he couldn't prevent."

"Why would he commit treason?" I asked.

"Money. The Germans have offered him much more than Her Majesty for those designs."

"But the Admiralty has them."

"He could sell them twice. The Germans were willing to pay for an identical copy slipped to a so-called burglar. Gattenger could make a fortune and not appear to be a traitor. It pains me to tell you, Georgia, but the government found a letter from the Germans offering Gattenger a large sum of money for a set of the drawings. They believe Gattenger agreed. He was seen talking to a German agent two nights before the murder. Gattenger is staying in prison, charged with murder and treason."

As much as I wanted to doubt the government's evidence, the set of his jaw deterred me from questioning him further at that moment. I knew the futility of contradicting him when he was in a mood. At least he didn't appear to like the current situation, either.

Now I knew what the evidence was that Fogarty had heard rumored.

"I don't believe it." Phyllida walked out of the room, shutting the door softly behind her.

I turned and looked out the open window. Heat lay on the city like a shroud. There wasn't a breath of air anywhere. No one would want to do anything more energetic than read, and here I was, away from the bookshop every afternoon. "Will we be going anywhere tomorrow night?"

"I'm certain we will. Why?"

I shrugged, wondering how long I could keep up with both the bookshop and the investigation.

The duke walked up behind me. "Georgina," he said softly in my ear, "is Lady Bennett's sister going to present a problem?"

"I hope not. Is the Viscount Chattelsfield truly on the executive council to the governor? I can't look it up until tomorrow. And is Mr. Monthalf supposed to have been an important enough personage to know him?"

"Yes, but keep on with whatever story you've given so far."

I swung around, my skirt twirling around my legs, and looked up into his eyes. "I'll have to. Wish me luck."

His smile was warm as he said, "Luck."

After the duke left, I went upstairs to undress for bed. When I reached my room, Emma was waiting.

"Here's your nightgown. And I saw Sumner."

I was instantly alert. "What's happened?"

"Nothing to make you jump like that. Sumner is my gentleman caller, which you allow as long as my work doesn't slip, and he came by while you were out this afternoon. The bookshop is doing splendidly. Watch is being kept on the Germans so closely that a protest has been lodged at Whitehall. Von Steubfeld was told threats had been made against his life by anarchists and extra security was in place for his protection."

I was only interested in part of what she said. "How splendidly?"

"We'll see in the morning when you check the ledgers and the receipts. And you'll want to know that Sir Broderick was visited by a lady who attended the musical evening at Lord Francis's last night. She asked him if he'd ever heard of this mysterious Mrs. Monthalf."

Oh, dear. Was Sir Broderick up to date on the character I was playing?

"He told her he knew about Lord Monthalf's murders in

London, and while he knew part of the family had gone to the Far East years ago, he didn't know anything about what had become of them. Then he questioned her about what she'd learned." Emma was about to bubble over with excitement, which made her helping me get out of my dress difficult.

I put my hands on her arms. "Tell me what she said, and then help me undress."

She nodded. "She said you're an old friend of the Duke of Blackford's from India, and he is obviously smitten with you."

I wished that were true.

"They're buying your story. Your entrance into society is assured. Isn't that great?"

"Yes." It would be even better if we quickly found those plans so I could get out of society and back to managing my bookshop.

She slipped off my dress and began to unlace my evening corset. "You don't sound very pleased."

"Sir Broderick and the duke appear to have forgotten I have a whole life that doesn't revolve around espionage."

The yank Emma gave to the laces told me whose side she was on. "You've forgotten two things. You dragged Phyllida into this by promising to find her cousin's killer." The corset was tight enough to make breathing difficult. "And you have very good friends who know the business and will take good care of your bookshop. Trust them."

"I'm trying. I really am. But I can't do anyone any good if you break my ribs."

Emma considered for a moment whether I'd learned my lesson before she loosened my corset strings.

CHAPTER EIGHT

THE next morning I was up, dressed, and eating a light breakfast when one of the maids brought me a note addressed to Georgina Monthalf. I set down my tea and opened it.

> *Georgia Fenchurch, I know what you're up to.*
> *Stop immediately or I will give away your identity.*

I glanced around the empty dining room as if the writer were lurking in my house. Blast it. Someone knew my real name and my role in the investigation. I'd been careful to keep my real life separate from the people I was investigating, but someone had found out.

Sir Jonah Denby, who knew my real name and that I was involved in the search, could be the author, but he was supposed to be on our side. I hadn't heard from Sir Broderick on my request for information on Sir Jonah. I needed to telephone him from the bookshop.

Or someone had found out from Madame Leclerc, but who would go to all that trouble? And what about the German spies? Were they onto me already?

I considered my options. If I told Emma and Phyllida, Emma would shrug it off, but Phyllida would immediately insist we stop before we were hurt.

The worst the writer threatened to do was give away my real identity to everyone involved in the investigation. The only way I could imagine proceeding with this investigation was to wait to see what happened.

There was no point in telling anyone and upsetting them before it became necessary.

I stuffed the note up my sleeve with my handkerchief and finished my breakfast in time to travel with Emma to the bookshop.

We took a different route than the morning before, which was Emma's way of assuring we learned every street and alley and knew how to reach someplace safe if we had to escape an attack. On the way there, I told her what I'd learned about the baron and Lady Bennett going to Lord Harwin's.

"Could someone else be carrying the plans to Germany for the baron? Someone we're not watching?" Emma asked.

"Such as the Dowager Duchess of Bad Ramshed or someone in her party? I think the duke's going to learn more about that today, leaving us free to worry about the bookshop."

"You don't have to worry about the bookshop, Georgia. You have very good friends who are looking out for you."

I nodded. She was right. But I still worried.

It turned out I had good reason to. As soon as we opened the door, a half-dozen customers descended on us. Their spokesman, a heavyset woman in black with a choleric face and sweat already running down her cheeks, said, "Miss Fenchurch, why aren't you selling the two-shilling copies of *The Ruined Castle* by Mrs. Hepplewhite?"

The cheaply bound two-shilling editions were our best sellers, especially ones written by the gothic and adventure writers. "We are, Mrs. Appleton. Or we will be."

"Other shops had them on the shelves yesterday afternoon. If they hadn't sold out, we'd not be here today."

How many customers had I lost by not being here yesterday afternoon? "Just a moment. Let me check in the back."

I walked to the office, the half-dozen customers following. Two large boxes sat on the floor, unchecked against the inventory still attached to one of the boxes. I opened them and found Mrs. Hepplewhite's newest on top.

I grabbed a dozen. "Here we are. I'll take these up to the counter and we can take care of you immediately."

"You'll have to do better than this next time if you want to keep our business." Nevertheless, Mrs. Appleton led the parade to the counter.

"You're right. I do. And I will."

I'd almost reached the counter when Grace walked in. I set her to checking the inventory in the boxes and then getting the books shelved. The women left with their purchases, still grumbling but not as loudly.

I looked at Emma and sighed. "Don't worry?"

"We'll get it straightened out."

"Get what straightened out?" Frances asked as she entered the shop.

I took a deep breath so I wouldn't yell at her. "When orders come in from the popular publishers, we need to check the inventory lists and shelve the books as quickly as possible. Most of the time, unfortunately, they come in the afternoon, when Emma and I have to work on the investigation. Maybe if you put Grace onto that chore while you wait on customers, it won't put too much of a strain on you."

Frances stepped back and folded her arms over her chest, her hat still perched on her gray topknot. "Grace had to do something for Lord Barnwood yesterday afternoon, or I would have started her on those boxes in the back."

"Next time you're in that situation, call Sir Broderick and have him send someone to help you. Quickly getting new stock of these big sellers on the shelves is important."

"Everything around here is important, or so you tell me. If you don't like the job I'm doing, just say so." She was nearly spitting out the words and still dressed to go out.

I knew none of this was her fault. More selfishly, I couldn't work on this investigation without her good-natured help in running the bookshop. "Frances, I'm less familiar with the character I'm pretending to be than you are with running a bookshop. I know I'm putting a lot on your shoulders, but you have good instincts and you're doing well. Much better than I am. Don't think I'm not grateful." I lifted my hands palm upward. "But today I'm tired and confused and so far, our investigation hasn't gone anywhere. We're being fed lies and half-truths and gossip."

The anger left her eyes, replaced by concern. No matter which members of the Archivist Society were actively involved in the investigation, we were all distressed when things weren't going well and proud when we succeeded. "What's happened?"

"The baron is leaving with his lady friend in a few days for a house party at an estate in Gloucestershire. His lady friend lied about spending the afternoon with Clara Gattenger on the day she died. Ken Gattenger lied about arguing with Clara and the fire in the study fireplace on a hot evening. The police have evidence Gattenger was selling a copy of his warship plans to the Germans and there's gossip he's short of money. The police think Clara died in an accident while trying to stop Gattenger from handing off the ship design. And if the baron told the truth about not leaving England in the foreseeable future, he doesn't plan to touch the stolen plans himself. That means they could be handed off to anyone."

Frances nodded. "Oh, dear. You do have your hands full. How is Phyllida handling the possibility that her cousin was killed by her husband?"

"Badly. She refuses to consider it."

"What are you going to do?"

I sighed. "The only thing I can do. Keep watching the baron and his friends and hope someone slips. And try to get someone to tell me the truth."

The bell jingled over the door, marking the arrival of more customers for *The Ruined Castle*.

We ran from one task to another, one customer to another, for hours. I took a few minutes off to look up the Viscount Chattelsfield and Sir Jonah Denby. They were who they were reported to be. I didn't find the time to telephone Sir Broderick to discover if he'd learned anything more revealing about Sir Jonah.

About the time business slowed down in the shop, Blackford, along with Sumner, climbed out of his plain coach, the driver and footman dressed as workmen. "I see you managed to awaken early again this morning," Blackford said as soon as he walked in.

Ignoring him, Emma set down her duster and walked over to speak to Sumner. The ruined side of Sumner's face was exposed to view, since he wore the collarless shirt and cap of a workman. Grace leaned on her broom and Frances paused behind the counter. Neither reacted to Sumner's ugly scar, as if they were accustomed to seeing his face.

"I'd appreciate not being kept up so late, Your Grace," I replied. "What brings you here?"

He held up a single piece of paper. "I thought you might help me with this."

I walked over and looked at the sheet. It contained names, addresses, and descriptions of three burglars Fogarty had gleaned from his friends at Scotland Yard after showing them the drawing Gattenger made of his attacker. "I'd be glad to, but why aren't Fogarty and his friends at Scotland Yard checking this out?"

"These men, and their friends and family, can spot a bobby, or a retired sergeant, at a hundred yards. We are obviously not with the police."

There was no way you could disguise Blackford's aristocratic ancestry. "That's true."

"Let's go."

I caught Emma grabbing Sumner's hand and giving it a squeeze. He didn't pull away or look shocked before he turned to join Blackford. Good for her. I had no idea if Blackford paid Sumner well enough to support a wife, but I wished her well. Sumner was a decent, if frightening-looking, man.

When had they had time to build a closeness? I'd spent more time with Blackford than Emma had with Sumner, and we certainly weren't more than associates. I wished our relationship were different, but that was impossible. He was a duke.

And all he cared about was finding a set of ship blueprints.

"I'll be back shortly," I said to Frances and set my straw boater on my head. It wasn't every day I hunted a thief with the duke. The last time, I'd nearly died. I took a breath and straightened my shoulders as I walked out the door. I'd left my white cotton gloves from the bookshop on; they weren't elegant but they'd do for this trip.

We rode past the East End tenements into slightly better, newer suburbs. We stopped on a cracked and worn street near a factory where laundry hanging on the line caught the soot from the smokestacks. "Stay here, Smith. Sumner, take the alley. The house should be the fifth one down."

Then the duke helped me from the carriage and we walked down the narrow gravel road off to one side. The dead-end lane was too narrow to turn a carriage around. One side was the blank wall of the factory; the other, crowded with small brick row houses. Grimy children stopped their play in the dirt to silently watch us.

We stepped onto the stoop of the fifth house and Blackford banged on the door. It was opened by a tired woman with stringy hair and a dirty apron. "Go away," she said and started to shut the door.

Blackford stuck his polished boot in the way and said, "Jeremy North."

"'E's not here."

"I don't believe you."

"Believe what you like. 'E's not here. 'E's at work."

"The police say he doesn't work."

"Well, they know sod all, don't they?"

I thought I'd better step in before Mrs. North, or whoever she was, took a swipe at Blackford. "How long has he had this job?"

"Three weeks this time, so don't go messin' it up for 'im."

"What's he doing?" My natural curiosity showed in my voice.

She seemed more willing to speak to me than the duke. "Stokin' the boilers for that lot over the wall."

That had to be horrid work in this weather. "So he's been too tired to get into any mischief in the evening."

She nodded. "'E comes home, eats, and falls into bed. In this heat, with them boilers, 'e can't do nothin' else."

"Come along, Your Grace. He's not the one you're looking for," I said and turned away.

"What's this?" the woman asked. " 'Yer Grace'? Why'd a lord be looking for Jeremy?"

I faced her again. "There was a burglary and a woman was murdered. Jeremy North is suspected of the crime."

She shook her head. "It was never Jeremy. He could never hurt a fly. And the last three weeks, he's been shovelin' coal in this heat. 'E hasn't the strength. Talk to Mick Snelling. 'E'd be the man you want."

I knew Mick Snelling was another name on our list of three. "Why?"

"'E's been braggin' about making a real score. But 'e's lyin' low since he did somethin' he said was an accident. 'E's afraid to collect 'is coins from the man who 'ired 'im 'cause the bobbies are everywhere around the gentleman."

I slipped the drawing Ken Gattenger had done of his attacker out of my bag and showed it to the woman.

"Aye, that's 'im. Where'd you get that?"

"It's Mick Snelling?"

"Aye."

I glanced up at Blackford. He nodded and held out his fist, knuckles up, to the woman. She held out both hands.

"God bless you," I said and turned away.

"Bless you," the woman said, her voice suddenly cheerful.

"How much did you give her?" I asked when we'd all climbed back into the carriage.

"A few shillings. We may need her information again some time."

"You believed her?" I had, but the duke was much less trusting.

"North's alibi is easily checked. Snelling has been missing from his lodgings for the past few days, but his belongings are still in his room. Something must have frightened him to make him flee."

I nodded. Blackford had either been in contact with Scotland Yard or he'd talked to Adam Fogarty, the retired police sergeant in the Archivist Society. "What's our next step?"

"One of his mates let slip that Snelling has a sister near the docks. She lives above the Crown and Anchor, and I think we ought to go visiting." The duke tapped his weighted cane.

The area around the docks was more dangerous than any other part of the East End. "Sumner, are you armed?" I asked.

"Yes."

"And I suppose . . ." I glanced in the direction of the driver and footman.

"Oh, yes," Blackford replied.

Oh, dear. They were expecting trouble. "Why am I along?"

"I expect you to keep us from having to use any weapons."

Oh, dear heavens. I swallowed hard and prayed for the best. "Then I suppose you want me to enter the Crown and Anchor first."

"No. That would be too dangerous."

"Then how can I prevent violence?"

"By being nearby."

The duke was a decent man, a brilliant man. But he could be stupid. "You and I will call on Miss Snelling. If I understood the burglar's actions, he didn't strike until he felt cornered. I believe while she greets us, her brother will sneak out the back. Sumner, you and Smith will need to watch from different points, and please, be careful. Snelling knows if he's captured, he will hang."

"It'll keep her out of trouble," Sumner said as he held the duke's gaze.

"Very well," the duke said.

I gave Sumner the drawing. He nodded, and then he and the footman left the coach a block before Blackford and I rode up to the door. He helped me down, and then we walked into the grimy-windowed building.

It was more depressing inside than out. An oil lamp was lit despite the glaring sunshine outside. There were a few sailors staring into their glasses and one man stood behind the bar, but no women were in sight. I walked up to the barman and said, "I'd like to speak to Miss Snelling, please."

"Rose? You mean Rose?" he asked in confusion. Then he gave a belly laugh, showing a mouth full of rotted teeth. "Miss Snelling, indeed."

"Is that Rose's last name?" I asked, my eyebrows raised.

"No one ever uses it."

"I do. Now please call Miss Snelling."

He walked over to the bottom of the stairs. "Rose! Someone wants ya!" I was surprised his bellow didn't bring down the building.

There was a pause and then a woman's voice yelled, "Who wants me?"

"Miss Adams," I shouted in return.

"Why do ya wanna talk to me?"

"I'm not going to shout. Either come down and find out, or I'll deal with somebody else."

"Jest a minnit. I'm not decent."

The barman gave another loud laugh. "She's never decent. She's a whore."

"All the more reason for her to want to be dressed," I told

him and walked to the bottom of the stairs. I heard quick footsteps upstairs somewhere, but I couldn't tell where. If it was Mick
Snelling, he must have been climbing out a window. I only hoped
Sumner and the footman would be able to catch him and rescue
the plans for the warship.

The young woman slowly came down the stairs, glancing
upward over her shoulder once. She was slender and still pretty,
but her profession was already showing in a hardening of her
features. "What do ya want?"

We had the full attention of the drinkers scattered around the
room. All of their expressions were lethal. I stepped forward
toward her. "Miss Snelling?"

The barman snorted at the name.

"Yeah."

"I'm Sally Adams. I'm here to help you and your brother, if
you'll let me." I hadn't thought out my role, deciding to improvise
as I went along. I had nothing to offer her, and nothing less than
a hangman's noose for her brother if I was right.

"We don't need no help." She turned around and marched
back up the stairs.

I put up a hand to Blackford and followed her up the stairs.
The first floor was even more depressing than the ground level.
The odors of ancient urine and sweat and blood hit me as I
reached the rough wooden floor of the hallway in time to see
Miss Snelling dart through a door near the front of the building.

Knocking on the now closed door earned me a "Go away."
The doorknob refused to turn in my hand until I used a hairpin
on the lock.

I opened the door and dodged a thin pillow. Suspecting lice,
I opened the door wider and edged my skirt around the offending
object. The room was small, with a double bed, an armoire, and

a wooden chair. There was no masculine clothing in sight. Mick hadn't been staying with his sister. Then who belonged to the running footsteps I had heard from up here?

"Where's your brother been staying?"

"None of your business." She dropped onto the bed and lounged on it. She probably hoped Blackford had followed me here. I certainly hoped he'd followed my direction to wait.

I glanced around the room. The dirt-streaked window sat open and I walked over to look out. Part of the street was visible, but there was nothing to break Snelling's fall if he'd gone out this way.

When I pulled my head back inside, I saw a chocolate box from the most famous chocolatier in London lying in the corner, as out of place as a ruby. I hurried toward it, over Miss Snelling saying, "'Ey! What are you doing?"

Miss Snelling reached the box at the same time I did and she smashed me against the wall. My shoulder took the brunt as the decrepit plaster stood firm. I swung around to see her dive back onto her bed clutching the chocolate box.

Forgetting my fear of lice, I dove after her and knocked the box out of her hands. It flew across the room.

The chocolate box was empty. The woman collapsed back onto the bed with a sigh. "He took it with him."

"The plans to the ship?"

She made a face at me.

I leaped off the bed and began a search of the room, which brought the prostitute to her feet. "'Ey! This is my room. Get out."

"I came for the ship plans your brother stole. Give them to me and I'll leave."

"They're not here."

"Where's your brother's room?"

"Not here."

I gave her a disbelieving frown.

She shook her head. "I don't know where he's hiding. Not here."

"Your brother's in a lot of trouble. If Scotland Yard catches him, he'll hang. If he gives those blueprints to the man who hired him, the man will kill him to cover his tracks. I'm here to offer him, and you, a way out." If she bought my story, I had to think of a solution.

She dropped back onto the bed. "I know he stole those plans for someone, and I know he's in a lot of trouble. Some lady fell and hit her head. When he saw what happened, he ran. And if he doesn't hand over those blue papers, the man who hired him will find him and kill him."

"There's a way out," I said as the plan came to me.

"What?"

"I have the name and address of a man who can give him a second set of plans, doctored plans, to give to the man who hired him. Then he can get two sets of coins, one from us for switching the plans and one from the man who hired him."

By the calculating glint in her eye, I knew I had her interest. "What if this man realizes the drawings are fakes?"

"He won't. Not until months of work have been done on them. By then, your brother and his money will be long gone. Away from the law and anyone looking for him." This time I smiled.

"Who's this bloke and what's his address?"

"His name's Stevens. He pretends to be a butler, but he's really a mastermind. You'll find him at Blackford House on Park Lane. He'll be the one who opens the front door. Tell your brother to say the duchess sent him with the plans." And Stevens would know what to do because Blackford would instruct him.

"How do I know this isn't a double cross?" She studied my face, disbelieving.

I held her gaze as I walked over and held out my hand. "Rose, if you want to keep your brother alive, you have to trust me. This is his best chance."

She stared at my hand and then shook it. "You're the first person who's seen a way out of his troubles."

"Your brother needs to get in contact with Mr. Stevens soon. Everyone's looking for him."

"Don'tcha think I know that."

"Stevens will give him more than enough money to stay out of sight. Your brother will just have to find a way to deliver the doctored plans and get the rest of his money without getting caught by the police or murdered by the man who hired him. That'll be up to him."

I gave her a curtsy and left, shutting the door behind me. I paused long enough to rub my shoulder, certain I'd have a bruise by later that night. When I reached the bottom of the stairs, Sumner and Blackford were in close discussion. I joined them and looked from one man to the other.

"Outside," the duke said.

We climbed into the carriage and took off. "What happened?"

"Thought we had him cornered in a boardinghouse down the street, but he slipped out the window over the rooftops like he did at the Crown and Anchor. The man's a cat," Sumner said with obvious admiration in his voice.

"He definitely took the designs for the warship. I told his sister if he'd take the real designs to Stevens, he'd get a doctored version to give to the man who hired him and some coins to make his escape. Snelling is to say the duchess sent him. I told her Stevens was a mastermind posing as a butler."

The duke snorted. "Stevens would agree with your assessment. Good thinking, Georgia. I need to put your plan into action."

"Do you think he'll fall for it?" Sumner asked.

"I don't know," Blackford said, "but if he comes to Blackford House, he'll find everything just as Georgia described, including a doctored set of plans. I'm sure the Admiralty can produce that quickly for a good reason. And you've given them a good reason." He gave me one of his happy smiles, the ones I saw when the two of us had done well together. A smile that told me he was pleased. A smile that might someday say he loved me.

Except he couldn't. He was a duke.

"You'll let him go?" Sumner asked.

"I don't expect Stevens to capture him, and he won't see anyone at Blackford House but Stevens. Even if he gets away, we'll have what we want. The plans to the warship."

"And evidence Ken Gattenger is telling the truth," I added. "Will it be enough to let him out of prison?"

"No. Snelling could double-cross Gattenger as easily as the baron. Without Snelling testifying that Gattenger wasn't involved and the plans were taken by force, Scotland Yard can still say the prisoner is guilty of treason and murder. I'm sorry."

I leaned toward Blackford, every muscle tensing. "That's not fair. There must be a way to prove Ken Gattenger innocent."

"Possibly we'll catch Snelling handing off the doctored plans. Possibly the Germans will admit Gattenger had no hand in this. We won't know what evidence we'll have until we finish the investigation." Blackford gave me a reassuring smile. "You've done well. Shall we take you back to the bookstore now?"

"Yes. I have a lot to take care of today." Too much. I was grumbling and didn't care if the duke heard my temper. Before, I'd always been able to keep one eye on the bookshop as I carried out investigations. I didn't like the direction this case and my shop were headed.

CHAPTER NINE

I scarcely had time to glance at the receipts for the bookshop before it was time to take a stifling omnibus back to Mayfair. The heat wave seemed to have intensified, baking the horse manure almost as soon as it hit the pavement. If it weren't so hot, I could have walked the distance in less time. While Emma readied my outfit for the afternoon, I ate a light lunch. After Emma dressed Phyllida and me, we left to call on Lady Peters.

Her Mayfair town house was smaller than ours, but better located on one of the attractive squares that dotted that part of London. She rose to greet us when her butler opened the door to her parlor and announced us. "How lovely. I was afraid you wouldn't come."

"We were honored by your invitation," I answered.

We curtsied to each other and then she had us sit on satin-smooth jewel-green chairs. "Your home has a marvelous view, Lady Peters," Phyllida said.

"Please, call me Rosamond. Yes, we get a little breeze from

the trees in the park, and lately, we're grateful for every breeze we can find."

Why was this woman going out of her way to befriend us? "I'm Georgina, and I'm grateful for the invitation, since I know practically no one in the city. And now it sounds as if everyone in polite society will be escaping London."

"When does the Duke of Blackford intend to leave? Or shouldn't I ask? I've heard you and he are old friends, but I suppose I shouldn't listen to gossip."

Good. The story we'd concocted was getting around. "Oh, that isn't gossip. That's the truth. We were friendly when we were younger, but we haven't seen each other in years. I have no idea what Ranleigh's—I mean, the duke's—plans are. Did he mention them to you last night?"

"No. He didn't seem to be able to talk about anything but you. He seems quite smitten."

"As Sir Henry appears to be with you."

Rosamond laughed a carefree, tinkling sound. "Sir Henry is in love with half the females in London. One of us serves quite as well as another."

"Oh, dear. A male coquette." I smiled broadly, and Phyllida, bless her, tittered.

Lady Peters didn't. "I shouldn't speak so dismissively of him. He seems quite interested in you. Particularly since the duke hasn't frightened him off."

I shook my head. "Neither has more than a passing interest in me. I'm new here, and that makes me exotic for ten minutes. By the time cooler weather comes in, both of them will be on to other pursuits."

"And you? What will you do then?"

I'll be back in my bookshop, if my friends haven't made too many mistakes like this morning's. "I'm at Lady Phyllida's disposal. We might travel a little, see the sights of London, I don't know. This is all so new."

"You didn't grow up here?"

"I sailed to join my father in India as soon as I left the schoolroom. Having not lived in London leaves me at a disadvantage when it comes to polite society. So tell me, why has Lady Bennett taken such a special dislike to me?"

Rosamond Peters smiled, but her eyes narrowed. "I'm sure she hasn't."

"You don't believe that." I decided to strike a blow for my supposed honesty in not knowing important people in Singapore. "She seems quite upset that I wasn't the social equal of her sister the viscountess in Singapore."

She shook her head. "It sounded as if you'd never heard of her family, in whom she's quite proud."

I'd managed to check some sources at the bookshop, so now I could speak with authority. "I meant I didn't move in their circles. We'd never been formally introduced. She should be honored rather than insulted. But beyond that, she doesn't like me."

"Lady Bennett has had many conquests in society over the years. Both before and after old Lord Bennett's death. Perhaps she feels guilty when she sees you because the last time your cousin and Kenneth Gattenger broke their engagement, it was because of her."

"What?" I thought Phyllida would slide off her satin-slick chair.

"He came to regret it quickly enough and strove to make amends with Clara, but Gattenger and Lady Bennett did have an affair immediately after Lord Bennett died."

Gattenger and Lady Bennett. I shook my head. "I can't believe that's the reason for her animosity. Clara's gone. It can't make any difference now."

Lady Peters smiled. "Being more than a few years older than you, perhaps she fears you'll attract the attention she wants. Especially as she once made an effort to gain the Duke of Blackford's eye and failed."

I was glad to hear he had better taste than that.

Glancing around the room, a painting over the fireplace caught my eye. The woman was definitely Rosamond Peters with a toddler on her lap. "Your son?"

"The current Lord Peters. He's four years old now and growing quickly. He's spending the summer with his aunt and uncle and their children at their family estate." She smiled at the portrait.

"You're brave to share him with the family after losing your husband." I didn't think I could bear being separated from my young children if I ever had any.

"I miss him terribly, but it's better for him. London is so hot and unhealthy."

"Did your husband get to know the child? He's been dead that long, hasn't he?" Phyllida asked.

Good for you, Phyllida. She was turning into a first-rate investigator.

"Sadly, no. His father died a few months before his birth."

The parlor door opened and the butler announced Lady Bennett. I glanced at Lady Peters as we all rose and curtsied. Rosamond's eyes flashed with a strong emotion. By the hard set of her lips, I suspected it was hatred.

Still, she was all graciousness as she invited her guest to come sit with us.

"I'd have thought you'd be packing for your trip to the countryside. Although it's so much easier now that we don't have skirts a yard wide, with underskirts and petticoats and hoops and underpetticoats," Phyllida said.

"I hope we don't ever go back to those styles," Rosamond Peters said with a laugh that sounded forced to my ears.

"I leave all my packing to my maid," Lady Bennett said. Apparently she was smug about everything.

"You trust your maid to decide what you'll wear to every event while you're gone? I could never do that," I said and hoped no one repeated this to Emma. Her taste was much better than mine.

"Well, of course I oversee her work," Lady Bennett said. "Oh, Rosamond, don't tell me you plan to stay in London in this heat wave."

"I'm also going to Lord Harwin's, Lark. Celeste Harwin was a childhood friend of my husband's, and she offered to rescue me from this oven."

"Lark. What an unusual name," Phyllida said. "I knew a woman who called her daughter Lark. Caused an unholy ruckus when it came time for the bishop to baptize her."

Lady Bennett turned cherry red. Rosamond Peters had a hand over her mouth, trying to keep the laughter from leaking out between her fingers. And I had my mouth half-open, wishing I could question Phyllida further on this oddly named baby girl.

"Are you Genevieve Hollingsworth's daughter?" Phyllida asked. "How is your mother?"

"She's dead," Lark Bennett snapped.

Phyllida reached out and patted her hand. "I am so sorry. She was a wonderful woman. A determined woman."

Lady Bennett aimed a calculating look at Phyllida. "How did you not know Mother had died? It created a sensation fifteen years ago."

Oh, Phyllida, don't blow our story, I said with my eyes. Phyllida looked at me and said, "I'm sorry, Georgina. I'm sure Edgar didn't tell you about my brother, who was executed for murdering a score of prostitutes. It happened before you two met, but for years before he was captured, my brother kept me prisoner in my own home. I only received the news and the visitors he allowed." She turned and faced Lady Bennett. "I heard nothing about Genevieve's passing. I'm sorry if I brought up a painful memory."

Lady Peters said, "How terrible, Lady Phyllida. You must have suffered terribly from society gossip."

"No. I left. It saved me from being pitied. I can't stand pity." Then Phyllida gave the ladies a bright smile and said, "Where do you recommend traveling to avoid the heat?"

Lark Bennett gave a relieved sigh and said, "I can't believe the Duke of Blackford hasn't arranged a house party to entertain you and Mrs. Monthalf."

"If he has, he hasn't told me," I replied.

"He's probably just awaiting confirmation from his butler," Lady Peters said. "I shall miss seeing you while you're in— Northumberland, isn't it?"

I'd seen his manor house within the castle walls, and I really didn't want to go there again. I also doubted he kept the house fully staffed with a butler.

I needed to stay close to Baron von Steubfeld and Lady Bennett. A country house party would be isolated enough to keep out policemen and Archivist Society members and busy enough to hide the passing of the stolen warship plans. How was I going to crash a country house party?

"I wouldn't think Ranleigh would go there except to administer his estate. He seems more accustomed to life in London," I said.

"But London won't cool down, not even for a duke. When they suspended Parliament, most of the peers fled," Lady Peters said.

Lady Bennett looked me up and down before saying, "Are you and the Duke of Blackford an item? Forgive me for saying so, but you two don't seem to be well matched."

"In what way?" I asked, neatly lobbing her remark back at her.

"He's going to have to marry a highborn young lady to give him an heir."

"I can assure you neither of us has been discussing marriage. Have you been discussing marriage with von Steubfeld?" I tried to sound interested and hoped she'd tell me more about her relationship with the baron.

She laughed. "We just enjoy each other's company. He came into London looking for an attractive widow to have on his arm for society affairs, and I like being surrounded by the mighty at diplomatic receptions."

"Really? Your relationship developed as simply as that?" I said in pretended amazement, trying to get her to continue.

Lady Bennett turned to Lady Peters. "Tell her. I see you at diplomatic social events all the time."

"I've only attended one or two."

"One or two a month is more accurate." Lady Bennett raised an expressive eyebrow.

Lady Peters shook her head. "I've been invited by friends on a few occasions, but hardly with the same frequency as you have." She looked uncomfortable with the direction of the conversation as she glared at Lark Bennett.

"You're far too modest," Lady Bennett said. "The French ambassador is quite fond of you."

Rosamond Peters blushed. "He's an old family friend, soon

to be recalled to Paris. And I'm sure you'll be upset when Baron von Steubfeld is sent to another embassy."

"I won't have to worry about that until Christmas season. He's assured me he has to stay here until then."

"Why?" Phyllida asked. "How can he possibly be sure?"

I was mentally applauding her innocent question when Lark Bennett said, "He said his work won't be finished until then."

I suspected her of involvement in the theft of the plans until she looked directly at me and said, "Once he leaves, I'll look for my fun elsewhere. Next time, I may set my sights on a duke."

I wanted to laugh. If she knew the real relationship between the duke and me, she wouldn't feel nearly as envious.

AFTER MY UNINFORMATIVE visit with Lady Bennett at Lady Peters's, I planned to go to our borrowed quarters and sleep while Phyllida paid calls on a couple of old tabbies. I sent her on in a carriage while I walked in the blazing heat. After such a strenuous occupation, I was sure I could sleep well.

No such luck. Blackford arrived just as I entered the front door into the relative cool of the foyer. He followed me up to the parlor and then said, as I shut the door on the servants, "You look like hell."

"I walked back from Lady Peters's."

"In this heat? Not advisable."

"I needed to think." I collapsed onto a sofa and waved him into a chair. "Sit."

Never one to listen to a mere mortal, he walked over and pulled the bell rope. A maid immediately appeared. "Tea, please, with lots of sugar for your mistress."

It must have been his ducal tones. The woman didn't look in

my direction. She simply left to do his bidding, shutting the door behind her.

I raised an eyebrow. "Why am I going to need sugared tea?"

"This investigation is entering a new phase. I discovered Sir Henry is attending Lord Harwin's country house party, along with the baron and Lady Bennett."

"I think Sir Henry is following Lady Peters to the Harwins'."

"Or maybe Lady Peters is following him," Blackford said.

I shrugged. "And Lady Bennett has nothing to do with this investigation. She's after the invitations and the glamour. In fact, she hinted today that you might be her next conquest." It might be impolite to repeat her boasts, but Blackford should be warned. I told myself that wasn't jealousy, but rather a concern for any man subjected to Lady Bennett.

He brushed my words aside. "I won't be her anything. Now, we need to keep an eye on them. Or rather, you do. I'm too obviously involved in the hunt for the blueprints. So we'll be leaving Friday morning for a stay at Lord Harwin's."

"We will what?"

The maid entered with the tea tray as I shrieked out the last word. She looked from me to the duke with widened eyes, but she set down the tray without spilling and fled the room, shutting the door quietly as she left.

"I suspected you'd need heavily sugared tea," Blackford said as he fixed a cup and handed it to me.

I took a sip. It was sugary, but it revived me from a state of sputtering disbelief to full-blown fury. "How did you manage to get us invited?"

"I applied economic and social pressure. Lord Harwin enjoys my help in finding the best investments for his dwindling fortune, and Lady Harwin enjoys mentioning the presence of a duke at her home. Then I simply invited the three of us, and your maid and my valet, to stay with the Harwins for a few days. Don't worry. They have plenty of room."

Was no one immune to Blackford's charm and power? "How long are we going to be there?"

"Four or five days. Phyllida will of course go with us, as will your maid, Emma."

I set down the cup with a clatter. "Who's going to manage the bookshop?"

"Whoever's managing it now."

"Emma and I are spending our mornings there, taking care of problems." Such as not shelving *The Ruined Castle*.

"I wondered why you looked so exhausted. Ladies are supposed to sleep all morning."

"I'm not a lady. Remember?"

"It's too late to back out now, Georgina." He stressed my assumed name.

He was right. I was going to have to trust the Archivist Society to take care of the shop. I took another sip of tea and said, "What's the plan?"

"We're going to the Royal Albert Hall tonight for a concert. All of society will be there. We will make a show of being surprised when we bump into the baron and Sir Henry, and then I'll casually mention we're going to spend a few days with Lord Harwin to get out of London's heat."

"We're not sitting next to them again, are we?"

"Not in the Royal Albert Hall. There, the best seats are in the private boxes. I found out what box the baron reserved, and obtained one on the other side. We'll have a good view of his seats, plus ours is close to the center and therefore more prestigious."

Of course it is. "How will we run into the baron? He'll be on the other side of a very large building."

"Oh, he'll come to us. Everyone will. I've invited Lord and Lady Salisbury to sit in our box. They accepted."

My gulp of tea lodged painfully halfway down my throat. I managed to swallow without choking and said, "You've invited the prime minister and his wife to sit with us? I have to perform as Mrs. Monthalf in front of the prime minister?"

He smiled. "Think of this as playing your role on a larger stage."

"What's next? Dining with the queen?"

"No. That wouldn't help with the investigation."

Dear heavens. He was serious. My Georgina Monthalf disguise would have to be very good. "How will attending a concert with the prime minister help us find out if Clara Gattenger died in a struggle to save the blueprints and where those warship plans are now?"

"The best way to clear Ken Gattenger's name is to seize those drawings during the handoff from the burglar. When the baron arrives to greet Salisbury, which he is almost obligated to do, I'll tell him we're to join his little country house party and that we'll travel down to Gloucestershire with him. Start the party early."

"He's going to resist it."

"I know. That's why you have to convince Lady Bennett it would be great fun." He gave me a patently false smile.

I raised my eyebrows in response. Spending more time with that lady would not be fun by anyone's definition. Her sister's husband could arrive at any time and denounce me, and my supposed late husband, as a fraud. "You'll be able to do that better than I can. You're the one she's after."

"Perhaps I'll have to sweeten the offer."

"How?"

"We'll see."

I hated it when he became enigmatic. However, I could under-stand his strategy. "You're going to disrupt their plans as much as possible to try to force them to make a mistake."

"Yes. Left to their own devices, they would have had those drawings in Berlin by now."

"And the concert with the prime minister is tonight?"

"Yes."

I was ready to slide down in my seat. "I need to get some sleep first."

"Too late for that now." Blackford spun around as the door opened behind him. "Ah, here's Lady Phyllida. What have you learned?" he asked, kissing her hand.

"No one can quite decide if you're lovers yet or not. Oh, good. Tea." She poured more tea from the pot into my empty cup and drank. "Good gracious, the gossip that flows around this town. I'd forgotten how everyone knows everyone else's business. Gen-evieve Hollingsworth, Lady Bennett's mother, went completely bonkers before she died. Ran naked in the snow and caught pneumonia."

Blackford cleared his throat, but I suspected it was to hide a chuckle.

"Oh, dear. Excuse me, Your Grace. I also heard the last Lord Peters was so paralyzed with a wasting disease for over a year before he died that no one can imagine how he fathered a child when he did. Of course, no one questions the little boy's paternity out loud. So unfair to the child."

Blackford huffed out a breath. "But it would be wrong for the child to have the title if there's any truth to the rumor."

Phyllida ignored him and continued. "It appears everyone

knew about the liaison between Lark Bennett and Ken Gattenger, including Clara. She gave him a very hard time before she took him back. Meanwhile, Lady Bennett had moved on to the first secretary at the Russian embassy."

"Is she a spy?" She certainly had affairs with the right personalities for espionage.

"Not one of ours. And Whitehall's been keeping an eye on her," Blackford told me.

"They've been wasting their time. She's a light skirt with high expectations," Phyllida said with her nose upraised.

"She may be both," I suggested. Lady Bennett was having affairs where she could be learning secrets to pass along. I'd have to consider her as part of our current problem as well as a danger to my disguise.

I was growing weary of listening to gossip and being the subject of rumors. "We're going to Lord Harwin's country house party on Friday," I told her.

"That will certainly tip the balance toward the two of you being lovers. Are you staying for dinner, Your Grace?"

"No. I'll pick you up for the concert at the Royal Albert Hall. Tell her the rest, Georgina," the duke said as he bowed and walked out of the parlor.

"We're sharing a box with the prime minister and Lady Salisbury."

Phyllida leaped up. "Oh, dear. There's not a minute to lose. Anyone who wasn't looking at us before will be now. What do you wear to sit in a box at the Royal Albert Hall with a duke and a marquis who happens to be prime minister?"

CHAPTER TEN

L EFT to my own devices, I would have been dressed in plenty of time. Instead, Emma and Phyllida worried over every detail of my costume and I still wasn't ready when the duke arrived. Emma proclaimed me "as good as could be hoped for" while Phyllida said she'd "hoped for more."

I told Emma to fix my hair because I was attending in what I had on at that moment. It was my finest gown, an icy green with a scandalous neckline, delivered from Madame Leclerc's that morning, worn with low-heeled pumps and a simple necklace and earrings.

As Phyllida reached the door, she said, "You shouldn't keep a duke waiting. I'll be in the parlor with him, since some of us are ready."

I rolled my eyes at her and told Emma to hurry. Emma grumbled, but she worked miracles with a bunch of hairpins and a bit of ribbon and a brooch. She pronounced me ready and I grabbed a lacy white shawl before I flew down the stairs to the parlor.

The duke rose when I entered the room. "Your cousin has been telling me about the gossip concerning Mrs. Gattenger."

I nodded, knowing Phyllida must have found the rumors disheartening. Her silence told me she was upset. She'd not said a word to Emma or me about what she'd heard concerning Clara during her visits. "Did you learn anything useful for the investigation?"

Phyllida and Blackford exchanged glances, and the duke nodded.

"The consensus is Kenny killed Clara. Today I heard of two different disagreements between them in public. Oh, Georgia, I don't believe it. They always seemed so happy." Phyllida looked ready to cry.

"No one can know the inside of a marriage, except for the husband and wife. And there could have been any number of tiffs that meant nothing." I gave her a quick hug. "Tell us about them."

Phyllida brushed an invisible wrinkle out of my dress. "One was at a musical evening. Kenny said something innocuous that Clara didn't like. She walked off and didn't speak to him the rest of the evening. The other was at the theater. Some family comedy, but at the end, Clara was seen to have tears pouring down her face. Kenny tried to comfort her, but she pushed him away."

How odd. "What was the play?"

"The ladies couldn't remember. But these episodes are going to count against Kenny, aren't they?"

Blackford took Phyllida's hand. "If I were the prosecutor, I'd use them to paint a portrait of a troubled marriage. But I think our best bet is to keep an eye on Sir Henry. If Georgia will question him, I think we'll find he's the man who hired Snelling and he plans to turn around and sell the plans to the Germans."

Both Phyllida and Blackford stared at me as if waiting for me to do my job.

Annoyed with their attitudes, I turned to leave. "Let's not keep the prime minister waiting."

"I refuse to believe Kenny had a hand in Clara's death. It's impossible. Remember that, Your Grace, while you carry out your investigation."

Once we were in the carriage I asked, "What do you plan to discover tonight?"

The duke smiled, but his eyes stayed grim. "I have no idea. We'll keep an eye on the baron and listen to all the maneuvering around the prime minister. We'll see if we can uncover any clues."

When we arrived at the Royal Albert Hall, we went straight to our box and waited for the arrival of the prime minister. The duke went out to meet him, leaving Phyllida and me on our own. I saw the baron and Lady Bennett arrive in their box with another man, wearing a uniform identical to the baron's, and the Dowager Duchess of Bad Ramshed and her daughter Lady Magda. None of them looked our way.

"The Germans have arrived," Phyllida hissed.

"Have you learned any more about them from your afternoon visits?"

"The woman is a relative of the kaiser's wife. Everyone says she's a terrible dragon, so it's not just my opinion from meeting her at Lady Bennett's. I was given all the particulars when I paid my calls this afternoon. Several people called on her and were treated to a litany of all the things wrong with Britain. Apparently she's leaving tomorrow, having visited with her doctors."

Alarm bells rang in my head. "What's wrong with her?"

"Rheumatism."

Nothing unusual in a simple case of rheumatism, but could she be the mode for moving the blueprints to Germany? She had such a reputation and had such a powerful family that no one would want to search her carefully for the ship plans.

"What I don't understand is how Lark Bennett could put up with someone as stuffy as her. Her mother never would." Phyllida stared across the space to the box a distance away where Lady Bennett sat with the Germans.

Perhaps Lady Bennett would pass the ship blueprints to the dowager duchess and the baron would never have to touch them. I didn't like the possibilities that kept springing to mind.

I heard noise behind us and turned around as Sir Henry Stanford entered our box. "Sir Henry," I said with a smile as I rose. "How wonderful to see you again." Wonderful for him, maybe. His suave smile made me nervous.

"I called today, hoping to find you at home, but you were out." He brushed his lips along the back of my glove in the European manner.

"Yes. We called on Lady Peters. It was kind of her to invite us." I sat and waved him into a chair. "Please sit, Sir Henry. We have a few minutes to talk before the performance."

He sat and leaned toward me in a familiar manner. "I wondered if you ladies would like to accompany me to an art exhibit tomorrow evening. I realize it's short notice, but I'm leaving town the next day."

"How extraordinary. So are we. We've been invited to Lord Harwin's for a few days." I tried looking delighted.

He smiled. I hoped he was buying my act. "Extraordinary. That's where I'm headed."

"We won't have time to go out tomorrow evening, but perhaps we can ride down to Gloucestershire in the train together."

"Of course." He glanced at Phyllida. "If I could have a private word with your cousin?"

"Of course." Phyllida turned toward the stage and Sir Henry beckoned me to the rear of our box.

"I know what you did last night, and it won't do you any good." He kept his voice to a murmur.

Blast. The maid must have spotted me before I reached the bottom of the stairs. Trying to brazen it out, I said, "What do you think I did?"

"Rummaged through my study. I don't keep anything of value there. Too easy a place for someone to search. And I asked around in the city. No one is handling the business affairs of Mrs. Edgar Monthalf. There is no money, is there?"

"Of course there is. How else would I be able to afford these dresses and jewels?"

"When your bills catch up with you, you'll be hounded out of London." His breath brushed my cheek as he continued to murmur. It made my skin crawl.

I stared at him, uncertain how to answer. The truth was the last thing I could tell him.

"If you want me to keep your secret, here's what you're going to do." He gripped my upper arm and I gasped. "You're going to visit Gattenger tomorrow and find out if his ship will sink or float. And you will tell me tomorrow afternoon when I call on you. Five o'clock."

"That's too soon."

He gave me a cruel smile. The smile of a killer. His grip on my arm tightened. "You'll do it, or I'll expose you as a thief and a fraud."

He let go of my arm and said to Phyllida, "Lady Monthalf, it was lovely to see you again. I hope you enjoy the concert."

I wanted to rub my sore arm, but I wouldn't give him the satisfaction of knowing he'd hurt me any more than he'd frightened me. "Sir Henry, what do you—" I was ready to tell him off.

Instead, I was forced to stop in midsentence as the duke entered, joined by a pleasant-looking woman and a man with a ferocious beard. Phyllida immediately rose and curtsied. I followed her example.

Sir Henry, his mouth dropping open for a moment at the sight of the prime minister standing in front of him, pressed his lips together and bowed.

The duke made the introductions, saving Sir Henry's for last as he said, "And before he leaves, this is Sir Henry Stanford."

I was amazed at how gracefully Sir Henry bowed to the prime minister and his wife and maneuvered around me without coming within reach of the duke, all in a small, crowded area. Gracefully enough to be the burglar?

No. We knew Mick Snelling was the burglar from Ken Gattenger's drawing. We just didn't know who'd hired him, or how they planned to exchange the blueprints for cash, or if the person who'd hired Snelling was only a middleman, putting the drawings up for bid.

The possibilities bothered me for the entire first half of the performance. That, and hearing the duke and the prime minister call each other Ranleigh and Cecil. I felt completely out of place.

Phyllida shot me little glances of worry. She'd no doubt heard the tone of my talk with Sir Henry, if not the actual words. I gave her confident smiles in return, while inside I knew I had to deal with yet another problem.

When intermission came, Lady Salisbury murmured, "Prepare yourselves for a great deal of curtsying. By now, everyone in the hall knows the prime minister is here, and there will be a line around the building wanting to greet him or ask if he's enjoying the concert. Anything to come to his attention."

"Is it as bad as all that?" I asked.

Voices in the entryway to our box caught our attention. "Yes," she answered as we rose and curtsied to a duke and duchess.

The parade of British aristocracy and foreign diplomats continued for the entire intermission. Mrs. Monthalf was gracious. Inside, I was overawed.

Near the end, Baron von Steubfeld and Lady Bennett appeared with a count and the Dowager Duchess of Bad Ramshed and her daughter. The duke introduced them to the prime minister and Lady Salisbury. I slid in next to Lady Bennett and said, "So nice to see you again. The duke says we're to be guests at the same party in the country. I look forward to improving our acquaintance."

"Perhaps you'll do us the honor of traveling with us in the Duke of Northumberland's saloon car," Blackford added, more to the baron than Lark Bennett.

"Oh, how lovely," Lady Bennett immediately exclaimed, "we'd love to travel in such a civilized manner," leaving the baron no choice but to nod agreement as he looked daggers at Blackford.

After all the well-wishers had gone and the orchestra readied to strike the first note, I whispered to the duke, "I invited Sir Henry to travel with us."

His reply was a low grumble. I'd have thought he'd be glad.

"At least the Dragoness of Bad Ramshed won't be with us," Phyllida said.

"No, she won't be there," the duke said, eyebrows rising. " 'Dragoness'?"

"A difference of opinion," I muttered.

I nodded off a few times in the second half. The heat of so many bodies, my long hours, and the strain of acting a role all evening were taking their toll. Phyllida elbowed me twice and the duke, who sat behind me and to the side, took to running a finger down my neck in the most sensual manner. Unfortunately, all I wanted to do was curl up and go to sleep.

We left the hall and saw the prime minister and his wife off before the duke escorted us around the building looking for our carriage. A confusion of horses and vehicles circled the round structure, each jockeying for better position or to park in front of a different doorway. As we moved along the outdoor walkway, nodding greetings to the famous, Blackford said to Phyllida when we reached an open exit, "I don't think you should walk any further. The carriage should find us in a moment."

Phyllida glanced up at him with a puzzled frown, looked around, and said, "I suppose you're right."

At that moment, the baron and Lady Bennett walked outside with the others who'd sat in their box.

Lady Bennett was holding a large chocolate box from the most aristocratic candy maker in the city. A box like the one I'd seen in Rose Snelling's room. A box that could hold the folded warship drawings. I moved closer to take a look, saying, "Oh, what a fortunate lady you are," when I was shoved roughly from behind.

The momentum carried me into Lady Bennett, knocking her off her feet. The duke and the baron did all they could do to keep us from landing in a sprawled heap on the pavement. The dowager duchess shrieked and grabbed her daughter. I managed to shove on the candy box, sending two pounds of the most exquisite chocolates rolling in all directions under our feet as the box spilled open.

"Oh, look what you've done," Lady Bennett exclaimed, her tiara slipping to one side and her evening cloak twisted around her.

"I am so sorry. Some ruffian shoved me. Where is he?" I glanced around, suspecting I'd recognize a face, but everyone in sight was well-heeled and middle-aged.

"There he is. You must catch him," the dowager duchess screeched in a thick accent and pointed.

"No. It wasn't him," Phyllida said. "I'm afraid he's gone now."

"He must be an anarchist. We must stop him," the count exclaimed and took two steps forward, only to collide with Phyllida.

She grabbed on to his lapels, murmuring, "An anarchist? I'm so frightened. You must stay here and protect us."

"I don't know who it was. I was too busy trying to catch Mrs. Monthalf and Lady Bennett," the duke said and glanced around.

If he'd really been trying to catch me, I was certain I'd never have collided with Lady Bennett. And the whole affair was carried out so Phyllida was never in any danger of being injured.

Fortunately, by the time Lady Magda calmed her mother, Phyllida stopped rejoicing over everyone's lack of injuries, and I stopped apologizing, the baron's coach had arrived and he left with an aggravated Lady Bennett straightening her outfit and the dowager duchess snapping orders at the others. Everyone was scraping chocolate off their shoes.

Moments later, the duke's coach arrived and we climbed inside. Once we were moving, I asked, "Was that Sumner?"

"Yes."

"How did he know about the chocolate box?"

"He was watching them from inside the hall. Lady Bennett was given the box by a man he didn't know. A man not in uniform or livery."

"How could he have told you?"

"He came into our box in the second half. Didn't you hear him?"

"No."

"You must have been sleeping."

"I would have been, if you hadn't kept waking me."

"I heard the whole thing. That's why I knew to stop the count. Your friend needs to move faster next time if he wants to get away," Phyllida told him. She was enjoying her role too much.

"If he'd moved any faster, he'd have called attention to himself in that crowd," the duke replied. "Don't go to the bookshop tomorrow, Georgia—er, Georgina. You need to get some rest."

"I can't, Your Grace." I snapped the words at him. "I have to get everything ready for my absence. My several-day-long absence. Along with Emma's and Jacob's absences, I might add."

He brushed the air, as if shoving away a pesky fly or my argument. "Sumner is filling in for Jacob admirably. I'm sure your Mrs. Atterby is doing well. Things are going splendidly. You need to get some sleep."

"No, Your Grace." Frances was doing well, and Sir Broderick was aiding her admirably. Still, it was my bookshop. My responsibility. And my livelihood.

"Lady Phyllida, can you reason with her?"

She smiled at him. "It hasn't worked so far."

He leaned back in his seat, his arms folded over his chest, and grumbled. "All right," he said at last. "Do what you have to do tomorrow. The next day, whether you and your shop are ready or not, we will be leaving from the train station."

"Including Emma?" I was hoping she could stay behind. She knew almost as much about the bookshop as I did.

"Of course Emma. Someone has to snoop around the servants' quarters. And you and Phyllida can't attend a house party without a lady's maid."

All I could do was pray my bookshop survived my absence.

"There's something else I need to tell you, Your Grace. Sir Henry threatened me with exposure. He found out I really don't have a fortune being managed for me in the city."

He murmured something, then said, "What made him suspicious?"

"A maid saw me coming from his study after I searched it."

"You were gone from the table too long," Phyllida said. "Sir Henry said he was afraid you'd gotten sick and left the table. I think he got suspicious when I dragged him back into the dining room."

"He wants me to find out from Gattenger, by five tomorrow afternoon, if the ship will float or sink. If I don't—"

Blackford said, "We'll see Gattenger tomorrow morning and find out. Do you want me to turn up at five minutes after five tomorrow?" If Sir Henry had been present at that moment, the duke's expression said he'd run him through with a sword.

"No, Your Grace. I'll deal with him better alone."

When Blackford dropped us at the house after the concert, Emma was waiting in my room with one of the maids. The heat had dissipated in the night, enough that I wasn't clammy with sweat. Despite my lack of sleep and a desire to collapse onto my bed, I let Emma talk as she undressed me.

"This is Mary," she said, gesturing as she undid my hairdo. "She's working here because the duke sent Gattenger's help to his housekeeper to keep employed until either Gattenger is freed or the end of the quarter."

"Mary." I nodded my head and my loosened hairdo slipped, releasing a cascade of curls down my back. I'd spoken to Elsie the day I'd gone with the duke to see the site of the crime. I'd not seen Mary, and hopefully, she'd not seen me.

"Mrs. Monthalf. Emma said since you're kin to Mrs. Gattenger, I should tell you what I know about her murder. Well, not her murder, but her life leading up to her murder."

I studied Mary. She was small boned and thin, a few years younger than Emma, with lovely brown hair and eyes. I could picture her slipping into dark corners to stand undetected or dressing as a street lad to follow a suspect in an investigation. My imagination runs away with me sometimes. I had no idea if she had the intelligence or talent to carry out those roles.

I gave her a gentle smile and said, "I'd be interested in what you have to tell me, Mary."

"Well, ma'am, I know Elsie always said the Gattengers got along well, but I didn't see it that way. I had my day out on a different day than Elsie, so I was the one who heard the row they had a week before the mistress's death."

"Which day was this?"

"Tuesday, ma'am. My day out was on Thursday."

"Tell me what you heard, please, Mary." Would she echo the gossip Phyllida had heard?

"I was plaiting the mistress's hair like Emma's doing to you now, and the master came into her room. She said, 'Get out, Kenny,' and he said, 'I love you, Clara.' Then she said, 'That's twice now. I don't think I can bear it a third time.' Then she burst into tears."

"Bear what?"

"I don't know. I do know I'd had to get the doctor the Tuesday before."

"Why?"

"I don't know. The master sent me because the mistress was ill. Next day, we were having to bleach blood out of the sheets and all of their nightclothes."

"Had that happened before?"

"No, ma'am, but we had to get the doctor for the mistress often enough. And she bruised easy. She was talking once, and not watching where she was going, and smacked into a door. The whole side of her face was bruised. She couldn't leave the house for almost two weeks on account of how she looked."

"Did you see her run into the door?"

"Not me. No. Just the master."

I'd heard of men who took out their anger on their wives and children. I hoped Ken Gattenger wasn't one of them, but what Mary said worried me. Now I had two reasons to talk to him again before we went to the country. I hoped I'd get to sleep on the train to Lord Harwin's. There wouldn't be time to get any rest before then.

CHAPTER ELEVEN

I'D barely gotten to sleep before Emma came in to get me up and bathed. "I need to get a message to Blackford before we go to the shop today," I told her.

"We can have Mary take it. She knows where the house is, since she worked there a short time before being sent here."

"You've gotten to know her in the few days we've been here." I'd noticed how easily Emma made friends. Much quicker than I did.

She shrugged. "It's my assignment, although I've enjoyed it. I've gotten to know all the servants. The same assignment I'll have at the country house party. Tell me it'll be cooler there."

"It must be. It's out in the country." Truthfully, I had no more idea than Emma did. I was as much a city girl as she.

"This came for you, shoved in the letter slot before anyone rose this morning."

I took the note from Emma, noting the same printing as on the first note. Inside, the message was just as brief.

*Georgia Fenchurch, you've been warned. Stay in London
and away from Lord Harwin's.*
   Otherwise, you will die.

Passing the note to Emma, I said, "Someone knows who we
are and what we're doing."

Emma handed the paper back by one corner, as if she found
it contaminated. "Are you going to tell the duke?"

"No. If we tell Blackford or anyone else, Phyllida will eventually find out, and she'll insist we stop. She wouldn't want to
chance us getting hurt." I gave her a steady gaze. "And we promised her."

Emma nodded. "We won't say a word to anyone. Agreed."

I wrote a note to Blackford over my tea and toast, sent Mary
off with it, and left for the shop with Emma. When we arrived,
Frances and Grace had the front door open to any errant breeze
that might pass. Walking into the office, I found the window
open, the papers filed, and the space free of boxes of unshelved
books.

Grace and Emma were reorganizing the books as they dusted,
and Frances was assisting a customer. Once Frances was free, I
joined her at the counter and said, "You have this place running
like a well-oiled machine."

"It's Sumner and Mrs. Hardwick who've made the difference."

"Mrs. who?"

"Mrs. Hardwick. Sir Broderick's assistant while Jacob is
working on this investigation. She has Sir Broderick busy on
cleaning and reorganizing his house. She even had him ride down
in the elevator yesterday to work on the parlor, stripping the
sheets off the furniture and bringing the room back to life."

"Good heavens." Sir Broderick had had the elevator installed when he was first recovering from his injuries. In the dozen years since then, I'd never known him to use the machine. Mrs. Hardwick had managed this miracle in a few days. "It sounds like the woman has been a tonic for him."

Frances grinned. "She has. You'll like her. Everyone does."

"And Sumner?"

"He loves this place. Works hard shelving books and avoiding customers when he's not running antiquarian books between here and Sir Broderick. He's also our connection to Jacob. I can't wait to hear what he has to report today. Jacob thought he might have figured out who the traitor is in the Admiralty."

Two women came in at that moment. One headed to the latest novels and the other to natural science. With a smile, Frances and I headed to separate parts of the shop. I had just finished with the woman in the literature section when Blackford strode in.

His boots gleamed in the already stifling sunlight pouring heat through the front windows. The creases in his pants and the starch in his collar had not yet wilted. Come to think of it, I'd never seen the duke wilted. He must have ice water in his veins.

He nodded in the direction of Emma and Grace, then in the direction of Frances and her dithering customer, and then approached me. "You have another reason to question Gattenger again?"

"Yes. I need to know why Clara was seen frequently by her doctor, and what happened that caused her to lose a lot of blood only a week before her death."

The duke's eyebrows rose. I was glad to see I could surprise him. "All right. What has Jacob learned?"

"We're waiting on Sumner."

"Not any longer." His gravelly voice came from behind me. Sumner, the ruined half of his face hidden by a bowler hat removed from his head but not yet lowered, headed toward Emma.

She smiled broadly. "Good morning, Mr. Sumner."

"Miss Keyes. Miss Yates," Sumner replied, bowing slightly to Emma and Grace.

"What's the news from Jacob?" Emma asked as Blackford and I moved closer and Frances moved her customer farther away.

"The clerk he thought was the traitor has a well-to-do grandfather who sent the lad to school and got him the job in the Admiralty. He explained his ready cash to Jacob without realizing the point of a conversation on families. He also mentioned a fellow clerk who's been secretive lately and suddenly moved to nicer lodgings. Jacob's going to follow up on him today." Sumner delivered what was for him a lengthy speech as he gazed only at Emma.

"I hope you told Jacob to be careful," she responded directly to him.

"Is he your sweetheart?" Sumner asked with what could have passed for laughter rattling around in the rough edges of his voice.

"No. We come from the same neighborhood. Jacob could have been my brother."

"Sumner. A word," the duke said, and Sumner followed him to a corner of the shop. They kept their voices lowered so that I couldn't overhear their conversation.

Then Blackford put on his white cotton gloves and strolled to the counter. "I'll be by at eleven to take you to Newgate Prison. Now, let's see if you have any antiquarian volumes that interest me."

I showed him a beautifully bound and preserved quarto of the New Testament. I knew there was no point in giving him a sales pitch. If he liked it, he'd buy it on the spot.

One of our most annoying customers, Mrs. Rutherford,

pranced in the open doorway, her maid holding a parasol over her mistress's graying curls and massively flowered hat. The lady carried her yapping lapdog in a basket. Emma moved to wait on her and I turned back to the duke.

He examined the volume closely under the electric lights, shrugged, and handed it back. "Any Shakespeare? I'm more interested in sonnets than parables."

I had an octavo, barely held together any longer, of *The Merchant of Venice* published at the time of the Restoration. Carefully taking it off the shelf, I held the volume out to him.

The duke stared at it for a moment and then took it, quickly becoming absorbed in his examination. "I'll give you thirty pounds for it," he said, not looking up.

"Fifty. It's very rare."

"It's in horrible shape."

The book had been eaten by book worms and attacked on one edge by mold. The ink had faded. I knew what he said was true. "Not as horrible as most copies that age. They no longer exist."

Beyond him, I saw Frances whisper to Grace, and then both of them looked intently in Emma's direction. At the same moment, I saw the stray cat we called Charles Dickens wander in the open door. He headed straight for Emma's skirt.

Grace began to move toward him in one direction and I crossed the shop in another. Mrs. Rutherford's maid had put away the parasol and was now carrying the basket with the dog.

Dickens marched up to the maid and meowed loudly, which set the flat-faced dog to barking madly, her tufts of hair shaking with every move as she hopped around. The maid looked down, saw the cat, and jumped, jostling the basket.

The dog must have seen that as a sign to jump down. She landed first on the maid's dress, then bounced over to her mistress's skirt, and finally back to the maid's skirt above her shoes. Once on the floor, she lunged at Dickens, barking and hopping.

Dickens held his ground, staring at the dog. The dog yapped, her flat face coming within striking distance, the fur on her ears quivering. The cat hissed. Suddenly, a brown paw swung out, claws extended. The dog howled and dashed under Mrs. Rutherford's skirts.

The woman shrieked, holding up her skirts in a shocking display while trying to locate the dog.

The maid rescued the dog, Grace grabbed Dickens, and I rushed in to make peace with Mrs. Rutherford.

"My dog has a bloodied nose," she exclaimed, once again holding the dog basket and petting the shivering dog.

"I'm so sorry. You're very wise to keep her in a basket where she's free from unfortunate incidents." Such as being stepped on or kicked. Dogs did not belong in bookshops. Neither did cats, but Dickens was a good mouser.

"You should keep animals from coming into your shop."

I smiled. "Then I should have to ban your dog."

"Saucy girl."

"I'd have to ban Saucy Girl." I'd love to. The racket the dog made when left alone in her basket was nearly as bad as when Dickens struck.

"No. You're being a saucy girl. The dog's name is Jane and she's a well-mannered house dog. You're keeping a feral cat."

I restrained myself from throwing her bodily into the street for her insult. Instead I said, "Dickens isn't feral. He's a working cat, performing a valued service for the shopkeepers on this street. If we didn't have Dickens, we'd be overrun with vermin."

Seeing her face turn crimson, I added, "You'll need to have

Jane return at a time when we're certain Dickens isn't working
in the immediate area."

"How will we know?"

"I have no idea. I've not figured out his work schedule yet."
I was keeping both my temper and a straight face with difficulty.

"Well, I hope you teach that cat some manners."

"I'm sure Grace is dealing with him most severely. Now,
Emma, will you see what Mrs. Rutherford requires."

I returned to waiting on the duke, certain Grace was in the
office spoiling Dickens.

Blackford looked up from the ancient volume and continued
our discussion as if it hadn't been interrupted. "That's why you
keep old books behind the brass grille, so air will flow around
them. That's why you installed electric lights, to keep gas and oil
smoke from damaging them. That's why you keep them at torso
height, so there won't be as great a temperature change as at floor
or ceiling level. You have a soft spot for the written word. You
can't stand to see old books dissolve into dust."

He smiled then and reached for his wallet. "And I should
never forget you know this business as well as you know how to
step into character and run an investigation. Forty."

"No. Fifty. It *is* a very rare edition."

Carefully turning it over in his hands once more, he said,
"Done."

"I'll wrap it for you." I took a piece of brown paper and carefully began to cocoon the volume. "I think it matters to you, too.
That old things don't turn to dust."

"My title's older than that book. I feel comfortable with old
things." After he paid me and took his parcel, he gave me a slight
bow, glanced at Mrs. Rutherford, and then turned back to give
me a wink. "Everything all right now, Miss Keyes?"

Emma dropped into a curtsy and said, "It is, Your Grace. Mrs. Rutherford, may I present the Duke of Blackford?"

Mrs. Rutherford smiled, simpered, and fussed with her hat as the duke nodded to her. Then she gave a deep curtsy, nearly dropping the dog out of its basket again. "Pleased to meet you, Your Grace."

"Good day, Mrs. Rutherford." Then he walked out of the bookshop, Sumner on his heels.

The duke knew the power of his title. Mrs. Rutherford fussed the rest of her visit, but she also was heard to giggle.

Blackford had been gone less than five minutes before Sir Jonah Denby arrived, swinging his cane as he walked up to me. "How is the investigation coming, Miss Fenchurch?"

I motioned him to join me in my office away from customers. Once we were in the privacy of the crowded space, I asked, "Have you been sending me threatening notes?"

His green eyes widened. "Good heavens, no. I'm on your side."

"The Duke of Blackford is working with Whitehall, and he swears he's never met you, much less told you what I'm doing." I'd found a few mentions of Denby working for Her Majesty's government. He had to be legitimate, and yet—

"Our government is a large organization. I doubt even someone as comprehensively involved as the duke has met everyone. And I'm only a minor functionary. Now, tell me, what has happened?"

"Someone is threatening me in an effort to stop us from finding the blueprints."

"I would never do such a thing, I assure you. All I want is for the blueprints to be found and returned to the Admiralty. Now, do you have any news to report?"

I now knew from my reference books that Sir Jonah Denby worked in Whitehall, lived in London, and belonged to respectable clubs. Not someone likely to steal warship blueprints, but I would also say that of Sir Henry Stanford. I'd also not been able to find a connection between Denby and von Steubfeld or Gattenger. But why did Denby say Blackford had told him about me one day and then as much as admit Blackford didn't know him on another? "We think we've identified the thief and hope to follow him to the person who hired him."

"You've identified the thief? Wonderful," Sir Jonah said. "Who?"

"We're not mentioning his name to anyone. You'll have to trust us to do our jobs."

"Can you catch him?"

"We will. And we'll retrieve the plans." I gave him a hard stare. "Now, what is your role—" I began, but Sir Jonah cut me off.

"Good work, Miss Fenchurch. Thank you." With a smile, Sir Jonah stepped quickly the length of the shop and out into the street.

When the duke arrived to escort me to Newgate, I told him about my latest visit from Denby.

"We're meeting with some people from Whitehall tonight. Hopefully, he'll be there. If not, we'll get to the bottom of this. Don't worry." Blackford's lack of concern relieved me. I forgot Sir Jonah as I climbed into the carriage.

The prison was as bleak as I remembered it, but the heat wave had lasted long enough to have penetrated the corridors. Putrid smells rose up from the stones. Sweat rolled down my shift. The hair at the duke's neckline began to curl, the only sign that he perspired.

Gattenger had shrunk, his hair limp on his head, his skin graying as if he'd already died. I sat across the table from him again and stared at him. He didn't look in my direction.

"Why did you call the doctor so many times for cousin Clara?" I began.

"Guard, take me back to my cell," Gattenger said.

"No," Blackford said in that ducal tone that froze people in place.

"Was she ill, Kenny?"

"No. I don't think so. The doctor didn't think so. I don't know."

"Did you beat her?"

He looked at me then, a ferocious gleam lighting his eyes. "No. I'd never hurt Clara. I'd rather chop off my arm. I loved her."

"Why was she bruised? Where did the blood come from?"

"I asked her when we were first dating if her father beat her. She wouldn't speak to me for a week. It turned out she bruised easily. She had since childhood. And the blood—oh, God." He burst into tears and buried his face in his arms on the table.

"The blood, Gattenger," Blackford said.

When I realized, I couldn't believe it had taken me so long. "She was with child, wasn't she, Kenny? The blood came from a miscarriage. That's what the doctor will tell us, won't he?"

He straightened, wiping at his eyes with his fingers. "Two. In the year we'd been married, Clara had suffered two miscarriages. She wanted a baby so badly. She felt she'd failed me, while I couldn't care less. I loved Clara. She was all I needed."

"And when the maid heard her tell you she couldn't stand a third time, she was sending you from her room so she couldn't get with child again." The poor woman was probably distraught.

"Yes."

"And those stories about the two of you fighting in public, that was her reaction to something that reminded her about the miscarriages."

"Only the first one. We'd not had a chance to go out in the evening after the second one before she—" He pinched the bridge of his nose and then took a breath. "She lost a lot of blood and was very weak."

"Being the daughter of a lord, she'd consider giving you an heir of more importance than you put on it," Blackford said, more to himself than to Gattenger.

Lady Bennett might see me as a rival in a contest to become the duke's paramour, but he'd soon need to marry and produce an heir to the dukedom. And neither of us would be considered for the position of duchess.

"Poor Clara. Fearing she'd failed me, when in the end, I failed her." Gattenger shook his head.

I broke in then. "I have another question. Why did you take the drawings of the new warship out of the Admiralty that night?"

"Why did I? It was such a mistake. It cost Clara her life."

Before Gattenger could go off on another round of self-pity, I said, "You said there was a question about a calculation. Why take the drawings out that night? Why not work on them in the Admiralty or take them out another night?"

"Sir Henry said he was certain I'd made a mistake, and if I didn't correct it immediately, he was going to the Admiralty Board the next morning. He'd tell them my design was flawed and not worth bidding on. I couldn't let him. Not after I'd failed to give Clara the baby she wanted. I couldn't ruin her economic standing, her home, her position in society."

"Had the Admiralty paid you for the design?"

"In part."

"And you needed money. You were desperate for money."

He hung his head. "Yes."

I pushed harder. "Desperate enough to take German money in exchange for a copy of the plans."

He looked into my eyes then and slowly shook his head. "No. I thought I would, but then I backed out. When I didn't have to worry about the baby anymore."

"So they offered you money, and you accepted. But then you changed your mind. Did you tell them no?"

His posture straightened. "Of course I did. And I never agreed. Not really. I said I'd think about it."

"What did they do when you turned them down?"

He sank down again. "They threatened me. They said they'd destroy me."

I glanced at the duke. "Who did?"

"I don't know who he was. A large man with a German accent. Lethal looking. He stayed in the shadows."

My excitement must have shown in my voice. "When did this happen?"

"Two nights before—that night. While I was walking home."

"And then Sir Henry Stanford forced you into taking the drawings out two days later?" Blackford shook his head. "Sir Henry's not smart enough to figure out any flaws on his own."

I ignored the duke and leaned my face close to the prisoner's. "You were afraid Sir Henry was right, weren't you?"

Gattenger nodded.

"Why? Did you have doubts about your design?"

I had Blackford's attention now. He leaned forward over the table, no doubt so he could hear every whisper Gattenger might make.

Gattenger murmured his words with his eyes shut. "Yes. The people at the Admiralty took my drawings before I'd conducted tests on scale models. Before the ink was dry on the blueprints. Before I'd checked and rechecked all my calculations over and over. I was so excited about my new design I told them about it immediately, and they paid me and took possession of all my drawings then and there.

"The balance of the big guns may be off, or I may have over-loaded the ship with heavy weapons. I'm just not sure." He slammed his fist on the table.

"You're afraid the ship will sink." Blackford leaped to his feet and made a quick circle of the room.

Gattenger looked up at him and said, "I'm not sure. I took a set of the drawings home to get all the figures I'd need to run the miniaturized tests."

This didn't make sense to me. "Why did they take the draw-ings before you were ready to hand them over?"

"The Admiralty got wind of a German plan to beat us to the punch with a new warship. They took the designs, copied the blueprints, and began bidding for building the first ship. They want to conduct sea trials as soon as possible. The Admiralty wants Britain to be first."

"So you don't know if the plans as you designed them will work."

"I'm not even certain the ship will float. Not anymore. Not since Sir Henry voiced his doubts. Sir Henry Stanford knows ships."

Beside me, Blackford snorted. I dipped my head and shook it. This nightmare just got worse. Not only were we chasing after a set of plans the Admiralty hoped had been destroyed and the

Germans would pay a ransom for, but the designer didn't know whether the ship would even sail.

"How long will it take you to decide if Sir Henry was right or not?" Blackford asked.

Gattenger shrugged. "Two days at the most. Probably only a few hours."

"Can you decide with only a full set of the plans to work from? No scale model tests?"

"The tests would just prove my suspicions. Yes, I should be able to check to make certain the ship will perform as designed."

"I'll try to have someone from the Admiralty bring you a set of plans and wait while you work on them. I'm not promising anything, but I'll try." The duke rose. "I need an answer to this question of the seaworthiness of your warship as badly as I suspect you do."

"Thank you. I'll do the best I can." The two men shook hands.

"God bless you, Mr. Gattenger," I said as I stood. As far as I was concerned, if the ship would sink, we ought to let the Germans steal the design.

I walked with the duke on the long trek down confining hallways, pleased when the last clank of a gate locking sounded behind me. The sun beat down on us mercilessly, but I was glad to be out in untainted air.

The duke helped me into the carriage and, once he was settled across from me, said, "Sir Henry doesn't have the knowledge to tell if that ship will sink or not. Did the Germans or someone else put him up to it? Or did he use his doubts as a ruse to get Gattenger to take a set out of the Admiralty so he could steal them?"

"Either way, we need Gattenger to check his blueprints before five this afternoon. I have to tell Sir Henry something."

"I need to talk to my contacts in the Admiralty and arrange for someone to take him a set of the blueprints and then wait. You're going to have to lie to Sir Henry."

"I don't know anything about warships. How do I lie convincingly?"

"You'll manage. I'm amazed at how competent you are, Georgia. Are you sure you don't want me to show up a little after five?" He leaned forward in his seat and took my gloved hand in his.

Even through the fabric and leather, I felt his warmth and his strength. We exchanged smiles before I said, "No. I'll be fine."

"Then I'll drop you off at the bookshop and stop by the town house at seven."

"No chance of an early bedtime tonight?"

He shook his head. "You must learn to sleep through the morning. We have a dinner party to attend and then I'll take you to my home. A few hours later, I'll return you to your town house."

"But people will think—" My drooping eyes flew open.

"Precisely."

CHAPTER TWELVE

AFTER I gave final instructions on how to run the bookshop in my absence for the fifth time, I asked Frances, "Does your family have any problem with you leaving for the entire day every day?"

"Don't worry, Georgia. My son is too busy to notice and his wife is happy I'm not there to interfere with running the hotel. She's stopped mentioning how nice it would be if I moved to her family's farm." Frances patted my arm. "We'll be fine."

"Grace, any sign of Lord Barnwood returning soon?"

"My employer refuses to set foot in London until this heat wave ends. So hurry back. We'll miss you, and we're more than willing to share this weather. You know how misery loves company." She laughed as she fanned herself with her hand and left to wait on a customer.

"Georgia, go. Sir Broderick is phoning us daily to make sure we have everything we need, and Archivist Society members are stopping by at odd moments to run errands and lift boxes. The shop will be fine."

I gave her a brave smile, but inside, I didn't want to leave. "Thank you. All of you."

I tried to linger, but Emma dragged me out of the shop. She led me back yet another route to the town house for a cold lunch in the large, gloomy dining room. The furniture was dark wood and the walls were papered in a washed-out rose on a charcoal background. The lace curtains blocked any sunlight that might have cut through the dimness. The room matched my mood.

"More calls today?" I asked Phyllida.

"No one would be home. Along with the rest of what's left of polite society in London, we're going shopping on Regent Street and Piccadilly. And we'll need to take Emma with us to carry packages."

"And the money will come from where?" I couldn't afford a shopping spree on Regent Street. Those shops were well out of the size of my purse. And I needed to question people, not look through store windows, so I could return to my own shop.

"The duke has set up an account in my name at various businesses. There will be no trouble about it."

"Phyllida, he's coming by tonight to take me to Blackford House. Alone. I suspect there'll be trouble tomorrow." I was tired, hot, and upset. I was not in the mood to pretend to have an affair. I would either leap into bed with him or scratch his eyes out. Possibly both.

"Georg—ina," Phyllida said, stopping herself at the last moment from calling me by my real name, "the duke is a gentleman. Relax."

I'd dealt with the duke before. I was not about to relax.

"We have lots of stops to make. Milliners, glovers, parasol

makers, shoemakers, hosiers, jewelers, perfumers. All places where we will be seen, and where we can watch anyone we want to keep an eye on. All for the price of a pair of hose."

She smiled, and I realized I had a lot to learn to play my role convincingly. For me, shopping was something I had to fit in quickly between other errands.

But not today. After lunch, Phyllida, Emma, and I climbed into a hired carriage and rode to Regent Street. We started at the top end where Regent Street crossed Oxford Street in a mad confusion of wagons, omnibuses, carriages, hansom cabs, and all their horses. Pedestrians had to look sharp to keep from being run over. We dismissed the carriage and walked downhill toward Piccadilly in the general direction of the Thames.

The small, tasteful displays in the windows and the number of maids and footmen trailing well-dressed women let me know this neighborhood was out of Georgia Fenchurch's league. It was nice, for a day, to be Georgina Monthalf.

We walked two blocks on those crowded sidewalks before Phyllida met someone she recognized. "Lady Ormond," she said as she curtsied to the sharp-faced woman who today was leading a girl still in the schoolroom and a footman in livery.

"Lady Monthalf," the other replied. "I heard you were in the prime minister's box at the Royal Albert Hall last night."

"Actually, he was in ours. Or rather, the Duke of Blackford's."

"He's a friend of your cousin, isn't he?"

They reminded me of two dogs circling each other, sniffing.

"Yes, he is." I gave her a decent curtsy.

Outranking me by title and age, she gave me a small nod. "How are you finding our unseasonable heat?"

Phyllida's tone was aristocratic as she said, "Actually, we're leaving for the country tomorrow. Lord Harwin's invited us."

Surprise and speculation shone in Lady Ormond's eyes as she glanced at me. Her features kept their polite, distant expression. "Oh, we shall be neighbors, then. We're going to Gloucestershire also, to the Marquis of Tewes's estate. This is my granddaughter, Alicia, up from the country for a short visit. We've been doing a round of the shops."

Alicia gave us a nice curtsy and almost managed to hide her twelve-year-old boredom.

Once we passed by, I murmured to Emma, "This is going to complicate things for our burglar if he comes down from London to pass on the drawings. I imagine every inn near Lord Harwin's will be booked up with people escaping the London heat to take the waters at the spa."

"It might also make him stand out more when we question the landlords of the inns."

"And the pubs," I added. The burglar would have to be somewhere when he wasn't trying to contact Baron von Steubfeld. Or whoever he planned to contact with the ship plans.

When we saw Lady Bennett in Fortier's Jewelers, we walked in. Emma waited by the door while Phyllida and I stood on either side of her. "Lady Bennett," I said.

We curtsied and the shop assistant behind the counter bowed. "What brings you in here, Mrs. Monthalf? Shopping for jewelry?" Lark Bennett asked.

"Wouldn't that be fun," I said, trying to hide my alarm at spending money on anything in so expensive a shop. "What are you getting?"

"The clasp on this necklace repaired." It was a pearl choker with diamonds strung through in an intricate pattern. "I want to take it with me tomorrow. Thank you, Henry. The work is perfect." She pronounced his name in the French fashion.

"Thank you, madame." The clerk had a slight French accent.

"Is Fortier's a French company?" I asked.

"It was, but we've been here since the Revolution." He gave me a small smile. "Everyone who could afford our workmanship came to England."

Lark Bennett picked up the small pile of bags and the hatbox she was carrying. The gold writing spelling out *Gautier's* flashed in a sunbeam from the window.

The bell over the door chimed, and from years of habit, I turned to see who'd come in. Lady Peters strode three steps into the shop, blinking in the change from brilliant sunshine to shadow. As soon as she saw us she froze. An instant later her face took on a welcoming smile. I wondered if I was the only one who saw the look of fear or dismay cross her features before she set her expression in place and stepped forward to greet us. She'd worn a similar expression when Lady Bennett had called on her the day we'd been there.

We went through a round of curtsies before I said, "Lady Peters, have you ever seen anything as exquisite as Lady Bennett's necklace?"

"I've seen her wear it before. Truly lovely." Rosamond Peters's tone was smooth but less than enthusiastic.

"Have you been lucky in your purchases today?" Phyllida asked.

"So fortunate my maid has had to load them into a carriage, since she couldn't carry any more. So many last-minute details before going to the country. And you?" Lady Peters, too, carried a hatbox from Gautier's.

Phyllida drew a cloak of highborn aristocratic reserve about her. "We've barely started. Mrs. Monthalf hasn't been shopping in London before, so we are making a circuit to familiarize her with all the city has to offer."

Well done, Phyllida. She was growing into her role. "Are you shopping here today, Lady Peters?" I asked.

"I'm dropping off a chain to have the clasp repaired." Lady Peters brought out a gold chain with a gold heart-shaped pendant. On the pendant was etched a finely detailed rose.

Phyllida oohed and aahed over the jewelry. The shop owner took the chain and logged it into the large book on the counter before he handed the pendant back to Lady Peters.

"You should hold on to this, milady," he said with a small bow.

"Yes, of course." Lady Peters glanced around. "Oh, Lady Bennett, I see we shop at the same milliner."

Their hatboxes were identical. "Is there anyone in London designing prettier hats?" Lady Bennett asked.

"And a lady can never have too many hats." Lady Peters dropped her pendant into her purse. "I'll see you ladies tomorrow at Paddington Station."

After a round of curtsies, we followed Lady Peters out into the wilting sunshine. She walked away before Lady Bennett said, "I'm off home. Enjoy your shopping, although I imagine this doesn't rival the markets in Singapore. My sister says the Chinese market there has better silks and spices than we get in London."

"I haven't seen any silks or spices here to make a comparison," I replied. "Good day." I didn't want to fake knowledge of the Far East that I lacked. Lady Bennett would no doubt check every statement I made when her sister arrived.

Free of the two ladies, we continued down Regent Street to Piccadilly. When we passed Hatchard's bookshop, I looked in the windows with the eye of a rival proprietor, but I didn't dare go in. The staff at Hatchard's knew me as Georgia Fenchurch of Fenchurch's Books.

We followed Piccadilly to Old Bond Street, looking in the

windows of more shoemakers, hosiers, and glovers. I noticed two more hatboxes from Gautier's carried past us, drawing Phyllida's attention. She led us into shop after shop as we climbed the grade up to New Bond Street. I bought a pair of short white kid gloves and some sheer hose. Emma nudged me as a signal to buy her some thin white stockings.

When we reached the milliner's window, Phyllida enthusiastically rushed us into Gautier's and found a straw hat with a wide, floppy brim that made her look rakish. Gautier packed her purchase in the same eight-sided brown carton, flat on the top and bottom, that we'd seen several times that day. The only flourish to the container was the name of the store printed on the sides in shiny gold.

We walked up the sidewalk slowly, while I looked for a hire carriage to take us back to the town house. Behind me, I heard a yelp. I turned to see Emma fall to the ground, her packages flying. A young man scooped up Phyllida's hatbox by the string handle and ran down an alley.

"Stop him!" Phyllida screamed. "Help! Police! Somebody stop him!"

There were few pedestrians out in the heat and Phyllida loved that hat. Abandoning my role as a well-bred lady, I held up my skirt and took off down the alley.

The young man was fast, but he wasn't clever. I saw him look over his shoulder at me and dart off to his left. Thanks to Emma's childhood training in the East End, in the cool of the mornings she'd dragged me down every shortcut between the town house and my bookshop. I knew he'd gone down a dead end.

I hurried to the turnoff and then slowed down, catching my breath. Our robber was trying to pull off the grilles over doors and windows, searching in vain for an escape.

Emma ran up to my side, her plain black uniform dirty and her hem torn.

"You okay?" I asked, stalking toward the foolish young man.

She nodded and moved farther to my left. Her knife was in her hand.

The young man saw the knife, dropped the hatbox, and tried to run past us. Emma made a feint with her knife while I slammed my fist into his face. He went down in a sobbing heap.

Emma put her knife away and retrieved the hatbox while I kept a hand on his collar. "What do you want with a hat?"

"The gent said to steal a case jest like that 'un from the lady and bring it to him. 'E didn't say nothin' about being chased by ladies with knives."

"What gent?"

"Dunno. Kept his face hidden behind a white cloth." The robber wiped at his bloody nose with a dirty kerchief.

"So he was dressed as a gentleman?"

"More like a shop assistant, but real clean."

Looking at the young man, I wondered what his standards were for clean. "Did he pay you?"

"Half."

"Well, that's all you'll be getting," Emma said cheerfully as she helped me pull him to his feet and march him between us back to New Bond Street.

The bobby on the beat turned away from Phyllida and came down the alley to meet us. He put handcuffs on the prisoner and marched him toward the nearest station, saying, "You ladies shouldn't chase after criminals on your own. You might get hurt."

"'Ere. They're the ones with the knives. I'm unarmed," our young robber said.

"Tell it to the magistrate," the bobby said.

"Do you need us to come with you as witnesses?" I asked.

"If you don't mind sending your maid with me to speak to the magistrate, we'll get her home after," the bobby said.

"Of course. Emma?" I held out my hand, and she gave me the hatbox.

"What's in there?" the bobby asked.

"A very stylish new hat belonging to Lady Phyllida Monthalf," Emma replied, while I felt the weight of Emma's wicked blade slide across the bottom of the box.

"'Ey, not 'er. She's got a nasty-lookin' knife."

"No, I don't," Emma said, giving the thief a big smile. "You can search me for one if you want. You won't find a thing. He's lying."

Our young robber knew we'd pulled some sort of switch and shook his head in frustration. The bobby was trying to be gallant to Emma, asking her name and saying he hoped she hadn't been hurt as they walked off.

I turned to Phyllida. "We need to find a carriage to take us home after our excitement."

"Thank you, Georgina, for rescuing my new hat." She clutched the box to her.

"And I'm certain it will look lovely on you." Baron von Steubfeld stepped out of the small crowd that had gathered to watch the commotion. "I was just dining in the Grosvenor Club across the street. My carriage will be here in a moment. Perhaps I can give you ladies a ride home?" He bowed.

"That is most kind of you, Baron." Phyllida curtsied.

I followed with my own curtsy. "That would be lovely."

His carriage, with the German embassy seal on the side, pulled up nearby and the three of us, and all our packages, fit into the interior. Like everything else in London, the black leather seats were hot enough to iron our skirts and scald our skin.

"I'm so glad you're traveling with us to Gloucestershire," I said, sounding lame to my ears. "I've never been to Germany, and I hope you'll tell me more about it."

"That would be my pleasure. We have much to delight the tourist. Magnificent scenery. Medieval castles and cathedrals. Museums. Folk festivals. You must come to Germany sometime. Both of you."

"But it's not so modern a country as Britain, is it?"

"Never. It is more modern. Our military is the greatest in Europe. Our industry surpasses Britain's. But those are not the things that would interest two ladies." He smiled at me through that ferocious mustache, and I returned the smile.

"Tell me," he continued, "what caused the scene in the street just now?"

"A robber knocked over our maid and stole my hatbox," Phyllida told him.

"You are unhurt?"

"Yes, quite unhurt."

"That is fortunate. And he stole nothing else?"

"No."

"How odd." The baron fell silent.

It was an odd thing to steal, but it was a good size for holding all the plans to Gattenger's new ship. If the baron truly thought it was odd, maybe he wasn't in on the theft. Who else had spies in London?

The French and the Russians, surely. Perhaps the Austrians. Could I get him to talk about the other diplomats? "Do you have any diplomatic events in the near future? I imagine full dress uniforms with loads of medals would be uncomfortable in hot weather."

"They are, but there are no events scheduled until the queen returns from Osborne House."

"Do you see other diplomats in London outside of formal events?"

"Of course. I was just dining with the first secretary of the Austrian embassy while you had your scuffle with a thief." He gave me a tight-lipped smile that seemed to dare me to ask anything else.

Once we arrived at the town house, I took a cool bath both to wake me up and to remove the dust and sweat that clung to my skin. Then, while Phyllida bathed, I helped Emma pack for our trip the next morning.

"The magistrate didn't question me closely and let me go with his thanks. He paid no attention to our robber's claim that I had a knife." She gave me her angelic smile, all blond innocence and big blue eyes.

If I'd been the magistrate, I'd have believed her, too. Emma's looks let her get away with almost anything, particularly when she was trying to get around a male. Eight or eighty, it didn't matter. They all crumbled at her feet.

"Do you think the theft had anything to do with the anonymous note?" Emma asked.

"If it did, it was very poorly done." I looked at Emma and shrugged. "I think our correspondent is brighter than to use that foolish young man."

"I think you're right," Emma said while she folded one of my dresses. Then I saw her nibble on her bottom lip. "I've never been outside of London."

"It's all right, Emma. I seldom have, either. But the trains go out there, and we'll have Blackford there. And Sumner part of the time. It's not like you have to sleep in the fields and forests at night. You'll be safely inside."

She gave me a dry look. "Inside may not be any safer. But I'll do whatever needs to be done to find out who killed Clara Gattenger, and so will you."

"I was only trying to make you feel better." I folded a petticoat with more vigor than necessary.

"I know. And I'll be glad when we go home, too."

I nodded. We understood each other.

There was a knock on the door and then we heard male voices. "Oh, blast. It's five o'clock. Sir Henry is here to extract his first pound of flesh."

Emma was immediately on alert.

I patted her arm. "I'll explain when I come back upstairs."

A moment later, a maid brought up a calling card on a tray. Sir Henry.

"Thank you. Have him wait in the parlor. Tell him I'll be right there."

The maid curtsied and went downstairs.

"Emma, keep Phyllida up here. I'm going to have to lie, and it's imperative that Phyllida is ignorant of the lies I tell him."

"You have a plan?"

I nodded.

"Good luck."

She tidied my hair and then I walked down to the parlor. I shut the door to the hall and faced Sir Henry, who'd risen when I walked in.

"This is quite a nice house. Rented with Lady Phyllida's money, I suppose?" Disdain dripped from his voice.

"I paid my share. Edgar didn't leave me completely without resources."

"If I were to contact the authorities in Singapore, what would I learn?" He moved forward to stand improperly close to me. The gleam in his eye told me he was gloating.

"That my husband's death saved him from a great deal of embarrassment."

"Financial problems?"

I nodded.

"What would I learn about you?" He ran the back of his hand along my cheek.

I turned my face aside. "That I left quickly for England with funds that Edgar might have had to explain."

"And you should still be wearing mourning?" he asked, apparently buying the impression I gave that I'd escaped Singapore and arrived in England without bothering about full mourning.

"I spoke to Ken Gattenger," I answered. I wasn't going to give him anything specific about my life in Singapore. I had nothing specific to give.

"What did he say?" he asked, immediately focused on his own interests.

"The ship will float. There's nothing wrong with the calculations."

Sir Henry grabbed my upper arm in the same place as the previous night and pulled me against him. "You'd better not be lying."

"I'm not. Now let go of me." I didn't add, *You make me feel soiled*.

He had a cruel smile on his lips as he studied my eyes. "The blueprints are correct as they're written?"

"Yes. Let go of me," I hissed out from between my teeth.

He let me go but he blocked my path to the door. "I'd hoped to get you to invest in my shipyard, but you can't do that without money. Does Lady Phyllida know you're broke?"

I decided to let him think he had a bigger hold over me than he did. "I'm not broke."

"Close enough."

I shrugged.

"What a pity." He sneered, ruining his good looks. "But handy for me. I'll have another task for you to carry out at Lord Harwin's. Until tomorrow. And remember, I'm very good at uncovering secrets. If you try to deceive me, everything will be revealed."

Laughing softly, he walked out of my parlor and down the stairs. I heard the front door open and close.

I stood there rubbing my arm with a shaking hand. I wasn't worried about Georgina's secrets. I was worried about Georgia's secrets and those of the Archivist Society. Sir Henry could be a dangerous man with all the digging he'd done into my background. But somehow I knew he hadn't written my threatening letters. He received too much enjoyment from bullying me in person.

CHAPTER THIRTEEN

RETURNING to my room, I filled Emma in on Sir Henry while she helped me dress. Once Phyllida rose from her nap and joined us, we changed the topic.

I had no idea what Blackford had in mind when he called for me later. I wore a new Georgina Monthalf gown of turquoise satin with emerald earrings. He looked me over intently before he said, "Exquisite."

"Am I really going to Blackford House after dinner?" I hoped he was teasing.

"Bring a dark cloak so it looks like you're sneaking out for an assignation."

"What am I really doing?"

"Visiting my house so that it looks like we're having an assignation."

"Should I take my maid?"

"Not unless you want everyone to think we engage in shocking, rather than scandalous, behavior." He shook his head. "Besides, I'd like to keep Emma's name out of this if you don't mind."

"Because she's a young innocent?"

"And because Sumner might take offense. We need him on this investigation, Georgina."

So he had seen the growing interest between Emma and Sumner. I thought he was completely oblivious to the concerns of others.

"Have you heard anything from Jacob?" I asked.

"Sumner arrived at my house earlier and said Jacob's been rebuffed by the clerk he now thinks is the best candidate to be in the pay of the Germans."

"How will we get any news while we're out in the country?"

"I booked a room in the closest inn for Sumner to use while we're at Lord Harwin's. We'll shuttle messages back to London through him. If worse comes to worst, I have a code set up with my man of affairs to use in a telegram."

I was impressed. "You've thought of everything."

"I'd better. Britain's security rests on keeping those plans out of the hands of the Germans."

I shook my head slightly so the dangling emerald earrings brushed my neck. "The life of Ken Gattenger rests on our finding the plans and the thief, who might not be in the employ of the Germans." I thought of Sir Henry. "We have to consider that possibility."

"What happened with Stanford this afternoon?" He studied my face as he reached out and took my hand.

"I told him Gattenger said it would float. Has he checked that out yet?"

"He ran through a set of blueprints at the prison this afternoon. All the calculations say it should be a success."

"Good. I admitted I was broke, that Edgar died while under suspicion of financial chicanery, and I told him Phyllida doesn't know. He thinks I'm at his service for any more errands he may have in exchange for his silence. He told me there would be one at Lord Harwin's."

Blackford smiled. "Involving the blueprints?"

"I don't know."

We rode to dinner in his unmarked carriage. I wondered how often he'd taken a woman to Blackford House in this manner. Dragging my mind away from our supposed purpose, I said, "We had some excitement earlier today. Phyllida's new hat was stolen."

The duke raised his eyebrows, but he didn't say anything.

"Some young thief knocked Emma over and stole the hatbox. Nothing else. Emma and I chased after him and caught him in a dead-end alley. The bobby arrested him, Emma gave a statement, and Phyllida and I rode home in a carriage belonging to the German embassy."

"Baron von Steubfeld?"

I nodded.

The duke leaned forward on the seat. "Why was he there? And what did he say about this strange crime?"

"He was having luncheon at the Grosvenor Club, and he didn't say much about the crime. He seemed puzzled by it. So was the thief, who was paid by a man whose face he didn't see to steal a lady's hatbox from Gautier's."

"If we assume he stole the wrong hatbox, who had the one he should have grabbed, and what was in it?" Blackford looked out the side window of the carriage and murmured as if he were talking to himself.

"I think a hatbox could hold the plans to the warship."

"Easily. Von Steubfeld wasn't carrying any packages, was he?"

"None. And both Lady Bennett and Lady Peters had hatboxes identical to Phyllida's. Could this be how they plan to get the ship designs to Germany? The dowager duchess and her daughter should be leaving for Germany soon. No one would be surprised if they carried a hatbox."

"They've already left. All their luggage was searched by agents of our government disguised as baggage guards. Nothing was found, and the ladies haven't yet realized we explored every inch of their trunks on the train to the coast."

"What about at their seats in the rail carriage with their possessions?"

"Neither lady carried anything large enough to hold the blueprints. Their servants were searched, discreetly, out of sight of the ladies. I suspect there will be a complaint filed with Whitehall by the German embassy on behalf of the dowager as soon as she speaks to her servants."

We pulled up in front of an elegant town house. "We'll talk later. Leave your cloak in the carriage." The duke climbed out first and then turned to me, his arms outstretched.

I'd planned to leave my evening cloak in the carriage. I certainly didn't need extra clothes in this heat to stay warm. Blackford's gruff tone clashed with the solicitousness he displayed for anyone watching as he lifted me down and ushered me into the house. At a distance, he appeared to be treating me like a lover.

Our hosts, Lord and Lady Fleetwhite, met us at the double doors as we were announced into the drawing room. The only thing I knew about him was he was important at Whitehall. I knew nothing about her. When I was almost immediately introduced to Mr. Goschen, the First Lord of the Admiralty, I felt like I had stepped into another world. Last night I had met the prime minister. Tonight it was a member of his cabinet.

There were two other, younger men in the room who were introduced as Sir William Darby and Mr. Frederick Nobles. I curtsied my way through the introductions, praying my shock and confusion didn't show.

One of the things Phyllida had taught me was the importance of having an even number of men and women at dinner parties. She said she learned the necessity of balanced numbers at social events at about the time she learned to walk. Since Lady Fleetwhite was the only other lady present, I knew something was not right.

We went into the dining room, where instead of being seated by order of precedence, I had the duke on one side and Sir William on the other. Lady Fleetwhite sat across from me, with Mr. Nobles on one side and Mr. Goschen on the other. Lord Fleetwhite sat at our end of the table. The other half of the table sat empty of place settings or decoration, putting us close enough together so that no one needed to raise his voice to be heard.

"I'm afraid we're not doing things by the rules tonight," Lady Fleetwhite said.

"More in the family style. How lovely," I replied with a bright smile. My mind was working feverishly. They wanted something from me, or more precisely, the Archivist Society. Since the Admiralty was represented, I knew Gattenger's blueprints for the new warship were the reason for this meeting.

Once the soup course had been delivered to our mysterious dinner party, the servants departed. I had eaten one spoonful when Lord Fleetwhite said, "I understand you don't believe Kenneth Gattenger killed his wife."

"I don't."

"Why?"

I took a deep breath as I set down my spoon. "A burglar could have come and gone from the study during the Gattengers' dinner without leaving a trace. However, they had a shortened dinner that night and went straight to the study. There's room behind the door for an enterprising thief to hide when the Gattengers entered the room."

Glancing around, I saw I had everyone's attention. The duke gave me an encouraging nod. "Gattenger says that's where the burglar hid, and it was only when Gattenger blocked his escape out the window that the thief, with the plans in one hand, struck him down. The shouting the servants heard could have been Mr. and Mrs. Gattenger shouting at the thief when they saw him, and not a fight between husband and wife."

"A convenient story," Sir William said. "The thief could have easily escaped through the house."

"With the household raising a hue and cry after him? This way, the burglar could escape unseen by any but the Gattengers. Kenny was down, no threat to him, and he apparently didn't realize Clara would try to stop him. He probably made the mistake of thinking a woman would have the vapors at the slightest hint of trouble."

Lady Fleetwhite looked down, her serviette raised too late to hide her smile.

"Yes, well," Sir William began and ground to a stop.

"We need to know what happened to those plans. That warship is increasingly important to our safety as a nation," Mr. Goschen said. I wondered if the worry lines etched into his forehead and around his eyes were new or from years of serving Her Majesty. The dark circles under his eyes were no doubt due to the current crisis.

"I think Clara grabbed for the plans and managed to tear at least the last sheet. I also think the burglar struck out at her to try to save the plans he was sent to steal. The piece that was found partially burned near her body could have fallen into the fire when she was attacked and killed. Her death may have been a tragic accident." Clara, who'd married beneath her class for love and died protecting her husband's work, had won my admiration.

"The thief has the plans minus at least part of the last page. A page with critical calculations," Blackford said. "You must be ready for an attempt to steal that last page. And we believe we've uncovered a traitor in the records room."

"Who?" Goschen demanded.

"We have someone planted in the records room who is watching the suspect. As soon as he is certain, he'll let us know," the duke said.

"So far, there's been no report of anyone tampering with or trying to steal the last page of those blueprints," Goschen said.

"We don't believe the person who ordered the theft has learned part of the plans is missing. The thief still has them, and he wouldn't know what was important and what wasn't," Blackford said.

"How do we know we can trust the discretion of the Archivist Society?" Mr. Nobles asked.

"Because you can," I answered as everyone else looked at him.

Mr. Nobles shut his mouth and gave one long nod.

The servants came in and cleared the soup course, replacing it with fish and green peas. Once they had left, I continued. "Ken and Clara Gattenger were happy together. They'd waited a long time to wed, and they enjoyed each other's company very much."

"What of the gossip I heard about their public rows? I saw one myself," Lady Fleetwhite said.

"They'd only been married a year, and Clara Gattenger had suffered two miscarriages. She was devastated by the loss."

Sir William and Mr. Nobles were both blushing. The other

men took a sudden interest in their fish. Lady Fleetwhite shook her head slightly as she glanced around the table and said, "Are you certain it was a love match?"

"Yes."

"What about his rumored affairs? One was with the current— friend of the German spy, Baron von Steubfeld."

"The Gattengers had a very long engagement, broken off twice, at which times Mr. Gattenger had affairs with other women. There were no affairs while their engagement was on-going or after they wed," I assured her.

"Apparently he loved his wife. If that is so, he would have found a way to destroy those plans without endangering her. I believe you, Mrs. Monthalf. Those ship designs were stolen, not destroyed by Kenneth Gattenger." Lady Fleetwhite gave her husband one sharp nod.

"Drawings that we must prevent from falling into the wrong hands," her husband said.

"How do you know they haven't already?" I asked.

Several of the men exchanged glances. Finally, Sir William said, "There is a branch of Whitehall that has ears in many places. That's not entirely accurate. They're not our ears, just ears who are sympathetic to our interests."

"For money," I said.

"Sometimes. Sometimes their interests are a bit more compli-cated. All of them, here in London or in Berlin, are certain the warship design has not reached the kaiser's government. They are very aware it is missing, but German telegrams indicate they don't know where it is."

"Are you certain the burglar was in the employ of the Ger-mans? We are not well loved by the French and Russians, much less the Austrians, the Spanish, the—" the duke began.

Lord Fleetwhite interrupted him. "The French now know they're missing, as do the Russians and Austrians. None of them seem to have been involved in the actual theft, but now their local agents are all scouting around, trying to get their hands on those papers by order of their governments."

"Sir Henry Stanford convinced Gattenger to recheck his equations on the night the burglar took the plans. He needs money. Do we have any idea which government could have paid him to make the theft possible?" The duke looked around the table.

His words ruined my appetite. At least I had eaten a few bites of the fish before the servants whisked it away, replaced by pigeons and beans in thick gravy. I didn't mind talking through this course. "Do the police have eyes on the Russian and French spies? Do we know the identity of everyone involved in trying to recover the ship's plans?"

"We know all the Russian and Austrian spies, although a large contingent of Russians with their servants just arrived in London for the announcement of an engagement between a member of the imperial Russian court and a member of the queen's extended family. There could be a new spy in that group.

"Unfortunately, the French and Spanish are more subtle. We don't know who their spies are or who might be carrying their messages back to their countries. And we have very little manpower to keep tabs on the foreign agents we know about, much less the ones we don't know." Lord Fleetwhite eyed me cautiously. "That of course goes no further."

Great. They didn't know the identity of everyone chasing the blueprints. I nodded my agreement. "Have the police found Mick Snelling yet?"

"No. He's gone to ground. He knows we're looking for him," Mr. Nobles said.

" 'We'?" I asked.

He blushed as he realized he'd slipped up. "I'm the Scotland Yard liaison to Whitehall, playing the role of an idle young man for this mission."

"We know the design will work. So now all we can do is wait," Mr. Goschen said. "And I don't like waiting."

"Are you speaking as First Lord of the Admiralty or a businessman?" Blackford asked.

Goschen gave a dry smile. "Both. We can't afford to have these drawings fall into foreign hands both for the safety of the country and for the good of our business interests."

"Kenneth Gattenger can't afford for us to fail to catch his wife's killer. He's facing a hangman's noose," I reminded them.

"You're Mrs. Gattenger's kin. Why are you so concerned for her husband?" Lord Fleetwhite asked.

That wasn't true, and they knew about my connection to the Archivist Society. What had Blackford told them about me? "I want the right man to hang for Clara's death. That man isn't her husband."

It wasn't until the roast course, leg of lamb with carrots and spinach, had been brought in and the servants had removed themselves, along with the nasty-looking pigeon dishes, that Lord Fleetwhite spoke again. "How do we know Gattenger wasn't a party to the theft? We have the letter passed between the Germans and him. He was seen talking to a German agent two evenings before the theft. He needed the money. Snelling might have been there by appointment."

"We know Snelling wasn't there by invitation because Clara was killed. Ken Gattenger would never have allowed that." My fork and the carrot on it went back on my plate.

"An accident during a falling-out of thieves."

I stared down the table at Lord Fleetwhite. "I asked Gattenger about the letter."

"You did what?" Fleetwhite raised his voice. Looking around the room, he lowered it to a conversational pitch. "He's not supposed to know we have it."

"Well, he does. And he admits he received it and gave them an equivocal answer. He needed the money for his wife and unborn child and so he considered selling the design to the Germans. Clara miscarried, and his reason for taking the money was gone. When he told them no, the Germans threatened him."

"Which Germans?"

"It was dark. He couldn't see the man's face."

"How convenient." Fleetwhite's mouth closed in a thin line.

"He tried to stop a thief from taking the ship's plans."

"After he'd agreed to sell them to a foreign power. He may have planned for the burglar to come into the study. As far as I'm concerned, he's guilty of treason and at least partially responsible for his wife's death. He can rot in jail until we get those blueprints back, and then he can have his trial." Fleetwhite tossed his serviette on the table.

Goschen nodded, as did Darby and Nobles.

I shifted forward in my chair, ready to disagree, when Blackford laid a hand over mine. I looked up into his dark eyes to see him give a small shake of his head.

"We'll need some police presence outside Lord Harwin's estate this weekend to capture Snelling with the plans," the duke told them.

"Nobles and I will both be there to help, but the police are already stretched thin watching the Germans in London and now the newly arrived Russians for this engagement party. There are rumors of anarchist activity. We'll have to use whatever forces the local constabulary can provide," Sir William said.

"I'll see how many Archivist Society members can get away from London for the next few days," I offered.

"Let me know and I'll make arrangements for their lodging and travel," Blackford said. I'm sure his smile was meant to be encouraging.

I returned the smile, feeling anything but reassured. "By the way, why isn't Sir Jonah Denby here?"

"Old Denby?" Sir William asked. "Why would he be here?"

"He's approached me a couple of times asking what we've learned so far."

"Why would he be interested? Denby works in the ceremonial office, coordinating events with the palace," Lord Fleetwhite said.

"You might ask him. He's been to see me. I didn't look for him."

"Have you ever met him before?" Sir William asked.

"No." The room became very quiet. I looked at their faces staring back at me.

"We'll talk to Denby tomorrow. In the meantime, don't tell him anything else. Just in case," Lord Fleetwhite said.

"Just in case?"

"Just in case he's another spy on the hunt for those drawings," Blackford said.

Dinner went on for another three courses, but I didn't learn anything new. I ate and drank sparingly but still felt sick from worry and weak from fatigue when we were released from the table. With the tepid thanks of three governmental departments, Blackford and I walked into the dark, warm night. I wanted to curl up on the hard carriage bench and go right to sleep, but Blackford had his plan to carry out.

"I think two hours will be sufficient for our tryst," he said.

I gave him the big yawn I'd been fighting throughout dinner.

He gracefully crossed the carriage to join me on my seat. Putting an arm around me, he said, "You have to learn to look at me with love in your eyes if we're going to carry this off at Lord Harwin's."

He tickled my ear and ran a finger down my neck, until another huge yawn got in his way.

"Oh, Georgia," he said, pulling me against his soft jacket and kissing the top of my head.

It was dark in the carriage and I was comfortable and safe nestled in Blackford's embrace. My eyes refused to stay open. He said something, but I couldn't make any sense of it. He jostled me, but my eyes stayed shut and my mind refused to work.

CHAPTER FOURTEEN

I awoke to light streaming into my room. Vague memories of riding in the duke's carriage to carry out a tryst sprang to mind as I leaped up in bed.

"Good. You're awake," Emma said.

"How did I get here?" I asked.

"The Duke of Blackford carried you in from his coach. It seems he couldn't wake you. He laid you down and wished us a good night."

"Blast."

"Apparently you destroyed your chance to begin your affair with him last night. He was put out that you're ruining his reason to have us invited to the Harwin estate."

"I'll just have to flirt harder today."

"I think it's going to take more than that." As she handed me a dressing gown, Emma added, "Were you going to, eh, er . . ."

"I will not be any man's mistress. Especially not a duke who will soon be looking for a duchess and getting rid of any inconvenient mistresses." The idea of Blackford tossing me aside was a physical ache in my chest. I enjoyed his company too much to dare complicate our friendship.

She put up her hands, palms out. "I'm sorry. Get cleaned up. It's almost time to go."

Was she sorry because I'd failed that night, or because Blackford would soon lose interest in me when the investigation ended?

"I need to send a message to Sir Broderick. Anyone available from the Archivist Society for the next few days must travel out there to encircle Lord Harwin's gardens. The police don't have enough manpower to watch for Snelling and those ship plans. I don't think Whitehall and the Admiralty believe Gattenger is innocent in the theft and the murder. We'll be practically on our own."

I wrote a note during breakfast and included Blackford's offer to arrange for lodging and transport. Emma gave Mary directions and sent her off to Sir Broderick's, certain she was plucky enough to find her way and honest enough not to read the note.

I'd rarely traveled by train, since I seldom left London. I couldn't guess how the Duke of Blackford would turn this unusual event into a surprise, but he'd promised Phyllida to do so.

Phyllida, Emma, and I traveled to Paddington Station with our luggage piled on the roof and back of a carriage. When we descended into the swirling mass of porters, passengers, and news boys, Phyllida took a step backward. She collided with our cabbie, who fell forward, shoving the trunk he held into a porter who was unloading more luggage. Then she swung around to apologize and stepped on the foot of an office worker racing past. I took her by the arm and led her to a quiet spot along the wall while Emma saw to the unloading.

"Is it always like this?" she whispered into my ear.

"Yes. Remember, you traveled away from London for long periods after—" I didn't need to say anything else to the timid woman to remind her of our story covering the years she'd lived with me. And I didn't want to mention her murderous brother and his capture ten years before.

Another carriage pulled up behind ours, and Baron von Steubfeld and Lady Bennett alighted. While a German valet and an English lady's maid saw to the luggage, they walked over to join us. I noticed the valet was a tall, beefy man. I wondered if he could have been the one who'd threatened Gattenger.

After we went through our round of curtsies and bows, Phyllida said, "I always have to stand to the side. Otherwise, large men in a hurry knock me over."

"The Englishman has no sense of order," the baron replied. After Lady Bennett's elbow discreetly hit his ribs, he added, "I hope you've not been injured."

"Not today," Phyllida replied. "Mrs. Monthalf takes good care of me."

Blackford appeared at my side. More curtsying and bowing. Then he said, "You're all here. Good. If you'll follow me?"

He led us at an angle through the vast station. Past family groups escaping the heat of the city with their entire households bunched together blocking the way. Past commuters hurrying into the furnace that was London from the slightly cooler suburbs. Past tiny shops selling papers, books, tea, and meat pies. My ears ached from the sound of so many rushing footsteps, shouting voices, and the clanging metal of carts. I tried not to choke on the pungent, smoky air.

Finally, the duke led our parade of passengers and luggage through a door to a landing with a long train parked alongside. A railway official directed the porters and the maids and the baron's valet farther along the platform. Emma gave me a nod as she passed. From where the duke stopped, we would enter the last car. Unlike a regular first-class carriage, with its row of doors along the side, this car had only one.

The duke gave me his hand, and I stepped up and inside. For an instant I froze, staring at the elegant parlor surrounding me. So this was the Duke of Northumberland's saloon car. Then I remembered the people behind me and walked across the room to where Sir Henry Stanford and Lady Peters stood to greet us.

More curtsies and bows. I didn't curtsy in my shop all day as much as I had that morning. "Isn't this lovely?" Rosamond Peters said. "It was clever of the duke to borrow this carriage from his friend."

I looked around me at the elegant furnishings. "I had no idea such rail carriages existed."

Sir Henry said, "The Duke of Northumberland owns several railroads. He uses this car when he's inspecting his lines, but at the moment he's shooting in Scotland. I believe this rail coach is unique."

I gave them both a smile. "Well, I'm certainly glad Northumberland lent the carriage to the duke. This will make travel so much more pleasant."

After Phyllida greeted the couple, I settled her in a sturdy-looking upholstered chair facing in the direction we'd be moving. I hoped the view out the window next to her would distract her because she was already turning pale. I took the other seat of the pair, planning to sit with her while we began our journey and then leave to question our fellow passengers. When she clutched my hand, I gave her a reassuring squeeze.

"You're certain this is necessary, Georgia?"

I frowned at the use of my real name. "You'll be fine."

Blackford must have seen the exchange, because he came over and knelt in front of Phyllida. "Should you feel unwell, there's a room with a basin and towels right behind you."

"Thank you, but with the movement of the carriage, I'm not certain I'll be able to walk."

"Then Mrs. Monthalf and I will assist you." Quieter, so only Phyllida and I could hear, he added, "We need your help, Phyllida. Remember Clara."

She lifted her chin and gave him a lovely smile. "I'll be fine." Glancing around the rail carriage, she said, "This is a tremendous surprise, Duke. Thank you."

He inclined his head. "Thank you for helping us, Lady Monthalf."

"Your Grace, has Stevens heard from Snelling?" I whispered.

He shook his head. "It was a good idea, but he was apparently more distrustful than greedy."

"At least we know the ship won't sink."

"I spoke to the Admiralty official who took Gattenger another set of blueprints to redo his calculations. He said it appears to be everything he'd hoped. An engineering marvel."

If the ship was an engineering marvel, then the ship's plans were worth all our efforts to reclaim them. I gave Blackford a relieved smile. Actually, every time I looked at him I wanted to smile.

We kept up a steady conversation to divert Phyllida. Once we had jerked into motion and crept out of the station, Blackford left us. I walked over to where Sir Henry stood alone by a window. "Not much of a traveler, is she?" he asked.

"Lady Phyllida finds the movement of the train upsetting."

"That's unfortunate."

"Only until she gets to her destination. Then she's ready to have a grand time."

"I heard you saved her from a robber yesterday." When I replied with a dismissive gesture, he said, "Don't be so modest. What happened?"

"Phyllida bought a new hat. It looks stunning on her. Some young thug grabbed it and ran. I ran after him, which was good because he immediately ran down a dead-end alley. A bobby came and took him away." Well, that was what happened, more or less.

"That was very brave of you."

"Or very stupid. I suspect the latter."

"Remind me not to carry out any crimes around you." He gave me a wide smile.

"Blackmail is a crime. And I suppose you'll force me to do illegal things to keep my secret secure." I returned a rigid smile showing teeth.

"Going through a gentleman's desk is considered a crime by the people we'll be visiting in Gloucestershire. Being penniless and untitled is another crime to this group. Remember, one word from me and you'll be snubbed by everyone, including the duke. You'd probably be thrown out of the house and sent back to London."

I couldn't carry out my investigation if I were sent back to London in disgrace, but he definitely didn't sound like my anonymous letter writer.

Wonderful. That meant two people in this investigation had figured out I was trying to deceive them. And I didn't know the identity of one of them.

"Besides," he added, "what I'll have you do will be easy enough for your tender sensibilities."

His scornful tone on "tender sensibilities" told me he didn't see me as a lady. I was only middle-class, but I was still insulted. "Did you put in motion the events that led to Mrs. Gattenger's death?"

The smile crumbled from his face, replaced by anger blazing from his eyes. "I'm deeply sorry about Mrs. Gattenger. She was your cousin, wasn't she? But Ken Gattenger lost his nerve when I asked him about the blueprints and said I'd go to the Admiralty Board."

"What do you think happened?"

"Isn't it obvious? Gattenger had doubts. He panicked and, in a fit of anger or cowardice, threw the plans in the fire. Probably planned to claim a burglar took them. Buy himself more time to correct his calculations while the hunt was on for his mythical burglar. Clara saw what he was doing and tried to stop him. What came next was a terrible accident."

I raised my eyebrows. " 'Clara'?"

Sir Henry lowered his voice. "We were friends for many years. Clara was the kindest, brightest lady of my acquaintance. A true beauty. Her death is a great loss."

The expression on his face told me everything I needed to know. "You were in love with her."

He took a step away from me. "I admired her. She was married. There's nothing else to say." Sir Henry stomped to the other side of the railroad carriage.

She'd only been married for the past year. What had happened between Clara and Sir Henry in the many years before her wedding?

I walked over to where the baron was pouring himself a cup of coffee into a delicate china cup from a silver urn. "Ah, Mrs. Monthalf. I see you've suffered no adverse effects from stopping a robbery."

"None, thank you. My cousin and I appreciated your taking us home in your carriage. That was very kind."

"Not at all."

"Have your guests departed?"

"My guests?"

"The Duchess of Bad Ramshed and her daughter."

He gave one deep chuckle. "They weren't my guests. Because they're relatives of the kaiser's wife, the embassy has a duty to smooth their journey. In the ambassador's absence, it becomes my responsibility."

"Does the duchess often need to have her journeys smoothed?"

"Did you meet her?"

"Yes. At Lady Bennett's."

He gave a wry smile as his diplomatic reply.

"Lady Bennett seemed to get along well with her."

"Lady Bennett loves royalty."

"She must be very useful when you have work to do and guests at the embassy."

"She is indeed. Now, if you'll excuse me?" He walked off with his coffee cup, leaving me to wonder how I'd be able to question someone who, as a diplomat, was so practiced at saying nothing.

The rail carriage began to shake and I took the chair next to Phyllida. "I'm sure in a little while the ride will be much smoother."

"How long is this trip?"

Blackford crouched down facing her, keeping good balance despite the jolts that whipped through the carriage. "Two hours or a little more. Is there anything you require, Lady Phyllida?"

"Distraction."

He smiled. "Are you familiar with the entire party who'll be at Harwin's estate?"

"Besides those in this carriage? No."

"There'll be a friend or two of the Harwins' son from Oxford, one or two young ladies the same age as Harwin's daughter, who was presented at court this past spring, and I imagine a few others. A bishop and his wife, perhaps, to keep us all on good behavior."

"It sounds jolly. How close is the Marquis of Tewes's estate?" Phyllida asked, holding the arms of her chair in a death grip as we rounded a bend in the tracks.

Blackford rested one hand on a chair arm to keep his crouched balance. "I believe the estates are adjoining. Have you been holding out on me, Lady Monthalf? You know more about where we're going than I do."

"Lady Ormond mentioned she was going there and that we'd be neighbors."

"Is this also jolly?" the duke asked.

"Not if you're visiting the marquis. Lady Ormond is an awful gossip."

Blackford patted her hand. "Thanks for the warning. Ah, we seem to be running smoothly now. If you'll excuse me?"

He rose and walked off with a grace I couldn't help but watch. Phyllida cleared her throat.

I turned my attention to her. "Are you doing all right?"

"Yes, thank you. Lady Bennett has been watching you watch the duke. The evidence of your liaison is obvious."

"What do you mean?"

"No one could mistake your gaze. Well done."

I hadn't been acting, but I wouldn't tell Phyllida that. "Good," I said with finality.

In a little while, Phyllida felt comfortable enough with the rocking of the train that I could walk over to sit on the couch with Rosamond Peters. "I feel cooler already," she told me.

"I've come to love London, but it will be nice to spend a little time in the country. Is it always so hot this time of year?" Georgia Fenchurch knew it wasn't, but this was just the sort of question Georgina Monthalf would ask.

"No. This heat wave has been far different from our weather the last few years. Tell me, where did you get the courage to chase after a robber? I've heard he knocked over your maid and stole some of your purchases, and you stopped him and had everything returned."

I laughed. "Where did you hear that?"

"Lady Bennett."

"Who heard it from the baron. He's the real hero of the story. He came to Phyllida's aid and gave us a ride home in his carriage once the excitement had passed." I looked over to see the baron in close conversation with Sir Henry while Lady Bennett flirted outrageously with the duke. Could the baron and Sir Henry be taking this opportunity to discuss terms for Sir Henry to sell Germany the blueprints?

I mistrusted every conversation I couldn't hear between our suspects. Finally, I turned back to Lady Peters.

She was saying, "But you chased down a robber? You ladies from the Far East are very brave."

"I only had to chase him a few steps. He ran into a dead-end alley. All I had to do was stop him until the bobby came, and my maid did most of that."

"How clever to have a useful maid. Minette would have expected me to save her."

"You have a French maid? However did you manage that?"

French maids were favored over English ones by anyone who could afford a lady's maid.

"I have family who helped me arrange it."

"Do you speak French?"

"Of course. Just as you must have learned to speak French in school. And now I guess you speak Chinese or some other Far Eastern tongue."

I shook my head. No sense in getting caught in a lie over that. "I never managed to learn a word. I'm a dunce at languages." Wanting to change the topic, I said, "You were carrying a hatbox when we saw you. It was a lucky thing you weren't the one the robber attacked. You were on your own, having sent your maid back. You could have been hurt."

"Do you think he was after hatboxes? How very odd." Rosamond Peters studied the thick blue carpet at her feet as she spoke.

"I know he was. He said he was hired to steal hatboxes."

She looked at me with a half smile. "Probably a rival milliner. They can be ruthless competitors."

"You don't believe that any more than I do."

Rosamond Peters laughed at me. "Georgina, you are such a mistrustful soul."

Sir Henry Stanford joined us. "What's so amusing?" His gaze told me to watch my step.

"Mrs. Monthalf has the measure of most of London. You must watch what you say around her." Her tone was light, but I wished she hadn't warned him to be careful of me. The more helpless he thought I was, the safer I'd be.

His eyes narrowed as he gave us both a smile, waiting to hear more. I wasn't going to enlighten him.

"Being near government and the queen, Mrs. Monthalf

believes we have all taken to being mysterious and deceitful," Lady Peters said.

I shook my head and laughed. "I don't believe I said anything of the sort."

"Then forgive me," she said with a nod, "I misunderstood you." She turned to Sir Henry. "Mrs. Monthalf said the most amazing thing. The thief who stole Lady Monthalf's hatbox told her he was hired to steal hatboxes."

"The heat is getting to people," Sir Henry scoffed. I thought he looked relieved. Perhaps I could eliminate him as the man who'd hired the hatbox thief, but he could certainly have orchestrated stealing the warship plans.

The duke came over from where he'd been talking to Lady Bennett, his face unusually red. "There have been strange incidents occurring in London lately. I challenge you to make sense of any of them."

"Stranger than stealing hatboxes?" I asked.

"Leading a goat through the cellars beneath Parliament."

Sir Henry chuckled. "I read about that. Bizarre."

The duke glanced over his shoulder. "Mrs. Monthalf, you might want to check on your cousin. Lady Monthalf looks unwell."

"Excuse me." I leaped from the sofa, but just as I did so the train swayed and I bumped into the duke. With masterly charm, he tucked my arm inside his and walked me to the chair next to Phyllida's.

I sat heavily and said, "Phyllida, are you all right?"

She gripped my arm. "Are we going to crash?"

"No. It's just a stretch of track that is bumpier than before."

"Please stay here with me."

"Of course." I smiled at the duke, who nodded in return and walked off.

"Learn anything?" Phyllida asked when we were alone in our area of the carriage. She looked at me intently, gripping my arm with one hand. She must have believed our journey would prove Gattenger's innocence, else she would never have withstood this train ride. She was terrified.

"Sir Henry was in love with Clara. Did you know about him? What did Clara think of him as a suitor?"

Phyllida leaned toward me and lowered her voice. "I'd seen Clara and Sir Henry together a few times before her marriage to Kenny. The last time she and Kenny called off their engagement, I thought she would marry Sir Henry, but he was disappointed."

"Were their feelings equal, or did Sir Henry love Clara more than she did him?"

Phyllida pursed her lips together for a moment. "Their loves were different. Clara loved him like a brother. Sir Henry's feelings were more romantic."

"Was Sir Henry angry enough at Ken Gattenger to hire the burglar to steal the blueprints?" I asked.

"But Clara was killed."

"Not the result that was expected or wanted. But what if Kenny was the one who was supposed to die?"

Phyllida's eyebrows rose to the ceiling of the train carriage. "Then the Germans might not have anything to do with the burglary and we've been looking at this all wrong."

CHAPTER FIFTEEN

WE both jumped when Sir Henry pulled over a chair and sat at my side. "I don't think I've properly expressed my condolences on the death of your cousin Clara Gattenger," he said to both of us.

"Thank you," Phyllida said. Her face looked like it would crumble at any moment, but her eyes were fearful as she looked at him.

"I accused Sir Henry of being in love with Clara. I should apologize," I said. It was a clumsy way to interrogate him again, but I needed to learn more without making him suspect I was more than a penniless widow and a chance thief.

"Please don't apologize. You're correct. I was a little in love with her. Had been for years. Not that anything inappropriate happened," he rushed to assure us. "She saw me as a friend of her father's. Nothing more."

"I'm sure we all loved Clara," Phyllida said and reached out a hand to Sir Henry. He grasped it for a moment and nodded over her fingers.

When he let go of Phyllida, I said, "I hope Clara's not the reason you haven't remarried. That's not something she would have wanted."

"No. I've grown used to having my freedom to come and go as I want. But, like my close relationship with Clara, I would like your friendship, Mrs. Monthalf." He gave me a fearsome smile, teeth showing.

"As I would like yours. I'm sure you and I and the duke and Lady Peters can all be good friends." I smiled, hoping he got the message that I wasn't entirely friendless.

Sir Henry smiled broadly. "I hope we're better friends than you are with them." He took my hand and clutched it.

When he didn't let me go, I said, "Tell me about your shipyard. You said it's the most modern in Britain."

He gazed into my eyes, looking uneasy. "Yes."

"Installing new machinery must have cost a fortune." I tried to pull free and failed.

"But it will be worth it in the end. I'll be able to build ships faster and better to satisfy my customers."

"Including the queen."

"Her Majesty's government is my biggest customer."

I jerked my hand free. "With your important position in the industry, of course you were called on to bid on building Gattenger's new warship."

"Of course."

"Did you discuss the bidding with Clara?"

"No, with Gattenger. He knew how keen I was to build the ship. If that warship lives up to expectations, it will make the reputation of both Gattenger and whoever is chosen to build the first models." He stressed the "if."

"And I imagine a tremendous windfall for the builder."

He nodded. "Only if it floats. Otherwise, the shipyard that builds it will be ruined."

I lowered my voice. "I told you, Gattenger said the design is sound."

He studied me for a moment. "I hope you aren't lying to me. That would be unwise."

"The Admiralty heard doubts and had Kenny check his calculations again. All is well." He moved as if to get out of his chair and I set a hand on his arm. "Did Clara know about your doubts?"

"No. I'd never tell her. When I talked to her the night before she"—he swallowed and swiped at his eyes—"was murdered, I'd planned to see Gattenger. Not Clara."

Across the railway carriage, Lady Bennett and Lady Peters laughed at something Blackford had said. Tamping down jealousy, I focused on Sir Henry. "You spoke to our cousin the night before she died?"

He looked embarrassed to have admitted it. Then he glanced around to make sure no one could overhear us. "Kenny wasn't there that evening. Being old friends, Clara kindly invited me in."

"So you two were quite alone," Phyllida said, for the first time looking fierce.

Sir Henry reared back. "It was nothing like that."

"You kept quiet to protect her reputation?" Phyllida sounded as if she were interrogating Sir Henry.

"Exactly."

"Where was Gattenger? Was he expected home soon?" I asked.

"Clara didn't know where he'd gone or when he'd come back. She seemed lonely. Frightened. It wasn't hard to see something was wrong."

"Did she tell you what was bothering her?"

"She only said she was distressed. She refused to give me any details. Said it had nothing to do with me, that it was personal. Between her and Kenny. If only I'd pressed her harder to tell me, perhaps I could have done something to save her."

"You think Gattenger killed his wife."

"Isn't it obvious, with something between her and Kenny upsetting her? Scotland Yard thinks so, too."

"You've talked to Scotland Yard about your talk with cousin Clara the night before her death?" I'd have been surprised to learn he'd volunteered any information. He seemed to want to use anything he discovered for his own benefit.

"Of course not. The police would see it as another nail in Gattenger's coffin. And Britain needs Gattenger alive designing ships."

"Could your doubts about Gattenger's warship design have led to her death?" I pressed him, not knowing how much longer I had until we'd arrive in Cheltenham Spa.

"If I thought I had done anything to lead to her death, even indirectly, I'd shoot myself. I adored Clara." The pain in his eyes spoke of his honesty. I hoped the pain was real.

"When you saw her that last time, did you tell Clara how much she meant to you?"

Sir Henry blinked at my question. "No. Never. Gattenger was the one who wandered before their marriage. Clara stayed true to him, although I told her how much I cared for her while she was still free to choose me. In the end, Gattenger returned to her and I lost the love of my life."

"I'd imagine Clara blamed Ken for their breakups if she blamed anyone. It usually is the male who's the pursuer," Phyllida said.

He glanced at Phyllida. "Not this time. Lady Bennett deliberately came between them, causing Clara to break off their engagement for the second time. That estrangement wasn't as long as the first one, only a few weeks, but I took the opportunity to court Clara again."

"'Again'?" I was beginning to sound like a parrot. Hopefully Stanford would mark my verbal clumsiness down to being a middle-class colonial.

"I also courted her before her original engagement to Gattenger, and then when they called it off the first time."

"How long ago was that?"

Sir Henry was looking at me suspiciously. "They were engaged eight years ago, and then broke up about three years later. Several months passed before Gattenger came crawling back to Clara. Poor woman forgave him both times."

"So you'd been courting Clara off and on for eight years. That shows a rare dedication." I tried to sound sympathetic. Truly, I thought he was a little mad.

"Clara was a very special woman."

Phyllida interrupted us. "It was Kenny who broke off the engagement both times after Clara refused to set a date for the wedding because of her father. She wouldn't leave him, and Kenny grew frustrated. Men do, I'm afraid, and so they begin affairs."

I glanced at Phyllida, surprised at her worldly insight. Either she hadn't been as cloistered as I'd thought in the days when the queen had a growing family or Emma and I had unwittingly provided her with an education.

"Gattenger's a good-looking man. He's always attracted women. Not always high-moraled women," Sir Henry said.

I'd only seen him in Newgate Prison and at Sunday dinners.

He'd always seemed pale and timid. Once I'd met Blackford, I discovered my tastes ran to dark and bold. "He is?"

"Yes, the man has that blond Greek god look that women find impossible to resist. Clara couldn't believe her good fortune that Gattenger chose her. I wish to God he hadn't," Sir Henry said with feeling.

Blackford walked over to us, glaring Sir Henry and me farther apart in our chairs. "We'll be in Cheltenham in fifteen minutes. Perhaps less."

"Oh, that is good news," Phyllida said with the most animation she'd shown all morning.

"We'll have a few more miles to go by carriage to reach Lord Harwin's estate."

As it turned out, Lord Harwin sent only one carriage for us, so Phyllida rode with Lady Bennett and the baron on the first trip. The luggage and the servants followed in a large, open wagon. Emma gave me a half smile as she passed on her way to the wagon, following a porter with our trunks. Being Emma, she would manage to sit on the bench next to the driver while the rest of the servants had to sit on trunks in the back.

The weather was noticeably cooler on the street in front of the Cheltenham railway station than it had been in London, sunny but breezy. While I stood there with the duke, Lady Peters, and Sir Henry, I watched as another coach pulled up. Lady Ormond and a couple I didn't know ignored us, and each other, as they climbed into the carriage, their faces stiff with suppressed anger. Their servants loaded the luggage into a pony cart that waited a short distance behind the first vehicle.

Looking past them to the opposite side of the street, I saw my parents' killer. He was here in Cheltenham Spa.

My gasp might have caught my travel companions' attention,

but I didn't glance their way. I darted out into the street between Tewes's carriage and a wagon being loaded with crates of fruit off a freight train.

My quarry was almost within reach. I could see his long nose, his thin lips, his silver hair beneath his top hat as he walked along the sidewalk. He appeared unaware of the woman dashing across the wide street as he strode along, a newspaper folded under one arm.

There was a carriage coming toward me in one direction and a wagon carrying barrels lumbering along in the other. This was a busy road, but I'd had plenty of practice crossing busy roads in London. I had time to cross. I'd just hurried out into the middle of the street, glancing down to avoid horse manure, when a sound to my left caught my attention.

A small, chariotlike carriage driven by a young dandy raced around the slow carriage, its horses urged on by shouts and the snap of a whip. It was nearly on top of me. I tried to back up, but not fast enough.

I looked at my parents' murderer. He'd noticed me now. His cruel, pale eyes widened in surprise as he stared at me.

An arm smashed against my waist and jerked me backward. Something struck my foot as the vehicle raced past.

I was nearly thrown onto the sidewalk. "What do you think you're doing?" Blackford snarled, staring down at me.

I adjusted my hat, which had slipped over one eye. "You've ruined everything," I snapped back at him. "Didn't you see him?" I was trying to look past him and the vehicles in my way to view the opposite sidewalk.

"Who?"

"My parents' killer."

Blackford stopped and blinked, as shocked as if I'd just

slapped him. He spun around and stared across the busy street. There was no one there. "I don't see anyone."

"He's gone now. You ruined it." I took one step forward and nearly landed on my face as my foot and ankle screamed *fire*.

By now, Sir Henry and Lady Peters had reached my side. "Are you all right?" Lady Peters asked.

Sir Henry handed me the shoe I'd lost in the street when the chariot raced past. "That was a close call with the curricle. Quick thinking, Your Grace."

I put my shoe on my aching foot, took a tentative step, and winced. "I've injured my ankle. I guess I can't have that first waltz with you like I promised, Your Grace."

"Whatever possessed you to run out in the road like that?" Lady Peters said.

I gave Blackford a glance and said, "I'm sure I saw an old friend of my father's. I was surprised to see him and wanted to let him know I was in the area. I could have had a nice chat with him if that crazy driver hadn't nearly run me over."

"Did either of you recognize the young pup?" the duke asked. "I have a mind to have a word with him about his driving."

"Who still drives a curricle in this day and age?" Sir Henry asked of no one in particular.

Blackford put an arm around my waist and helped me toward a bench by the front of the train station. "If you will sit still, perhaps we'll be able to continue our investigation," he muttered into my ear.

"He's here," I whispered back. "This is a small area compared to London. Someone must know who he is."

Blackford dumped me onto the bench and then Lady Peters came and sat beside me. "Is there anything I can do for you?" she asked.

"Besides salve my wounded dignity?" I smiled at her. "No, but thank you."

"Who's the man you wanted to meet? Perhaps someone knows where he's staying and we can send him a note to visit you," Sir Henry said.

"That's the problem. I don't remember his name. He was a good friend of my father, but at the time he seemed terribly old and stuffy. He left before my father died and I got married, so my name would mean nothing to him now. Hopefully we'll see each other again."

Rosamond Peters raised her eyebrows and said drily, "And if the fates decree that you don't?"

"Isn't that how life is sometimes? Chances slip through our grasp. I could be mistaken about the man's identity. He might not be my father's friend, although the likeness is uncanny." I gave her a look that was supposed to say I was unconcerned about failing to greet the unnamed man. Actually, I was seething.

He knew I was here now. Would he leave, ruining my chance to meet him? Or would he stay, possibly ruining our investigation into the stolen plans since he knew my true identity? Either possibility was troubling.

I shot discreet glances around me every so often, but I didn't see the man again. Lady Peters and I discussed the fashions of the ladies passing us. She told me Cheltenham Spa had been fashionable for over a hundred years, which explained the noble-looking buildings around us. She suggested while we stayed in the area we make an outing to drink the local mineral water at the Pitville Pump Room.

I agreed gladly. It would give me a chance to look for my parents' killer away from the estate where I'd be conducting the investigation.

The carriage from the Harwin estate soon arrived and we climbed in. Well, everyone else climbed in. I was hauled inside by Sir Henry and the duke like a sack of flour. Sir Henry seemed to find it necessary to place a hand on my bottom below my corset and squeeze. Knowing he could feign innocence, there was nothing I could do about the insult.

If it had been Blackford, I wouldn't have minded, but he would have treated me with respect. As it was, he'd climbed into the carriage first to lift me from above. After we were settled and began our journey, I made a point of looking out the windows on both sides. "I've not been here before. It's a lovely area, isn't it?"

"And a wealthy area with royal connections," the duke replied.

Somewhere in this town was my parents' killer. I hoped I'd glimpse him entering a home or a shop where I could return later and question the occupants, but he was nowhere to be seen. Disappointed, I watched the town quickly disappear and the rolling countryside spread out before us.

Lord Harwin's country home was a massive block of stone, added on to during different periods. We were greeted at the top of an imposing set of entrance stairs by his lordship and ladyship, a couple amazingly alike in their appearance. Both had dark hair liberally sprinkled with gray, untroubled blue eyes, and thin lips curved up in a smile of greeting.

I had made use of both a stone railing and the duke's arm to wince my way up the steps to curtsy before my hosts. Both of my hosts' jaws dropped in shock. "You've been hurt," they said in unison.

"A curricle nearly knocked her down in front of the train station," Blackford growled.

"Tewes's younger son. The boy is a terror with that old curricle of his grandfather's. He's already run over one of Knightdale's hunting dogs. He'll come to a bad end if his father doesn't take him in hand," Lord Harwin said.

"You need to get off that foot," Lady Harwin said. "Let's go into the red drawing room."

The red drawing room was nearby, relatively speaking. After walking down a hall wide enough to be a street, we entered a room three times the size of my shop. The entire house party seemed to have already gathered there, including the baron and Lady Bennett. They all stood as we entered, although more for the duke, who was taking most of my weight on my injured side, than for the rest of us.

I managed a curtsy for the room in general and then hobbled to the nearest sofa to collapse.

"Is it broken, you think?" Sir Henry asked. "That would be rotten luck."

I rubbed my injured ankle. "I think it's just bruised or sprained."

"Let's get you up to your room and I'll have ice sent up. Is your lady's maid a capable woman?"

I pictured Emma slicing a much larger man in one deft motion with her knife. "Very capable."

"Good. We'll hand you over to her until your limb has a chance to heal. If you should need a physician, have her let us know."

Lady Harwin gave me a faint smile and I nodded. "Thank you, my lady."

I rose unsteadily and had hopped two steps when Blackford muttered, "Oh, good grief," and swept me up in his arms. He strode out of the room to a chorus of gasps, including mine. My heart boomed in my chest. This was the most romantic thing I'd ever experienced.

Phyllida hurried after us, climbing the long staircase. "I'll show you where her room is, Duke."

"While you're at it, you might tell me how Georgina will carry out this investigation while holed up in her room," he said through clenched teeth.

"Are you angry?" I asked, my lovely fantasy of being carried off by Blackford dissolving into aristocratic dust on the antique Persian carpets.

"Yes."

"This isn't my fault. Who knew that young lord would speed through heavy traffic?"

"We're not here to find your parents' killer. We're here to stop naval blueprints from going overseas." I thought his teeth would crack from snapping out words with such violence.

"Now I'm here for both." One investigation was as important as the other for me. Really, finding my parents' killer was the more important. But it's hard to appear decisive and in control when you're being carried like a baby.

Phyllida opened a dark wooden door like any other on the corridor and the duke strode in, dumping me on the bed. Emma, hanging up a gown, spun around with widened eyes.

"Do something with your foolish mistress while I try to salvage our investigation." Blackford nodded to Emma, bowed to Phyllida, and then stomped from the room without a glance at me.

Emma blinked. "What happened?"

I brought her up to date, pausing only when a maid brought in a sack of ice wrapped in a towel. The cold numbed the pain enough that I soon tried to put weight on my foot. That turned out to be a bad idea.

Phyllida ordered me back to bed with a regal glare. This investigation was bringing out all the training she'd received as a child. How long had it been since she'd needed the protection living with Emma and me provided? I knew she could never go back to cheerfully cooking our meals and dealing with cleaners and laundresses. What would she do after we found out who'd killed her cousin? Wherever she went, I would miss her terribly.

"Emma and I will have to do the investigating in your place. Stay in bed and keep the ice on your leg. And please, heal quickly. We'll need you to assist us tomorrow." Phyllida swept from the room.

"I'll bring your dinner up on a tray. In the meantime, keep your foot elevated." Emma hung up the last of the dresses and readied me for bed.

I willingly let her take off my dress and unlace my corset. "What will you do?"

"I'll keep an eye on the baron's man, although that's going to be hard. They keep the female staff well segregated from the men in the attics."

"Is it hot and stuffy upstairs?" I felt guilty leaving her with all the investigating work and the chores of a lady's maid while I lay uselessly in this huge, cool, overly decorated room.

"It's not bad at all." Emma helped me put on my nightgown, plaited my hair, handed me a book from my luggage, and then left.

I sat on the bed, pounding my fist into the pillow. I had much to accomplish and no way to leave the room. My throbbing ankle was holding me prisoner.

CHAPTER SIXTEEN

I was laid up, isolated from the investigation and everyone in the house. Since I couldn't investigate, I could read with a clear conscience. I'd brought *The Ruined Castle* by Mrs. Hepplewhite. I loved a good gothic story as much as my customers did.

After a while, I heard noises on that floor of the mansion, telling me the others were dressing for dinner. Now would be the time to post someone on the main floor to see who was sneaking around. If I were trying to get ship drawings out of the country, this would be a good time to meet with my confederates. Everyone else, master and servant, would be busy with their own tasks.

And here I sat, on the bed in my nightgown, unable to walk around freely.

A tentative tap on my door made my heart leap with joy. Someone to question. "Come in."

My hostess walked in, already dressed in ropes of diamonds and pearls over an expansive bosom. "Has everything been done to make you comfortable?"

"Yes, Lady Harwin. And the room is lovely. Thank you for being so kind." Actually, "opulent" was a better word for the decor. I wondered if the reds that dominated the wallpaper, rugs, and bed coverings said anything about what she thought of my character.

"Anything for the duke." She glanced around. "Where is your maid?"

"She's also Lady Phyllida's lady's maid. She's probably helping her dress for dinner."

"What an odd custom. Sharing a lady's maid."

"We're two single ladies living together. It suits us."

Her eyebrows rose. "Both of you single?"

Blast. I'd made a mistake on something Lady Harwin would immediately notice. Widows could have affairs. Single ladies couldn't. She looked at me suspiciously.

"My husband is dead and I'm without male guidance. Lady Phyllida has never married. We both feel a little adrift, two solitary women." I smiled at her. "I should have used the word 'solitary' rather than 'single.'"

She looked down her nose at me. "Indeed you should. It gives the wrong impression otherwise."

"I don't want to do that. My apologies." I brought the conversation around to my interests abruptly. "There seem to be a large number of peers living in the area."

"There are three in the immediate area—us, Tewes, and Knightdale—plus a couple of baronets. Society is always lively when we've retired to our country estates."

"That is fortunate. The countryside must be dull when there's no one to visit."

"Indeed. We're having a ball tomorrow night. I hope you'll be able to get downstairs by then."

"So do I, Lady Harwin. I understand that young Mr. Tewes is responsible for my injury. I'd hate to miss your excellent hospitality on account of his youthful foolishness."

"I don't believe Lord Charles Wilson, which is his correct address, is the only one at fault in this accident. Running out into the street is a dangerous occupation." She gave that aristocratic sniff I was growing weary of.

Someone had already told her the circumstances by which I'd received my injury. "The roadway could have been easily crossed if it weren't for the presence of a young man speeding through town whipping his horses." The haughty displeasure I showed wasn't all an act. I had work to do. And the first thing was to learn the guest lists at these house parties. "I feel terrible that I haven't had the opportunity to meet your other guests. I'm sure all of them are fascinating."

"Besides the group you came down with, there's the Bishop of Wellston and his wife; two young ladies who are finishing their first season along with my daughter; the parents of one of the young ladies, Lord and Lady Stewart; and two classmates of my son from Oxford. The Stewarts stopped here on their way back to Scotland, and we'll be visiting them in September."

"How lovely." None of them likely to be after the drawings. But there might be more people in the area who wanted to get their hands on the ship's blueprints than just von Steubfeld. More people with a secret agenda than just Sir Henry. And my parents' killer was somewhere nearby.

We nodded to each other and Lady Harwin swept from my bedroom in a rustle of taffeta and lace. I'd just settled back on the bed when I heard another knock. "Come."

Lady Rosamond Peters opened the door a few inches and smiled at me. "I'm not disturbing you, am I?"

"Not at all. I'd love a diversion."

She strolled into the room, elegantly attired in green silk and emeralds. "Sir Henry and I were thinking. Since you don't remember your father's friend's name, perhaps we could ask around the neighborhood and see if anyone remembers him or you. What was your maiden name?"

Blast. I didn't need them messing about in either of my investigations. "It's really not necessary. It's not that important."

"It was important enough that you were injured trying to overtake the man."

"Through my own stupidity and the carelessness of that driver."

"Nevertheless, Sir Henry and I will see if we can't find the man. What was your maiden name?"

I couldn't tell her Fenchurch. "Smith."

Her face fell. "Oh, dear. There must be hundreds of officers in India named Smith."

I smiled. "Yes, it's quite hopeless. Thank you for thinking of me, though. And thank you for the visit. You look lovely. Enjoy dinner, and tell me all about it later. That way I can attend vicariously."

"What are you reading?"

"The latest Mrs. Hepplewhite. Gothic, but quite enjoyable."

"I've read two of hers. Now that I know she has something new out, I'll have to stop by a bookshop when we return to London."

I wanted to recommend mine but resisted. Keeping both halves of my life separate was necessary for my safety. And I didn't want thieves, traitors, and spies rendezvousing in my bookshop.

"They'll send your dinner up on a tray?" Lady Peters asked.

"I expect my maid will bring it shortly." Along with any news from the servants' hall. I hoped Emma had found a way to get the staff talking while playing her role.

"You certainly look lovely. Perhaps I'll have a tray sent up here, too," said a familiar male voice from the doorway.

Despite the role I was supposed to play as Blackford's lover, I felt my cheeks heat at his impertinence. "Please do. We could dine à deux."

Lady Peters laughed a tinkling sound. "That would certainly send tongues to wagging, but it sounds so romantic."

The duke's face froze in shock for an instant before he recovered and said, "It does, but I'm afraid duty calls. There's a matter in the House of Lords that will require Lord Harwin's vote, whether Parliament manages to meet again this year or has to wait until next. I need to convince him where his priorities lie."

"I hope by tomorrow evening I'll be able to join you downstairs. In the meantime, I'll have to be desolate without you."

Blackford shot me a look that said *Don't overplay your hand.* Then he smiled. "Georgina, dear, I can't last until tomorrow evening without seeing you. Perhaps I'll see you sooner rather than later."

"That would suit me well, Your Grace."

"There's no need of a chaperone here, I see." With an arch smile, Lady Peters curtsied to us and sauntered out of the room.

The duke shut the door behind her and walked over to the bed. My heart beat harder with every step closer. I knew he wouldn't do anything. He was dressed for dinner. Impeccably, regally, perfectly dressed. Still, a certain part of me wanted him to see me as a lover, an ally, a duchess.

"How long until your ankle will let you get around?" he murmured.

"I'm going to make it to dinner and the ball tomorrow if I have to crawl there," I assured him.

He glowered down at me. "Good. Because you are here for one reason and one reason only. To find the naval blueprints before they leave the country. We'll deal with this acquaintance of your parents once we accomplish our most important task. Do you understand?"

"Yes," I hissed back at him. I understood. I just didn't agree.

The duke had been gone about thirty seconds when Sir Henry entered my room without knocking. "I made sure the duke had left before I came in. I don't want to ruin your chances with a rich patron."

"How thoughtful of you." I gave him a dark look. "You can leave now."

He walked toward the bed. "We have business to discuss."

I pulled the covers a little higher as I watched him.

When he reached me, he grabbed my lower jaw in one hand. "What was that stunt about today? Because if you think you can lie about here and get away with not carrying out a job for me, think again."

I shoved his hand away. "My ankle is bruised. I hope to be walking by tomorrow night. Don't worry. I'll do what you want me to do."

"You'd better. Because a few words from me will ruin you."

I'd had bigger, stronger men try to bully me. Sir Henry didn't frighten me. Once we retrieved those blueprints, he wouldn't matter anymore. "I understood that the first four times you said it. I'm not stupid."

"Don't forget it." He grabbed me by the shoulders and pulled me out of bed. My feet hit the floor, one of them excruciatingly, and I slumped down, clutching the sheets. I managed to balance on my good leg before I hit the floor and held my other foot up as I stared at him, gasping with pain.

"Good. You're not pretending." He marched out of the room, leaving me to wonder exactly what it was he wanted me to do. I was very glad Clara hadn't married him.

I climbed back under the covers, slid my ankle onto the icy towel again, and picked up the novel by Mrs. Hepplewhite. I began to read until my lack of sleep during the preceding nights caught up with me.

When I awoke, night had fallen and cooler air came in the open window. I sat up in bed and listened to my stomach growl. After a few minutes, I stopped being annoyed about my stomach and started worrying about Emma. What if she'd followed the baron's man and been caught? I knew she carried her knife, but she could have been taken by surprise and overpowered.

Snelling was in the area. He'd killed Phyllida's cousin Clara. He could murder again.

When I heard the soft knock and saw the door open, I nearly jumped off the bed. "Emma?"

"No, it's me. Phyllida. What's wrong?"

"Emma never brought my supper tray, and I'm worried—"

Phyllida stepped back into the hall. "Duke."

Blackford entered the room behind her.

"Emma never returned with my supper tray. Where is she?" I controlled my voice with effort.

"She's not waiting for me in my room, either," Phyllida added.

"I'll have your tray sent up and send a note to Sumner in the village to start a search there. Lady Phyllida, if you could ask one of the maids to find Emma and send her to you, that will begin a search here. What's this?" Blackford bent over and picked up something from the floor near the door.

A note. He opened it and glanced at it before growling, "Someone's onto you."

I held out my hand. He walked the paper over to me so I could read it.

Georgia Fenchurch, you've been foolish. Now you and the Archivist Society members here will die.
   Their deaths, and yours, will be your fault.

I stared into his dark eyes reflecting light from the one gas lamp burning in the room. "This is the third warning I've received. The first two were in Mayfair."

"Warning?" Phyllida gasped.

"The only one who knew was Emma," I told him.

"Sir Henry?" Blackford looked like he'd rip the man apart.

"No. He's using what he believes to be Georgina's secrets against her. He wouldn't if he knew the truth."

"Who, then?"

"I don't know. And now Emma's missing." I gave his hand a squeeze. He squeezed back, and I felt a little relieved.

"I'll find her." The duke bowed to us and left the room.

"When did you last see her?" I asked Phyllida.

"She dressed me for dinner and then said she was going to the kitchen to get your tray. Goodness, Georgia, that was hours ago."

I didn't correct her use of my real name. I was worried, too.

"This note?" she asked, apparently afraid to say any more.

"Someone has known almost from the start that I'm Georgia, not Georgina. This person doesn't want the Archivist Society involved."

"Let's go home." She walked in a small circle, wringing her hands.

"No. Clara was brave, and she'd expect us to be brave to find her killer." When she sank down on the bed, I took her hand and gave her the same squeeze Blackford had given me.

We sat together until my tray arrived. I hadn't eaten all day, and I was famished. As I stuffed my face, Phyllida twisted the rings on her fingers. "She must be somewhere. Perhaps she's following the blueprints," Phyllida kept murmuring.

"Emma can take care of herself." I didn't know which one of us I was reassuring.

The maid came back to return the tray to the kitchen and I convinced her to act as Phyllida's maid for this evening. I also learned she was the one who'd turned on the gaslight near the bed in case I should awaken, which meant Emma must have been gone since before it grew dark.

Phyllida took the girl back to her room and I sat alone, listening to the creaks of light steps and murmured voices coming from under the door and through the open window.

I had dozed off again when I heard my door open. The lamp I'd left on showed Emma and the duke slip silently into my room. I sat bolt upright, my heart pounding from surprise and relief. "Where have you been?" I whispered as loudly as I could.

"When I went to gather your tray, I saw the baron's valet slip out the kitchen door. I followed him into the village."

"Alone?" Blackford demanded.

"Of course." Emma turned back to me. "He met another man in a tavern. I was watching through the window, wondering how I could learn what they were saying, when Sumner appeared. He went in and listened. He heard them argue about money, and then the other man, a young, thin man, said he'd bring it to the house and deal directly with the boss tomorrow night."

"Sumner identified the younger man as Snelling," Blackford said.

"Snelling is bringing the naval designs here tomorrow night to exchange for money. While a ball is going on." Oh, terrific. I looked from one face to the other.

"There will be so many excess people here, one more won't be noticed," the duke grumbled.

"Sumner is certain they didn't realize he was there and say that only to mislead him?" I asked.

"They were too busy arguing to notice much of anything. They were both faced away from the room. Sumner couldn't see their faces until they left," Emma told me.

"So who is the boss?"

"Sumner said Snelling never referred to the person who hired him as he or she. He did say he had an arrangement with one person and he'd give the drawings to that person directly in exchange for the money. He also told the valet if he works for the boss to report back that danger had raised the price."

"So we know the valet didn't hire the burglar for the baron. And the person who hired him could be male or female." I shook my head in frustration, my plaited hair swinging over my back.

"Sir Henry in a deal with the baron. Or the baron himself," Blackford said.

"Or Lady Bennett, who could have developed a taste for state secrets while bedding diplomats," I said. Since I'd learned she had come between Clara and Ken Gattenger, I disliked her enough to hope she was the guilty party.

"God help us if it's her," the duke muttered.

I leaned toward Emma. "What happened next?"

"I stayed in the shadows until the baron's man headed back

to the house and the other man, Snelling, went the other way. I started to follow the German, but Sumner caught up with me and walked me to the house," Emma told me.

"Did anyone here see Sumner?" I suspected the duke wanted Sumner's presence here kept a secret.

"I did. And only me," Blackford said. "He has his orders for tomorrow night. Are you going to be able to help us?" He gave me a dark look.

I looked at him with more assurance than I felt. "I'll stay in bed in the morning, then have Emma tightly lace up my half boot. You may have to let me lean on your arm, looking adoringly at you, if walking's too difficult."

He snorted.

I glared in reply. "I will be downstairs tomorrow night. You can be sure of it."

He strode up to the bed and looked down at where I sat, the covers demurely wrapped around me. His eyes darkened as I stared into his face and tried to gauge his mood. "I need your help on this, Georgia. I'm depending on you."

I held out a hand to him. "I'd never let you down."

He took my hand and grasped it firmly. "I believe you. Everyone from Gattenger to the queen will need you on your toes tomorrow." Then the corners of his lips lifted in a sly smile. "Figuratively and literally. I want to claim a waltz."

"I will be honored, Your Grace." I would dance with a duke. With the Duke of Blackford. For that, I would endure any amount of pain.

"I'll be busy with our host and the Foreign Office tomorrow. I'll see you at dinner. Good luck, Georgia."

"Good luck, Your Grace."

He still held my hand as he stared into my eyes. I gazed back with no desire to break our connection. His bare skin was smooth and lightly callused, warm against my hopeful fingers. I clung to his hand, breathing in his scent of brandy and expensive cigars. I didn't want this perfect moment to end.

Emma said, "I'm off to bed unless you need me for something."

The duke blinked and dropped my hand. "Good night, Emma. That was well done following von Steubfeld's man."

"Thank you, Your Grace." With the click of the door latch, she was gone.

He didn't move away from the side of my bed. "How sure are you that the man you saw today was your parents' killer?"

"Completely certain. It's the same man I saw in the spring. The same man I saw kidnap and murder my parents when I was seventeen."

"Have you any evidence he's the guilty party?"

"After Drake was arrested last spring, after you said good-bye, I received a letter from the man I'd been following. He didn't sign the note, but he was the one. He made that clear. He said he now knew we didn't have his Gutenberg Bible. He was leaving London for the time being, and perhaps we'd meet someday. He didn't say where he was going, but we know he sailed into Southampton from Cape Town a few weeks ago."

Blackford nodded once. "After we retrieve those plans tomorrow night, I'll help you find this killer."

I believed him.

I AWOKE THE next morning after sleeping well in the cool country air. Emma brought me a breakfast tray and then sat on the foot of the bed in a most un-lady's-maid fashion. "Where would be a good place for me to watch tonight?"

"You've seen more of the house than I have. Is there a safe place to watch from the gardens, or will there be couples strolling around?"

"There are several young people coming to the ball. I'd bet there'll be couples on all the paths and in all the parlors." She rose and looked out my window. "You and Phyllida have the same view of the garden facing toward the village, but yours isn't blocked by trees. I may camp out here in the window and keep an eye out for the man I saw meeting the baron's man last night."

"Will you be able to recognize him in the dark?"

She gave me a confident smile. "It should be a clear night with an almost full moon. I'll be able to recognize him. Will you be able to dance tonight?"

"We'll cinch up my ankle and it'll be fine." I returned her smile with an assurance I didn't feel.

She studied me for a moment. "Do you think the coach ran you down deliberately?"

"I don't know anyone who would do that." I hadn't left many enemies in my wake. They were all locked away. Or hanged.

"The person who left the notes might have hired the driver."

"He's the younger son of a marquis. He wouldn't need the money."

"He might," Emma said, "or he might owe your anonymous letter writer a favor or a debt. How many of the people here see us as a hindrance to their obtaining the blueprints?"

That was the question. Sir Henry had the wrong idea of what I was up to and thought he was using me. But someone in this group knew about my interest in retrieving the blueprints and wanted me stopped. The group I traveled with knew when we'd reach Cheltenham Spa.

Or could it be the mysterious Sir Jonah Denby? The men at

our dinner party the night before hadn't thought Denby would be interested in the ship design. He knew my real name, but did he know I'd come to Cheltenham Spa?

And if somebody had arranged this, how had they planned to get me into the street to be run over? I'd done that for them. I'd set myself up for what otherwise would have been a very chancy effort to stop me.

Too chancy to be practical. And whoever was behind the theft of the blueprints and Clara's death was definitely practical.

CHAPTER SEVENTEEN

A tap on the door was followed by Phyllida walking in, beaming. "Good morning. A few of the ladies are going to the pump room today to take the waters. Do you feel up to joining us?"

Emma and I exchanged a guilty look, since we'd just been discussing my getting run down deliberately. "I'd better rest my foot until tonight. I'd like to be able to dance, and I think the more rest I give it now, the better it'll be for the ball."

She shut the door and walked closer. "Is there something going on I should know about?"

I took her hand. My answer was as honest as I could make it when I said, "We don't want you mixed up in anything dangerous. But if someone should let something odd slip in the course of the day's conversation, please let us know."

She appeared to shrink into herself. With a timid voice, she asked, "How will I know if it's odd?"

"Phyllida, you know how these people think and talk and

move. You can spot the one false note in an entire symphony of aristocratic chatter. You'll know if something's off."

Her smile turned more confident. "When we return, I'll tell you everything I hear. Now, rest that ankle. The duke plans to waltz with you, and he won't take no for an answer."

He never did, but this time, I was glad.

The day passed slowly. Rosamond Peters and Lark Bennett came by my room separately to see if I could join them on their jaunt to the pump room to taste the spring waters. Lady Peters seemed genuinely concerned for me. Lady Bennett smiled like a snake who'd already bitten her prey.

Emma brought more ice for my foot. After my skin became cool to the touch, I tried standing. The injured foot ached, and I had a nasty bruise, but both feet bore my weight equally well.

I looked up from where I stared at the floor to Emma and said, "I can do it. The carriage struck me with a sharp blow, but I didn't twist anything. Let me keep ice on it for the day, and tonight I'll be ready for a dozen conspiracies."

"Good, because we have no idea what's going to happen."

"Emma, see if you can find out where the valets and lady's maids spend their time during dinner and the ball. You'll be able to tell quicker if the baron's valet is missing that way. And I suspect the baron won't want to get his hands dirty with the plans if he can help it." I put my foot back up on the bed with the ice.

"Do you want me to watch from wherever the servants gather rather than at your window?"

"Start with where they wait. If you don't have any luck there, then try my window. Do you know where Sumner is going to be?"

Emma shook her head. "The duke sent me into the house. I don't think he wanted me to know."

"The duke doesn't like to share information. Unfortunately,

it makes solving crimes more complicated for the rest of us." I didn't hide the grumble in my tone. Peers might think they were above everyone else, but that attitude created nothing but problems.

"I heard from Sir Broderick. Fogarty and three others are coming out here on the morning train. They'll be waiting on the road up to the estate and in the park for Snelling."

"All city dwellers. I wonder how they'll blend in on an estate." I was worried for my fellow Archivist Society members. We were all Londoners, and to us this rural area could be on a different planet. We would stand out, and someone wanted us dead.

Emma grinned. "Snelling has the same problem. He's a Londoner, too."

"Have you heard how much support we'll get from the local bobbies?"

"None. They seem to think if the Metropolitan Police can't handle spies, it certainly isn't their job. Lord Harwin will no doubt send for them if he needs someone to make an arrest."

"Wonderful. How did you find all this out?"

"Blackford's valet. He's a nice older man who worked for the duke's father originally. He passes messages discreetly without displaying any interest in what's going on."

With a sigh, I swung my legs over the side of the bed. "Help me get dressed and downstairs for luncheon. It's time I started considering where and how those plans could be brought into the house tonight."

I was tired of lying around. It was past time for me to get involved in this investigation.

I couldn't pull my half boot on, let alone lace it up tightly to protect my ankle. The only shoe I could get on my tender, swollen foot was my dancing slipper, so I wore the pair with an afternoon dress. The black satin slippers looked silly with the high-necked, accordion-pleated top in lavender and a simply cut skirt in the same color decorated with beige lace. I hoped either no one noticed or my skirt hid the slippers from view. Being thought a Philistine wouldn't help me escape notice as I hunted for the burglar and the naval plans.

I was able to climb down the stairs on my own with the aid of the massive banister and wandered the main floor without drawing attention to myself. The house was huge. Any hope of catching anyone doing anything in all these rooms seemed impossible.

I found the dining room almost by accident and discovered more than a half-dozen people seated around the huge polished table enjoying their first course. The men rose as I entered. I wasn't surprised to see the duke, Lord Harwin, Baron von Steubfeld, and Sir Henry Stanford. The presence of two other men, Sir William Darby from Whitehall's spy apparatus and Mr. Frederick Nobles, Scotland Yard's liaison with Whitehall, did surprise me. And I was puzzled to see an older man at the table with the youngster who nearly ran me down the day before.

"Mrs. Monthalf," the butler intoned.

The men all nodded to me.

"Well, I'm glad to see she hasn't suffered any lasting injury," the older man grumbled.

The younger man smiled at me. "So am I. Please believe me when I say I am grievously sorry for my actions."

He was too much of a young rogue, grinning boyishly at me, to believe him, but I decided forgiveness would pay better results. "All will be forgiven if I can dance a waltz with the duke tonight."

"I certainly hope so. You're far too pretty to be sitting on the sidelines," the young man said.

I smiled at the compliment as the butler produced a chair next to the duke and set a place at the table for me. Blackford said, "Georgina, this is the Marquis of Tewes and his younger son, Lord Charles Wilson. Gentlemen, Mrs. Georgina Monthalf."

As soon as I sat, a bowl of soup appeared silently in front of me and the men returned to their lunch. Sir William sat across from me, and I wasn't certain if I should know his name. "Excuse me. The accident seemed to have rattled my brains. Have we met?"

Sir William Darby flashed a glance at the duke and said, "I don't believe so."

The duke made the introductions. We made small talk through luncheon, when I learned that Sir William and Mr. Nobles were in the neighborhood and stopped by to pay their respects to our host, a friend of Sir William's father. Lady Harwin, leaving on the outing with her guests, had invited them to the ball that evening, and Lord Harwin had invited them to lunch.

I was amazed at how, in the rarified world of the aristocracy, everyone knew everyone else.

After luncheon, Mr. Nobles asked to see the garden. When the rest of the men went outside, Sir William delayed, fascinated by some paintings. I expressed an interest in the same paintings, and we began to study them together.

Even with everyone else outside, Sir William spoke quietly. "We have Snelling under watch in the village. When he comes out here tonight, we'll follow to see the handoff and then grab everyone at once. If it's one of the Germans, we'll be able to re-cover the drawings but we'll have to let the man go. Diplomatic immunity and all that."

" 'If'?"

"It could be an English partygoer who'll act as the middleman."

"Lady Bennett," I said. "Or Sir Henry?"

"Quite possibly."

"And our role?"

"Keep a close eye on the attendees at the ball. If one of them slips out of the room, follow them, but don't engage. We will handle that part of the plan."

"Four members of the Archivist Society will be out on the grounds, aiding the hunt for Snelling. If you don't move fast enough, we will engage." I stared at Sir William until he looked away.

When he looked back at me, he was smiling. "I believe you would."

"Good. Now, do you have any idea about what time this will occur?"

"All we know is tonight."

"Have you checked out all the guests at the other big houses nearby?"

"Everyone checks out, although"—he hesitated—"our inquiries didn't go very deep."

"So everyone at the ball tonight is a possible suspect. Wonderful."

Sir William glanced at me. "The only people we'll need to watch at the ball will be people with a connection to Baron von Steubfeld."

I gave up any pretense of studying the paintings. "We don't know for certain von Steubfeld's role in the theft. The Germans could be one of a handful of bidders. Stanford, or someone we haven't considered, might be trying to sell the plans for cash."

"Then we won't know who's behind this until Snelling makes his move." Sir William didn't look happy.

"Precisely." How I would love to learn who'd hired Snelling before the ball.

"We talked to Sir Jonah Denby. He knows nothing about the

missing warship blueprints. He's never heard of you. He seemed quite amazed that anyone would think he was interested in a theft."

"And you believe him?"

"Yes."

Sir William sounded so certain that I asked, "What does he look like?"

"Like any other midlevel civil servant."

"Does he have green eyes? Does he walk quickly? Does he have weathered skin?"

"He has pale skin and walks with a limp. He has a withered leg, so he's never been an outdoorsman. Uses a cane to get around." Sir William thought for a moment. "His eyes are pale. I don't remember the color."

A chill ran down my arms. "Definitely not the same man."

"Then who is he?" Sir William asked.

That was the question. He knew my real name, and he was out there somewhere following our investigation. Had he sent the threatening letters? I wished I'd sought a physical description of Denby earlier and not worried so much about his job and his associates.

The sound of a door opening and footsteps made me turn back to the painting. Sir William said, "I'd better get Nobles or he'll drag everyone around to look at every plant. He's fascinated by gardens."

"He was beyond me as soon as he said something other than 'rose' or 'daisy.'" Sir Henry came forward and nodded to us. Sir William returned the nod and retraced Sir Henry's steps.

I said, "I'd like to speak to you, Sir Henry."

"About Clara's death? Or other matters?"

"Yes."

He shrugged his shoulders. "Let's go into the library. We won't be interrupted there."

We walked down the hall, Sir Henry certain of our destination. After we entered, he closed the door and stood there, waiting for me to speak.

Sir Henry expected me to be meek as befitting a traditionally raised widow. That was far from my background, but I'd found it was better to conform to the other person's image of me if I wanted the answers to the questions I asked. I recited *Be meek* in my mind a few times before I looked at the Oriental carpet and said, "What do you want me to do?"

"Search Lady Peters's room."

My gaze flew to his face. "Why?"

"She has something of mine that I want."

"What is this thing?"

"A letter from me to a member of the Admiralty upper echelon, requesting a chance to bid on the new warship. In the same letter, I mentioned that his nephew had expressed an interest in a management position in the shipyard and I would be making my choice soon. I considered them to be two separate issues, but Lady Peters said the letter is open to interpretation."

I agreed with Lady Peters. Although Sir Henry would deny it, my interpretation would be bribery. "How did she get the letter?"

"She was being squired about town by Lord Hastings at the time I wrote the letter. She must have stolen it from him," Sir Henry grumbled.

Lord Hastings was in the highest levels of the Admiralty. Having heard its contents, I wanted to get the letter. Once I had it, I didn't plan to hand the letter over to Sir Henry. "What does this letter look like?"

"Two pages, good paper, embossed with my company's name. Go upstairs and do it now while the ladies are out taking the waters."

"Why do you think the letter is in her room? Why wouldn't she have left it in London?"

"She brought it along this week to exchange for Gattenger's blueprints."

I struggled to keep my voice calm. "You have the blueprints Clara was killed over? I thought you loved her."

"Oh, I did. Unlike Gattenger, I valued Clara. I adored her. I would never allow her to be harmed."

"But she was killed by the person who stole the blueprints. Did you hire the thief?"

He grabbed my arms, but not hard like he had before. "I didn't hire him. I believed Gattenger burned the drawings until you told me he was certain the ship was what he'd promised. That's when I went looking for the thief."

"You found him?" That was news. Blackford and I had had no luck speaking to him.

"Yes. It wasn't easy, but I caught up to him here, in Cheltenham Spa. I offered him a great deal of money, I begged, but none of it did any good. He said he'd made a deal and if he wanted to live, he'd carry it out. And he said he had the blueprints hidden well."

I tried to put awe in my voice. "That was very brave of you, meeting Clara's killer."

"I had no choice. Lady Peters won't return my letter without the blueprints. Since I can't buy them or steal them, I need you to retrieve my letter."

"Did he say who this dangerous man is who hired him?"

He made a face and dropped his hold on my arms. "No. It

doesn't matter. What matters is for you to go upstairs now while the ladies are still gone and get my letter."

"Why did you think Ken Gattenger would burn his warship design and kill Clara? You knew them. Ken told me his ship will sail and perform as expected. He's never been wrong before. Why didn't you trust him this time?"

"I overheard one of the clerks in the records room talking to another man. Those clerks know all about the mathematics of ship design. He found the design so flawed he was surprised the ship would float. That's when I asked Gattenger."

"The day the ship blueprints were stolen and Clara was killed?"

He nodded.

The clerk could be the one on the German payroll that Jacob was trying to identify. In that case, the conversation could have been set up to start questions specifically to get Gattenger to take a set of the blueprints home with him.

"Ken said you threatened him with ruin over a flaw in the design." Threatening someone with ruin seemed to be Sir Henry's usual method of operation.

"Gattenger is a genius, but since he married Clara, it's been hard to get him to focus. He looked panicked when I asked him. Why would he panic if there wasn't a problem? I decided I needed to force him to give me a straight answer as quickly as possible. The bids are due, and I couldn't risk spending money on something that wouldn't work."

One thing stood out in my mind. "Your shipyard is in trouble financially?"

"My shipyard has nothing to do with this. We all need to know how seaworthy this warship is for the good of Britain."

I pressed on the point I wanted him to admit. "Your shipyard is in jeopardy."

"Not in jeopardy," he hissed out between his teeth.

"On the edge of bankruptcy?"

"No. Not on the edge. Not really. The improvements I've made to the efficiency of the yard just haven't paid off yet. It's been touch-and-go. If I build his ship, I'll do it faster and better than anyone, but it has to work. If it sinks, my boatyard sinks with it."

His financial troubles gave him a strong motive to make Gattenger recalculate his equations rather than steal the plans.

Before I could ask another question, he had my arm and was walking me toward the door. "Get up there and get the letter."

"All right. You wait down here. Her maid may be up there and we don't want her to get suspicious. Why does Lady Peters want warship blueprints?"

"She wouldn't tell me."

I stopped him before he opened the door. "One more thing. How often did Lady Bennett call on Clara? Were they friends?"

"No. Never. Clara didn't like her. Lark Bennett stole Ken Gattenger away from her once."

I'd heard about Lady Bennett's romance with Gattenger. But Sir Henry was right. Clara was unlikely to have gone calling with the woman who'd ended her engagement at one time. "They went out together in Lady Bennett's carriage for an hour or two the day Clara died."

He paused, his hand on the door handle. "You're certain of this?"

"Yes." What did he know?

"I saw Lady Bennett's carriage at Lady Peters's that day. I had thought to call on that lady, to ask for my letter back, but when I saw Lady Bennett's carriage waiting, I decided not to go in."

* * *

I FOUND EMMA in Phyllida's room. "I need your help."

She scowled and hurried over to me. "What's happened?"

I gave her a brief explanation and then asked, "Do you know Lady Peters's maid?"

"Minette? Yes."

"Could you find her and keep her out of Lady Peters's room for a little while?"

"Yes. Wait here while I check Lady Peters's room. If she's there, I'll get her out and then you can go in."

Emma left and a minute or two later, I heard her voice through the crack in the door. A woman's voice with a French accent answered. I listened until their footsteps faded away, and then I slipped down the hall. No one was around, but I knocked on the door once before I entered the room.

Rosamond Peters's room was a model of tidiness. I quickly glanced in the drawers and wardrobe. Everything was so neat I could search her things in an instant and not ruffle anything. My search of the bed was equally unsuccessful. Nothing was tucked into the few books she'd brought with her. I pulled up the corners of the rug. Nothing.

The only place left was the lady's desk. There was a small stack of good notepaper, a pot of ink, and a couple of pens. The drawer was empty. Lacking any other spot, I looked in the notepaper. A few sheets down I found Sir Henry's letter.

I skimmed the contents. Sir Henry was a fool to commit both subjects to writing in a single document. I folded the letter and slipped from the room into the empty hall.

I'd barely shut the door behind me when I heard Emma's voice coming from somewhere nearby. Hearing the chatter she was infecting the air with, I was certain she was trying to warn me to get out. I crushed the letter into my palm and stopped to look around.

Emma and a dark-haired girl in a black dress came out from the servants' stairs.

"Ah, there you are," I said as if Emma had been playing truant. "Would you please tell the Duke of Blackford I'd like to see him right away? I'll be in my room."

"Yes, milady." Emma glanced at Lady Peters's maid and rolled her eyes. Then she headed downstairs and I went to my room, leaving Minette in the hall looking confused.

A few minutes later there was a tap on my door. Thinking it was Blackford or Emma, I stood by the window, soaking in the cool breeze, and said, "Come."

Sir Henry strode in. "Where is it?"

I stared straight at him, trying not to give away by a glance that I'd hidden the letter in my pillowcase. "I couldn't find it."

"I don't believe you."

"It's true. It's not in her room. Do you have any other ideas where she could have hidden it?"

He grabbed my wrist. "No, but you'd better. I can't get my hands on the blueprints, and if she ruins me, I won't hesitate to let everyone in on your attempted thievery, your husband's dishonesty, and your lack of funds."

I tried to wiggle away but failed. His grip would leave a bruise as bad as the one he'd left on my shoulder. "Let go of me."

"Not until you agree to do as I say."

I struggled, not wanting to scream and have Sir Henry ruin my false identity before we recovered the blueprints. "I'm trying to."

"Trying isn't good enough. Get me that letter, or I swear I'll destroy you."

CHAPTER EIGHTEEN

"Y OU need to consider your words before you threaten this
      lady again," came from behind Sir Henry as Blackford
strode into the room.

Sir Henry dropped my arm.

"Your Grace," I said, curtsying with relief that I was no longer alone with my blackmailer. "How much did you hear?"

"Enough to know this scoundrel needs to leave immediately
if he values his life."

"Stay out of this, Blackford. She's not your sister," Sir Henry
said.

"She's a woman I care about. Leave her alone."

"Mrs. Monthalf isn't under your protection or control. You
don't get to order her around like you did Lady Margaret."

Blackford's expression grew steely.

"He blocked practically all of Lady Margaret's suitors as not
being worthy of a duke's sister. Now he's trying to have the same

control over your life. Beware, Mrs. Monthalf," Sir Henry said, turning his back on Blackford.

"You'd better leave, Sir Henry." I tried to put a note of regret in my voice, but I really couldn't wait for him to go.

He gave me the stiffest of bows and stormed out of the room, shutting the door with more force than necessary.

"I have something for you." I took the letter out of my pillowcase and handed it to Blackford.

He read it quickly, then looked it over again more slowly. "How did you get this?"

"Sir Henry wanted the letter back from Lady Peters, who obtained it from Lord Hastings. He says her price to return it is the stolen ship blueprints."

"I don't believe it."

"Neither do I. Why would she want ship blueprints?"

The duke gave me a thunderous look. "Why were you searching her room for him?"

I gave him a smile, but his expression made the corners of my mouth droop. "You know why. Sir Henry has me doing his dirty work because he learned Georgina Monthalf is broke and he can ruin her."

"I'll take control of this," he said, putting the letter in the pocket of his dark brown vest. "Play him along, but don't get caught alone with him."

"Gladly."

"Now, Georgina, would you like to sit in the garden with me?"

I put on my straw boater before I gave him my arm. As we walked slowly downstairs, I couldn't get over the change in his dress. He looked relaxed in his beige lounge suit, even though his collar was still stiff and of course he wore a necktie, which matched his vest. Perhaps it was like me being relaxed in my work clothes, although I still wore a corset.

I was beaming at our spending time together without searching anything or questioning anyone. I gave his arm a squeeze. He gave me a contented smile.

He put on a brimmed hat of soft felt as we stepped outside and then angled the hat to give him a rakish air.

I blinked at this change in the duke. "You look so different."

"We're in the country," was his explanation. "There's a bench over there in the shade. Can you walk that far on your ankle?"

"If I can't, you can carry me." I gave him a grin.

Wonder of wonders, he laughed. A deep, booming laugh.

We sat down on the dust-free bench. Apparently the staff cleaned the outdoor furniture daily. "We need to hold hands to keep up appearances," Blackford said.

I gave him my hand. "Gladly."

"You should wear that color more often. It makes your eyes a brilliant violet." Reddening, he turned to face the immaculately trimmed garden. "It would be nice if all of life were like this, but then I guess we wouldn't appreciate it."

"Thank you for arranging this trip."

"Finally forgiven me for taking you away from—" He stopped as we heard footsteps coming toward us.

Looking over our shoulders, we saw one of the footmen approaching. "Your Grace," he said with a bow, "Lord Harwin would like a word with you."

"Of course. If you'll excuse me, Mrs. Monthalf?"

I nodded to him, and he was off. The sun went behind a cloud as he left.

The garden was lovely, but I didn't see it as I sat enjoying the shade and wondering why Lady Peters wanted ship plans and why Lady Bennett took Clara to see her shortly before Clara's death.

"May I join you?" a German-accented growl asked.

"Please, Baron von Steubfeld. Isn't the garden lovely?"

"Yes, it is."

He sat and we studied the garden in silence for a minute before the baron said, "Perhaps you and Lady Monthalf and the Duke of Blackford can visit my country this fall. I think you would find it most enjoyable."

"I'm sure we would. I think Lady Monthalf and I could agree to travel then, but I can't speak for the duke."

"Can't you?" he asked, raising an eyebrow.

"I'm sure I can't."

I could have sworn his mustache twitched before he said, "I've been watching you. Your friendship with the duke seems to be all business."

I started to rise. "I beg your pardon."

"No, no. I meant no disrespect to a lady," he hurried to assure me. "Your friendship is like a partnership, all quick meetings before and after you question people. It doesn't seem to allow much time for romance."

The baron had apparently been watching me as I watched him, and his interest made me uneasy. "I'm not related to the peerage. While I would love a deeper friendship with Blackford, he has to marry someone more in line with his station."

"Ah, the English. So concerned about their petty titles."

"And the Germans aren't?"

"We admire and reward—what is the word I want?—spunk. That's it. Spunk. And you are a young lady of spunk. If the duke were German, I'm sure he would marry you."

"But he's not."

"No. But you must think of your future. Come to Germany and see if anything or anyone there attracts you. Or if you, as a widow, can find ways to strengthen your bank account for the years ahead."

"Even if something appealed to me, I'm English, not German."

"These are labels only. Think about it. Travel can open your mind to all sorts of possibilities." He rose. "If you'll excuse me, I have to make sure the embassy has not fallen apart in my absence."

We nodded to each other, and as he walked off, I was left wondering if he'd invited me as a diplomat to travel in his country or begun to recruit me as a spy. Or, good heavens, did he proposition me?

The air was so pleasant, smelling of flowers and fresh breezes, that I lingered on the bench. I was shocked to see the figure of the man I'd known as Sir Jonah Denby quickly coming around a tree, heading in my direction. "How does the investigation go?" he asked.

"Who are you?"

"Sir Jonah Denby, at your service," he replied with a bow. "Surely you remember me."

"I do indeed, but I've learned you're not Denby. Who are you, and why do you care about stolen blueprints?"

He stared at me for a moment, and then the bluster in his tone evaporated. "May I please sit?"

I nodded and he dropped onto the bench. Sweat trickled down his weathered cheeks.

"I'm Lord Porthollow, one of the three bidders to build Gattenger's ship. Sir Henry seems to be in a state over the theft, and I wanted to find out why."

I saw his motive in a heartbeat. "You're hoping he stole the design and will be caught and eliminated as competition in the bidding."

He nodded. "I'm sure my bid can beat old Fogburn, but Sir Henry is sneaky. I wanted to keep an eye on him, find out what he's up to, and who better to do that than you."

I couldn't risk him giving away my true identity. "First off, you need to know I'm not here as myself."

"Ho, ho. So I'm not the only one with a nom de guerre." He tapped his cane twice on the ground.

"I'm Mrs. Monthalf for this investigation. Don't mess it up for me. Or are you the one who sent me threatening letters?"

"Why would I do that? I need to find out what you've learned. Did Sir Henry steal the blueprints?"

"We don't know. Personally, I favor someone else as the brains behind this."

"Is it a dastardly plan?"

I thought about what I'd learned. "Yes."

"That's Sir Henry all over. Tricked me out of deals a time or two."

I shook my head. "You seem able to hold your own against Sir Henry. You fooled me. How did you find out I was involved?"

"Inspector Grantham. When he came to see me, he let slip about the Archivist Society involvement. I asked around until I found someone who'd met you on a previous investigation."

We were hired by word of mouth. It would make sense that we'd be discovered that way. "Thank you for your honesty, Lord Porthollow."

He rose from the bench. "Thank you, Mrs. Monthalf. I'll see you at the ball tonight."

"Where are you staying?"

"At the Teweses'. Attended Oxford with him. This visit would be a pleasure without one of his guests. Name's Lady Ormond. What a tartar. Avoid her."

He strolled away, presumably back to the nearby estate, while I was once again amazed at how aristocrats all knew each other.

LATER THAT AFTERNOON, I still hadn't seen Blackford again. I was resting my foot while reading in Lord Harwin's library and enjoying a cup of tea. At the sound of voices, I went out to greet Phyllida and the group who'd gone to see the local sights.

They all exclaimed over my recovery and then headed in different directions. I followed Lady Bennett down a hall and saw her enter a doorway. Moving quickly without jarring my foot, I opened the door to find myself in the blue parlor. The dark blue draperies were pulled to block out the sunlight, leaving the blue-patterned rug, blue-upholstered furniture, and light-blue-papered walls in shadow.

If she hadn't moved, I never would have seen Lady Bennett, since, dressed in a blue gown and hat, she faded into the corner. "What do you want?" she snapped.

I approached until I was within a foot of her. Her eyes were red rimmed. I tried a caring approach. "I saw you were upset. What's wrong?"

"As if you didn't know."

Her snooty tone wiped away any compassion I might have had for her. "Does it have anything to do with Clara Gattenger's death?"

"Her again? Why should I care about her?"

"You came to her house, spirited her away, and brought her home again only a few hours before she was murdered. When she returned, she demanded a fire in her study on the hottest day of a very hot summer. The only reason would have been to burn something."

"So?" She yanked off her gloves, one finger at a time.

"Whatever she burned, she received from you. What was it, Lady Bennett? Or should I call you Lark?"

"I hate that name."

"What did she burn, Lark?"

"It had nothing to do with me."

"You were the one she was seen with. It had something to do with you."

She shoved aside the blue draperies and looked out on the lawn. "I wish to heavens I'd never gotten involved."

"Too late. What are you involved in?"

Whirling around, she faced me. "Baron von Steubfeld asked me to inform Clara about a rumor that circled around the peerage a few years ago. I thought it was a wild guess, a slander. He told me it was fact. I wanted nothing to do with his plan. I thought it was cruel. But he insisted. Said it was the price of attending diplomatic balls." She dropped her gaze. "He said it was the price I must pay for dancing with the devil."

I wasn't going to let her off easily now. "What was the price? Come on. You must own up to it."

She sat down on a sofa in a dim corner of the room, and I walked over to sit next to her.

"He called on me after luncheon that day and said I must go straight over to Gattenger's house and take Clara to see Lady Peters. I was to force Rosamond to tell Clara about—about Lord Peters."

"Her husband?" I was completely confused.

Fortunately, Lark Bennett was too immersed in her misery to notice, or she thought me stupid. "No. Her son."

After hearing about Clara's distress at miscarrying and Clara and Ken's on-again, off-again relationship, I had a terrible idea of what Lady Bennett would say next. "Tell me."

"Ken Gattenger is Lord Peters's father, from a time when Ken and Clara had called off their engagement."

"Dear heavens. How did you find out?"

"Von Steubfeld told me. And Rosamond as much as admitted it when she begged Clara and me not to spread the story for the sake of the child."

"And the fire in the Gattenger study?"

"Clara asked Rosamond for every letter, every keepsake Ken had given her. It was her price for keeping her silence. Rosamond left the room and returned in a few minutes with a small package. Clara returned home with it, vowing to burn the contents without peeking."

Her story made tragic sense in light of Clara's desperate desire for a child by Ken. It also made sense if the baron wanted their evening routine disrupted. Unfortunately, instead of driving the Gattengers to another part of the house while the blueprints sat unprotected in the study, the upheaval meant they arrived in the study sooner than usual. The baron had inadvertently made the burglar's work more difficult.

"And this is why you came in here crying?"

She looked shocked. "No. The baron told me he'd not be coming to my room tonight. He hinted he was going to yours. Isn't one man enough for you?"

My jaw dropped. I quickly shut my mouth and, before I thought of a suitable reply, opened it again and snapped, "Yes. No. I should hope he doesn't show up in my room."

Her smile brightened any hint of tears from her face. I, on the other hand, probably looked ready to do murder.

My expression changed the moment her words reached my brain. What was von Steubfeld going to do if he was too busy to entertain Lady Bennett in the dark hours of the night? This might be the clue we were waiting for; Snelling told the valet he'd meet the head man tonight.

"You know who he's going to meet. Tell me. Tell me her name." Lark Bennett looked ready to torture me for the information.

"I don't know. Why do you think he's seeing another woman?"

"I've seen him with a young blonde who dances in a London theater. And he's a man, so there may be more. As long as they're not women he can take to balls and receptions, I don't care. But someone here could replace me, and that I won't allow."

"I'm not that woman." I rushed out of the room and upstairs as fast as I could limp. I headed straight to Rosamond Peters's room.

Her maid, Minette, answered my knock and looked at me suspiciously.

"May I speak to your mistress?" I asked.

"Come in, Georgina," was heard from inside the room. Grudgingly, the maid stepped aside.

Lady Peters wore an elegant ivory dressing gown. "You may go, Minette."

The maid left, shutting the door behind her.

"Am I interrupting anything?"

"A hunt for something of mine that is missing. But I suppose you know about that."

I shook my head. "No."

"My maid is called down to the kitchen by your maid for just a moment, and when she returns, you are outside my room. When she checks, this item is missing, and as she peeks out the door, she sees Sir Henry Stanford go into your room."

"I was looking for my frivolous maid, and I can assure you I didn't invite Sir Henry to my room." I hoped Emma never heard I'd called her frivolous.

"What I lost is more valuable to Sir Henry than it is to me."

"Then perhaps he has it."

She shrugged. "Perhaps he does. Why have you come?"

"Lady Bennett just told me you saw Clara Gattenger on the day she died and gave her distressing news."

"It's distressing to me that Lark Bennett keeps telling people this story."

"Except it's not a story, is it?" When she didn't reply, I said, "Did you know Clara suffered two miscarriages in her year of marriage?"

"No." She looked at me through widened eyes. "That poor woman. I understand how much producing an heir means to the British aristocracy."

"Did Lord Peters know he might have an heir before he died?"

She rose, walked to the open window, and looked outside. Perhaps satisfied that no one was below us listening, she said, "Yes, and he was very happy. He wanted the title to continue, and he wanted me to be provided for."

"So he was content with his fate?"

"Quite content. He felt we'd accomplished all that we needed to do. All that we could do."

I repeated what Phyllida had learned. "Even though by this time his body had wasted away so badly that he was almost totally paralyzed?"

"Must you bring this up now?" she hissed.

"Unfortunately, yes, since it involves Ken and Clara Gattenger."

"I realize you miss your cousin, but knowing my secrets won't bring her back to life."

"I believe your secret was used to change the routine in the Gattenger household that evening. A change that was supposed to simplify a robbery but instead led to Clara's death."

"As if my secret hadn't led to enough pain already. Most of all to myself."

"How did your husband feel about your betrayal of him?"

She laughed, the brittle sound giving away her emotions. "Betrayal? Finding a suitable stud was his idea. Gattenger was one of his suggestions. I would never have done it if he hadn't insisted."

She walked over to me and held out her hand. "I'm a good Catholic. I loved my husband very much. But to make him happy, I had to defy the church and all that I believed."

I quickly wiped the shocked expression off my face and touched her hand. "The affair was Lord Peters's idea?"

"My husband was a traditional aristocrat. He wanted me to have a child, and I did. He was glad."

"And Gattenger?"

"Doesn't know. And doesn't need to know. A secret fails to be a secret if everyone knows."

I wasn't sure that was right, but telling even Gattenger wouldn't be fair to the child. "And the baron?"

"I don't know how he learned our secret and Gattenger's identity with such certainty. Bribed a servant, perhaps." She studied my face for a moment. "I beg you. Please keep silent. After all, it's a family matter."

"Of course." I wondered how Blackford would feel about dishonesty in the bloodlines of old, aristocratic families. I suspected he'd be displeased. I decided he shouldn't know.

There was one more thing I wanted to know. "Is Lady Bennett blackmailing you with her knowledge?"

"Yes. She wants me to procure something for her. I asked Sir Henry to get it for me. The item that is missing is part of the deal between Sir Henry and myself."

"I hope you find it." I left, certain from what Sir Henry had said that the thing Lark Bennett wanted was the warship blueprints. Why would she want them? And if the baron was the one who'd ordered the burglary, why was Lady Bennett trying to get them away from him?

I needed to dress for dinner and the ball while wondering what to do about all this new knowledge. Emma came into my room, Phyllida following her. "How is your ankle holding up?"

"Very well, thank you. I should be able to waltz or give chase, depending on what's required."

Emma smiled at my response. "Good, because it was the duke's acceptance of her invitation that made Lady Harwin decide to host a ball. The servants have been working hard the past few days on short notice to get ready for tonight. We could have cannon fire in the gardens and they'd be too tired to notice."

"Where will they be?"

"Except for the footmen serving dinner and the tasks surrounding the midnight refreshments, they'll be downstairs, out of sight and out of mind, and hopefully getting some rest."

"And the valets and lady's maids?"

"Wherever their masters and mistresses want them to be."

I winced. "So the baron's valet could be—"

"Anywhere the baron needs him," Emma finished.

But if von Steubfeld planned to meet Snelling, rather than trust the task to his valet, we could end up following the wrong man. I told them what I'd learned from Lady Bennett about the baron's nocturnal activities for that night.

"How can I help?" Phyllida asked.

"Where would you normally be?" My knowledge of balls was extremely thin. There wasn't much need for a middle-class bookshop owner to be aware of the protocol for a country house ball, and it was limiting my effectiveness.

"I could watch the dancing. I'm sure there will be a card room set up in a parlor. I could read in the library if there isn't a young couple using it."

"We have the ballroom covered. Too well covered. Could you move between the library and the card room? I don't expect the baron's valet or the baron to slip out from either of those rooms, but it will give you a clear view of the hallway."

"With a side door at the end of it," Emma added.

"And if I see one of them leave? What do you want me to do?" Phyllida sounded half-thrilled and half-terrified.

"Find me or the duke or Sir William immediately. I'll introduce you to Sir William as soon as he arrives. He's a handy young man who works for the Foreign Office," I added at Phyllida's confused expression when I mentioned Sir William.

"And I'm to wait up here?" Emma asked.

We needed a better use of Emma's talents. "How would you like to be Cinderella? You can't come into the house from the garden until after the ball starts, but there will be so many people there, you should be able to blend into the crowd." I gave her a wide smile.

"Nonsense. Emma could never blend in. Not with her good looks," Phyllida said.

"But what red-blooded man is going to question Emma's right to be at the ball? Especially if she's dressed the part," I asked.

Phyllida nodded in agreement. "You two are about the same size. Let's see what you have in your wardrobe that will suit our mystery guest."

"Do you have your good corset with you?" I asked as I looked at the gowns I'd brought with me. Phyllida had counseled me to pack everything I could because there was no way of knowing what I'd need. In retrospect, she was brilliant.

"Of course. I wear it with the plum-colored day dress that is supposed to be a castoff from you." Emma studied my gowns and selected the light blue. "You can't call me Emma, since someone will likely put two and two together."

"Eugenie," Phyllida said. "It sounds exotic. And I should be able to remember that, since it's close."

Not as close as Georgia and Georgina, and she'd had trouble remembering my false name. Still, if she felt comfortable calling Emma by Eugenie, I wouldn't complain. "Get anything you might need from your room and come back here. Once you're dressed for the ball, you'll have to stay here until dinner is nearly over and then you can slip into the garden undetected."

Emma nodded. "I'll float between the gardens and indoors?"

"Yes. There will be guests from other house parties and local gentry. Try to deflect any questions on which group you're with. Play mysterious."

"Any man who is spending all his energy trying to find out who you are is not involved in espionage. Ignore him," Phyllida added.

CHAPTER NINETEEN

EMMA left to get what she needed from her room while I went next door with Phyllida to assist her with her corset. When Emma returned, bread and an apple stolen from the kitchen tucked into her bundle, Phyllida was ready to have her hair dressed.

By the time we moved into my room, Phyllida was ready in a matronly wine-colored gown liberally decorated with black lace and ropes of pearls. She helped both of us into our ball gowns, mine dark green and Emma's the light blue. Both of the dresses were off the shoulder and showing a great deal of cleavage.

"Remember, there's a man in your life. You couldn't wear that dress if you were shopping for your first husband," Phyllida warned Emma.

"Perhaps I'm a merry widow," Emma said with a smile as she looked at her reflection in the full-length glass.

I thought of Rosamond Peters and Clara Gattenger and their secret. No one was merry in those events. "You'd better make up your mind on your story. You're going to be drawing men like moths to a flame."

Looking in the glass, I decided I looked nice. Maybe even pretty. However, Emma was breathtakingly beautiful.

"Maybe I'll avoid notice," Emma said as she began to work on my hair.

"I doubt it. Do you know where Sumner is supposed to be?"

Emma yanked on my hair. "He's gone."

"But why? He should get to see you in that gown," Phyllida said.

"Well, he won't." She gave a loud sniff.

I knew I'd risk being bald by the time we finished this conversation, but I had to find out. "What has happened? Where did he go?"

"Sumner's gone back to town. Blackford's orders. Jacob's going to approach the clerk he thinks is the leak in the Admiralty records room with new evidence the Archivist Society's uncovered. Jacob's going to try to force the clerk to confess. Sumner has been ordered to shadow them while members of the Archivist Society are watching the garden here."

"Far be it from me to correct a duke, but why didn't he have Fogarty or one of our other Archivist Society members tail Jacob?"

"He sent Sumner because he doesn't trust Fogarty to do the job properly." Emma made a face but didn't say another word. She finished my hair, did her own in a simple upsweep that Phyllida decorated with a few jewels, and pointedly stared at us, waiting for our departure.

I answered a knock on my door to find the duke, elegantly attired in evening clothes, waiting for me. I made a small gesture with my head and he entered my room, his eyes widening when he saw Emma.

"This is Eugenie, a mysterious guest. She'll enter the gardens while we're having dinner," I told him.

"She won't be the only one. The higher-ups in government refuse to believe any of this. Scotland Yard is overburdened with the arrival of the Russians and the anarchists. The local police refuse to get involved. So we have Archivist Society members watching the grounds." He strode over to where Emma stood. "You have your knife? Good. I'll have Sir William escort you around the gardens. At least we have Sir William and Mr. Nobles assisting us."

Then the duke turned to me. "Where did you get that bruise?"

Both my shoulder and wrist showed the results of Sir Henry's persuasion. At least I had covered my wrists with my twenty-button gloves. "Let me get my lacy shawl."

"Georgia."

"I think you can guess."

"When this is over, Sir Henry and I will have words." His tone made me think more than talking would be involved. I'd suffered worse during investigations before. Never had anyone threatened to avenge my injuries.

I put my hand on his shiny black jacket sleeve and marched out of the room, Phyllida following us.

The fantasy of every young girl is to walk down a grand staircase on the arm of a handsome, virile duke to attend a ball. I was nearly thirty and pretending to be someone I wasn't to stop an espionage plot, but I was living that fantasy.

The staircase was carpeted in acres of red with a carved banister. The Duke of Blackford was tall, dark, and manly. His formal evening attire was the deepest black with a blazing white bow tie and shirt. My dress, dark green with swirls of silk and satin, made me look like an alluring, elegant woman. I would carry the thrill of sweeping down those stairs like a princess until the day I died.

"You look ravishing, Georgia," the duke murmured, and I almost missed a step.

"Thank you, Your Grace."

"I will claim my waltz if I personally have to stop von Steubfeld from interfering. If he tries to grab those plans during the ball, I will shoot him." Blackford stared at me, his eyes darkening.

His words made my heart hammer against my corset. "I'll load the gun."

He grinned as he led me to the parlor where the guests were to meet before going in to dinner. As soon as we entered the room, Lady Harwin stole the duke away to introduce him to some local notable. My fantasy ended too quickly, but his words, *I will claim my waltz*, rang in my brain.

"The duke appears quite smitten," Phyllida said.

"He's playing his role well."

"No. He wasn't acting. There was no audience except me. And I do not count."

I glanced at Phyllida. She smiled serenely.

Time to get my mind back on business. "I'd introduce you to Sir William and Mr. Nobles, but I don't think they'll be here until the ball."

"There will be plenty of time, then, but what do we do if Snelling brings the plans while we're all eating pigeon or pheasant or some such?"

"We'll have to trust our friends. Scotland Yard has failed us." I knew we could handle this. The Archivist Society had to stop the sale of the naval designs and prove Gattenger's innocence.

"Scotland Yard has failed us?" Lady Rosamond Peters asked. "Whatever are you discussing?"

I jumped. "That young man who tried to steal Lady Phyllida's hatbox. If anyone is going to stop crimes like that against ladies while they're shopping, it has to be Scotland Yard. So far they've failed us." I hoped it sounded believable. I didn't have any better ideas, and I still had no idea what would happen tonight.

"Stealing a hatbox is such a strange crime. I doubt we'll hear of anyone else threatened in that manner," Lady Peters said. "I'm glad to see you on your feet again."

Good. She appeared to buy my excuse for mentioning Scotland Yard. "Either I heal very quickly or the blow was not as bad as first thought. Of course, my recovery could be aided by my desire to waltz with the duke." I gave Lady Peters a cheery smile and she laughed.

"You can hardly be blamed. I see the way he looks at you."

"You're teasing me."

"Not at all. I think he regrets letting you get away in India all those years ago."

I felt the heat rush up my face. Trying to deflect my wish that it were so, I said, "All those years ago? You make us sound ancient."

"You ladies look lovely," Sir Henry said as he came up behind Lady Peters. Thus began a round of mutual congratulations on our outfits that ended with us agreeing Phyllida would be the loveliest lady at the ball.

"Where are Lady Bennett and Baron von Steubfeld?" I asked as soon as I could steer the conversation in another direction.

"They're in Lord Harwin's study with him and a guest from Whitehall. Apparently there's supposed to be a bit of diplomacy carried out this weekend, away from London and all the usual formalities," Sir Henry said.

"I've heard the baron carries a message for Her Majesty," Lady Peters added.

"Then we're in exalted company this weekend," Lady Phyllida said as we all stared at the closed doorway that stood between the parlor and the study.

At that moment, the door opened. Lady Harwin, seeing that as her cue, told us to line up to go into dinner. She was escorted in by the duke, who sat next to her. I found myself near the middle of a very long table between a friend of the Harwins' son who was visiting from Oxford and an elderly barrister who'd been invited to even the numbers. Both men seemed interested only in eating and looking down my bodice.

In the long pauses between conversations, I was able to look out the windows into the sunset-lit garden. No one wandered into my view. This was fortunate, because I had no idea what the rules of etiquette said about the proper way to leap up from a banquet and dash after a criminal carrying stolen warship designs. Neither, apparently, did the baron, because he stayed seated throughout dinner.

Dinner was tasty, but I ate sparingly, afraid that at any moment I'd be called into action. Later, I couldn't recall a single dish served.

Somehow we managed to finish dinner without a hue and cry outdoors, and the guests for the ball began to arrive. Two of the first were Sir William Darby and Mr. Frederick Nobles.

With Phyllida trailing behind, I walked up to where they were handing over their top hats and canes. "Lady Phyllida, I'd like to introduce Sir William Darby and Mr. Frederick Nobles. I believe they're friends of the duke's," I added quietly.

"I'm so pleased to meet you. I'll be in the card room or the library during the ball, but if I have need of you, I'll be sure to call upon you gentlemen," Phyllida said quietly.

Merciful heavens. Phyllida was developing a taste for clandestine action. Perhaps she'd prefer a more active role in the Archivist Society.

"I would be honored to assist you," Sir William said as he bowed over Phyllida's hand. Then he looked at her and winked. Mr. Nobles bowed in the same manner, the edges of his mouth curling up under his mustache as he rose.

We headed into the ballroom at the back of the house. Blackford escorted Lady Harwin. "He'll have to have the first waltz with her," Phyllida whispered.

"I'd suspect there are any number of ladies he'll need to partner," I responded with what I hoped sounded like complete indifference.

She raised her eyebrows as she looked at me. I couldn't fool Phyllida.

The first dance was a country dance I had never seen before and begged off. Phyllida walked off with some older attendees to the card room, and I began to circle the room. Lady Bennett and Baron von Steubfeld took part in the dance, and I saw no activity outside in the terrace, so I felt I could relax my guard.

Lady Peters came up to me. "You're not dancing?"

"I didn't think I should risk my ankle on anything but a waltz. And you?"

"Don't tell anyone, but I find country dances tedious. You can't carry on a decent conversation with anyone."

"While you can have discussions on the edge of the room without a soul overhearing."

"You're never so alone as you are in a crowded ballroom," Lady Peters agreed.

I looked at the lines of dancers. "Sir Henry seems to be enjoying himself."

"Sir Henry enjoys himself everywhere."

"I never learned the country dances. Did you?"

"Yes. It was always part of the harvest celebration." Then she turned to look at me. "My parents liked to visit the countryside for the holidays. They found the city too somber."

"That would be a nice tradition to pass on to your son." I was waltzing around the topic I wanted to raise with her, not certain how to proceed.

"Did you and Mr. Monthalf have children?"

"No. Not being part of the aristocracy, failing to produce an heir didn't matter."

"Sir Henry told me what you admitted about your late husband. And how he made you search my room for the letter. You found it, didn't you?" Amazingly, Rosamond Peters watched the dancers with a pleasant expression.

I copied her mild behavior so that no one who glanced our way would see anything but two ladies discussing trivial matters. "Neither Sir Henry nor I have possession of the letter. On that, I give you my word."

"Not quite the same, but I'm content if Sir Henry doesn't have it. He can be overbearing."

I stopped myself from bursting out laughing. "Yes," I managed to say quietly. I couldn't stop myself from asking, "Why does Lady Bennett want the ship blueprints?"

"I don't know. I'd give her the crown jewels if it would keep her quiet, for the sake of my child."

As the dance came to an end, I glanced outside into the thickening darkness.

"Expecting someone?" Rosamond Peters asked.

"Vainly checking my appearance in the reflection." I gave her a smile and turned my attention to the room, where bowing and curtsying and offers for the first waltz were being exchanged. Across the room I spotted my ersatz Sir Denby, Lord Porthollow. He didn't seem to have noticed me.

Sir Henry came over, momentarily at a loss as to who to ask first. I excused myself, leaving the field to Lady Peters, and walked away. As I closed the distance to Lord Porthollow, I saw Lady Ormond approach him. She appeared to be lecturing him, and he appeared to be running.

He saw me and beamed. "A waltz, young lady?"

"Please." We waltzed away from Lady Ormond at top speed. "What is she upset about?"

"She's trying to force a match between her niece and Tewes's older son. Quite blatant about it. I told her to leave the poor young people alone. They'd have to spend the rest of their lives suffering from their decision. She didn't think I should have said that in front of the young people. I said someone should talk sense to them." He glanced over his shoulder. "She's been after me ever since. What have you learned?"

"Tonight perhaps we shall discover all."

"Good luck."

He left me on the far side of the dance floor and headed for the card room. Blackford waltzed with Lady Harwin. The baron waltzed with Lady Bennett. Sir Henry waltzed with Lady Peters. I circled the room until I bumped into Mr. Nobles. "Everything quiet?" I asked.

"Sir William is taking a turn in the garden. I'm minding the store in here."

Sweeping the room with my eyes, I said, "With a lot of goods on the shelves."

"Half a dozen peers, a few baronets, a churchman or two, plus their ladies, younger sons with the courtesy title of 'lord,' a few debutantes, and guests at neighboring houses."

"Quite a lot of goods in this store you're minding," I amended.

"Would you care to dance? We can watch them from the dance floor as well as here."

"Thank you."

Frederick Nobles escorted me into the center of the room and led me in a sweeping waltz, his hand placed correctly on the small of my back above my waist. He was light on his feet, and I was hard-pressed to keep up. I struggled so much that I nearly missed Baron von Steubfeld and Lady Bennett leave the floor and make their way to the French doors leading to the terrace.

"It's hot in here. Would you like to step outside and get some air?" I asked.

"What?" He glanced around to where I stared at the French doors. "Oh. Yes, I would."

We cut a tangled path through the dancers. Von Steubfeld and Lark Bennett had been outside for a minute or two by the time we reached the doors. Long enough to have lost us in the dark.

When Nobles opened the door, I discovered I needn't have worried. Past the light of torches hung from poles around the terrace, I could see two figures strolling in the garden away from the house parallel to the baron and Lady Bennett. A familiar pale blue dress reflected the moonlight. It was Emma, walking with Sir William.

Suddenly, branches snapped and bushes shook at the end of the garden beyond where the baron and Lady Bennett stood. Two men fell to the ground. "Gracious," I exclaimed as Mr. Nobles moved forward, saying, "Everyone all right?"

"Burglar," Fogarty said as he struggled to stand on his injured leg. He made a grab for his leaner, more agile adversary.

The second man moved into bright moonlight in the clearing for an instant, and I found myself looking at Mick Snelling. Before I could glimpse whether he was carrying a package the size of the ship plans, he bolted into the darkness and escaped.

Fogarty chased after him, leaving his bowler hat on the path. Lady Bennett looked over her skirt with an expression that said she was furious. Either she'd been splattered by mud or she didn't like Snelling taking chances on being caught. Mr. Nobles walked over and picked up the hat. "I say, we've had a bit of excitement."

His wide-eyed enthusiasm was so at odds with his usual demeanor I nearly laughed. Baron von Steubfeld, who'd been closest to the action in the bushes, looked at Nobles and in a tone that said the incident had nothing to do with him, asked, "Do you often have burglars at house parties?"

"They go where the pickings are the best," Nobles answered and strolled back toward the house.

Since I hadn't been spotted by the baron or Lady Bennett, I slipped back into the ballroom. The dance had ended, and the orchestra was readying for the next number. "What happened?" a warm baritone murmured in my ear.

"Your Grace. Mick Snelling was discovered by Fogarty in the bushes near the baron and Lady Bennett. There was a scuffle and Snelling escaped with Fogarty chasing him. The baron didn't seem surprised by any of this. Lady Bennett appeared annoyed." I looked up at Blackford, wondering if he'd come looking for me or if he was checking on the action in the garden.

The music began. "Georgina. Would you do me the honor?"

He led me out onto the dance floor and held me in an intimately tight embrace. While Mr. Nobles was a fine dancer and Lord Porthollow an energetic one, the duke held me so I couldn't fail to match him step for step. We gracefully moved as one across the shiny hardwood. My dreams of dancing with the duke had never been this smooth. This polished. This wonderful.

I smiled up at him and let him lead me where he wanted. He noticed my smile and squeezed my hand, whispering in my ear, "Was this worth waiting for?"

"Yes." I sighed. The feel of his breath on my skin was enchanting. I memorized the swirl of brightly colored dresses in time to the music. The one errant curl brushing his collar. The smell of his soap.

We twirled around the room once, twice, and then I made the mistake of looking toward the entrance to the room. There in the archway, standing with two other evening-dress-clad men, was my parents' killer.

"There he is," I whispered into the duke's ear.

"Who? Snelling?"

"No. My parents' killer. Come on." I pulled Blackford off the dance floor toward the doorway. By the time we reached it, the three men had vanished.

I stood in the hallway, looking in all directions. The duke said, "This way. Front entrance," and hurried me along. My dancing slippers slid from rug to rug on the smooth floor as I tried to keep up.

When we turned the corner, we saw the butler closing the front door. "Who just left?" the duke demanded.

"Sir Wallace Vance and two of his guests."

While Blackford spoke to the butler, I dashed around them and pulled open the door. A carriage was in motion, wheels grinding and horseshoes clomping on the gravel drive. All I could see was the back of a large, dark-colored coach.

"His guests' names?"

If the butler found my behavior and the duke's question

strange, he didn't hesitate or blink. "A Mr. van der Lik and Count Farkas."

"I didn't see them at the ball. Were they in the card room?"

The butler remained stoic. "I couldn't say, Your Grace."

Blackford took my hand. "We'll call on Mr. Vance tomorrow."

I sounded slightly breathless as I tried to pull him toward the door. "He might have left by then."

It would have been easier to move a mountain than the duke. "No, he won't. We'll meet him tomorrow. Come on, Georgina. We have more important business tonight."

Unfortunately, tonight was our best chance for catching my parents' killer as well as retrieving the stolen designs for the new warship. I'd vowed to find the ship blueprints and prove Gattenger innocent. That was the reason I was there. And I'd promised Phyllida I'd succeed in this investigation.

I'd have to ignore the man I'd vowed to catch a dozen years before. But only until the next day. Then I'd have the duke's assistance to confront Sir Wallace and his murderous guest. "All right, Your Grace. Lead on."

He took my arm and led me along the corridor. As soon as we were out of sight of the butler, Mr. Nobles stepped out of a doorway. "Snelling got away and took the drawings with him."

"Where is he now?" Blackford demanded.

"We don't know. There are Archivist Society people searching the town, but they've had no luck so far."

"He'll come back here," I said with certainty. "He wants to get his money and be free of those drawings. They've been nothing but trouble for him."

"I was surprised he didn't follow your suggestion to his sister and take the drawings to Stevens to get a second set made and get twice the money," the duke said.

"Stevens?" Mr. Nobles asked, his eyes narrowing.

"My butler. Mrs. Monthalf talked to his sister and suggested a plan for Snelling to double his money. It also would have meant we'd have the original plans and be able to pass on slightly altered, and useless, drawings in their place. He was spotted by one of my footmen loitering across the street, but after half an hour, he left and didn't return."

"A pity. It would have saved us all this effort," I grumbled. It would also have allowed us to chase after the man I sought tonight.

The duke must have read my mind, because he answered, "Then we wouldn't have needed to travel to the country at all and you wouldn't have seen your quarry."

"Who?" Nobles asked.

"A separate inquiry," I answered.

"Shall we try to dance an entire waltz?" the duke asked, taking my arm and ignoring Mr. Nobles.

"I'd love to." If Snelling returned now and destroyed my opportunity, I'd throttle him.

CHAPTER TWENTY

THE ball was lovely, fortunately lacking the reappearance of Snelling and the ship designs he'd stolen from Gattenger. Baron von Steubfeld danced with Lady Harwin, Lady Bennett, and an elderly dowager. Sir Henry danced with Lady Peters and then escorted her onto the terrace.

After our waltz, Blackford deserted me for the very eligible Miss Amanda Weycross, daughter of a lord and guest of the Teweses' daughter, followed by the equally eligible Lady Anne Stewart, daughter of the Scottish earl and his wife. I was asked once to dance by our host and then once by Mr. Nobles. Otherwise, I was on my own.

I walked over to join Lady Peters and Baron von Steubfeld in conversation. "The duke has chosen another partner?" the baron asked as I neared them.

"He can't dance every dance with me. It's not done," I told him. "And why aren't you dancing with Lady Bennett?"

"She was claimed by the Viscount Gathwite, and Sir Henry

decided to take a solo journey around the gardens, abandoning Lady Peters."

Sir Henry, who'd worried Ken Gattenger into taking the drawings home that fateful evening to restudy his calculations, therefore making them available to Mick Snelling. I had the sudden terrible feeling I'd misjudged Stanford and his connection to the thief.

The only thing I could think to say was, "Oh, dear. There were ruffians out there earlier. I hope they haven't returned. It might not be safe to be out there alone."

As an excuse, it was pretty weak, but I hurried toward the French doors leading to the terrace, aware of Lady Peters following me. Once outside, I looked around, hoping my eyes would quickly adjust to the torchlight and moonlight. I noticed the baron didn't join us.

Lady Peters stood next to me. "Do you really think he might be in danger? I'd hate for anything to happen to him, even as angry as I am at him at this moment."

Sir William and Emma walked up to us. "It's lovely outside," Emma said.

"Yes, it is. You haven't seen Sir Henry Stanford, have you?" I asked.

"We're afraid he might have run into difficulties," Lady Peters added.

"How terrible. We've not seen him, but we'll help you look. Shall we go this way?" Sir William said.

"Thank you. That would be helpful," I said and nodded to him.

He escorted Emma away, and I headed in the opposite direction, afraid of what I'd find. I suspected Sir Henry, but I didn't want to. If I caught him with Snelling, I'd raise an unholy ruckus out of disappointment and anger.

I rushed down one path and then another, Lady Peters trailing me. Reaching a dark bend in the path behind large shrubbery, I nearly tripped over a figure lying facedown. I turned him over, hearing Rosamond Peters gasp as we saw Sir Henry's face by moonlight.

"Is he—still alive?"

I felt for a pulse. "Yes. Run back to the house and tell our host to send some footmen to carry him inside."

"Do you think it's his heart?"

"No. I think it's the nasty blow to the back of his head that's felled him. Rosamond, please hurry."

She dashed away. I wished I had a lantern to show me the area around us. I'd like a clue to tell me who had attacked Sir Henry. Footprints, a shirt stud, anything to point to his attacker.

Thank goodness the first footmen Rosamond Peters brought carried a lantern. In the flickering light, his bloody head wound was visible. So were the scuffed footprints around him. Despite the dampness retained in the soil, the only firm marks matched the worn heels of Sir Henry's shoes. A rock tossed into a nearby flower bed had what appeared to be blood on one side.

Clues, yes, but leading where? His attacker could have come from the ballroom or from outside of the estate. I rose from where I'd bent over Sir Henry, checking on his condition and searching for clues, and let the footmen carry the wounded man indoors.

"Oh, Mrs. Monthalf, your dress is ruined."

At Lady Peters's words I looked down and discovered my dress had dirt spread a few inches up from the hem. Then I glanced at hers. "Yours is, too."

"I'll gladly lose a ball gown if Sir Henry recovers."

I nodded in agreement, then jumped as Lord Porthollow stepped into my path. "How is Sir Henry?"

"Unconscious. Did you see what happened?"

"No. I came outside to see what all the excitement was about. I was hoping you could tell me." He smiled, making deep creases in his leathery skin.

"I'm afraid I don't have anything to tell." I followed Lady Peters into the house by the side door where they'd taken Sir Henry. Muddy footprints lined one side of the carpet, as if a man carrying Sir Henry on that side had stepped in wet dirt. Then Lady Peters walked along the middle and left equally muddy marks. I checked, and my own slippers were not nearly as soiled as hers. What had she stepped in?

I put out a hand and stopped Rosamond. "When did Sir Henry go out into the garden alone?"

"It was such a nice night that we decided to talk outside. I told him I was angry with him for stealing that letter, and he blamed everything on you. We headed back toward the terrace, no longer friends. Suddenly, Sir Henry stopped and told me to go in. He'd follow me in a few minutes. When I suggested I could stay outside if I wanted, he shooed me indoors. I don't know if he saw something odd or planned to meet someone." She gave an indifferent shrug.

"Fortunately, you went in. Otherwise you both might have been attacked."

"Or unfortunately. I might have screamed and frightened off the attacker." She looked up the stairs where they had carried Sir Henry to his bedroom. "I suppose they've called a doctor, and we would just be in the way."

She turned and walked into the ballroom. I followed, hoping the duke had finished dancing with the lovely young aristocrats.

He had. "They're about to play the last waltz before we go into the supper room. Dance with me."

He escorted me onto the dance floor, and once again his masterful hold on me negated my waltzing inadequacies. "What happened?" he whispered in my ear.

This was to be a working dance.

"Sir Henry was attacked. He's still alive."

"Why Stanford?"

"If I knew who, I could tell you why. The plans were not in evidence." How I wished they had been.

"You think Stanford, and not the baron, was to retrieve the drawings from Snelling?"

"Possibly. He did convince Gattenger to take a set home to work on them the night Snelling broke in." And everything he told me could have been a lie.

"The attack on Stanford could be a screen for handing off the plans to someone else," Blackford said.

"Or Sir Henry saw something and had to be stopped from raising the alarm. I met Sir Jonah Denby here. He says he's really Lord Porthollow, interested in whether Sir Henry stole the blueprints, because if so, Sir Henry would be eliminated from the bidding and then he, Lord Porthollow, would win. He was outside when Sir Henry was carried in."

"Blast. There are too many possibilities. Too many suspects. I've been watching von Steubfeld all night and he hasn't gone far." The duke swung me around with a flourish and we waltzed in the opposite direction.

I managed to keep my feet under me as I considered our next move. "Maybe he knows Snelling won't be back until the supper is served. With everyone eating and drinking, he might think it'll be easier for him to slip away. Particularly since he must know he's under surveillance."

The duke raised his eyebrows before pulling me closer and

speaking directly into my ear. "We'll just have to keep an eye on von Steubfeld during supper. Afterward, the guests from the other house parties will be leaving. Lots of activity by the front entrance, and no one near the terrace."

I struggled to keep waltzing and think about the handoff of the ship blueprints, but the way Blackford's breath brushed my skin was claiming all my attention. "Except us."

"And Sir William, Mr. Nobles, Emma, the Archivists—"

Now I felt as useful as a horse pushing a cart from behind. "All right. Where should we be?"

His dark eyes were the color of a gloomy sky. "I don't know."

"Surely you must have some idea." I thought the duke always had an idea. Whether it was a good one was another matter.

"None."

"Then we must keep an eye on everyone, especially the baron, and go with our instincts."

"That's not logical."

I forced myself to sound more positive than I felt. I knew how important rescuing those naval blueprints was to the duke. "Sometimes we have to throw logic out the window and observe what is happening right in front of us."

The waltz ended and everyone moved toward the dining room. Including the baron.

We followed at the end of the laughing, colorful crowd like a sorrowful tail. I was frustrated at our lack of progress. I could only imagine what was going through the duke's mind.

Now that the music had ended, partiers found they had much to say to each other and stayed clustered in the dining room. Perhaps knowledge of the attack on Sir Henry had spread, keeping them together. When carriages began to arrive, the guests left in groups. They laughed, called farewells, and made a joyous racket. But they clung together for safety, and I saw several look over their shoulders.

As the last group left, Lord Harwin gave his butler orders to lock all the doors and wait for the doctor and the policeman to arrive about Sir Henry. Then he led the guests upstairs. Only a few men lingered in the smoking parlor. Von Steubfeld was one. Blackford was another.

Lady Harwin stopped me in the upstairs hall and asked if I was all right after the shock of finding Sir Henry unconscious in the shrubbery. I couldn't tell her I'd seen much worse, so I told her I hoped Sir Henry recovered quickly from his accident and walked off toward our rooms with Phyllida.

Emma was waiting when Phyllida and I entered my room. "Did you see Snelling?" I asked her.

"Only the once, early on. He's not come back, and none of the valets or maids left the house. Fogarty and some of the other Archivists are patrolling the grounds, but there are too few of them. Do you think the burglar will return as soon as the house is quiet?"

"I would. Did you see what happened to Sir Henry?" I asked.

"I didn't know anything had happened until Lady Peters ran past toward the house. Sir William and I walked in your direction, but by that time you had everything under control," Emma said.

"When had you seen Sir Henry before we discovered him attacked?" I took off my necklace and set it in the jewelry box.

A moment later, the duke walked in without knocking. I gave him a quick glance as Emma replied, "Earlier, deep in conversation with Lady Peters."

"Is that what they call it now?" Blackford asked.

I shot a look at him, and the edge of his mouth quirked up.

He continued to stare at me, and I couldn't look away. Something about the look in his eyes sent a tremor through my veins.

"Yes. They seemed to be arguing. Sir Henry walked away and Lady Peters gave a deep sigh and ran after him. I didn't see any more," Emma said. She and Phyllida stepped behind a painted cloth screen, and a moment later Emma's ball gown was draped over the top.

Had Rosamond Peters caught up with Sir Henry? And what were they arguing about? Sir Henry's letter or Lady Peters's son?

"The doctor's arrived. Sir Henry hasn't regained consciousness, so the doctor is having him watched during the night. He has every hope Sir Henry will be with us in the morning," the duke said.

"Will he know who hit him when he awakes?" I asked.

"Probably not. Not unusual in cases of head injury to have no memory of the attack," Blackford told me.

"If Snelling comes back tonight to meet with Sir Henry, he'll be walking around outside with the plans and no one to give them to," I said. "Emma, are you in your lady's maid costume?"

"Yes." She came out from the screen transformed into a servant.

"Help Phyllida get ready for bed and then slip down to the servants' entrance to see if anyone leaves that way. I'm going to hide behind the curtains and watch the rooms on this corridor."

Emma and Phyllida left my room, but Blackford blocked my path. "I'll watch the men's wing from the alcove with the suit of armor. Come and get me if you see anyone leave."

I looked up at him, my arms crossed. "Only if you promise to get me if anyone leaves from your wing."

"Of course. I wouldn't pass up the chance to sneak around in a dark garden with you." He smiled too broadly, and I discovered I didn't believe a word he said. Then he slipped his arms around my waist as his expression turned serious. "We're finally alone."

I smiled up at him, unsure what to expect. No matter what roles we were playing, he was still a duke.

He bent down, his eyes focused on my suddenly dry lips. I licked them in an effort to make them feel normal and watched his eyes darken. My insides twitched in response and my lips baked despite the cool evening air.

I slid my hands up the sleeves of his jacket, reveling in the softness. He shifted me against his chest and my hands snaked around his shoulders. Great heavens. Blackford was going to kiss me.

He never got the chance. I moved forward and pressed my lips against his in a rush of desire. I held the back of his head so I could get that last fraction of an inch closer to him. I might never get another chance to kiss him, and I wanted to know what his skin felt like against mine.

And then Blackford took charge. The kiss softened and gained electricity that shot down my spine and made my toes curl. For a moment, we were a pirate-raider and a princess, and the world stood still.

Then he pulled away and said, "I've wanted to kiss you for a very long time. Now I've discovered this might become habit-forming."

I smiled as if he had just given me the queen's jewels. "Some habits are good for you."

He released a long breath and swept one hand toward the door. "We need to catch Snelling. After you."

Sticking my head out of the doorway, I saw the hall was empty. Blackford left behind me and shut the door. I hurried toward the draperies over the window at the end of the hall. The hall seemed long enough to stretch across the width of London, but finally I reached the end and climbed behind the draperies without anyone catching me. Luckily, the maids did a good job cleaning and I didn't have to sneeze from the dust.

I peeked out from my hiding spot. The duke had already disappeared around the corner and I felt more alone than ever.

The window ledge was wide enough to sit on and draw my feet up, hiding me entirely from anyone who might see me in the weak light from the night lanterns. The glass windowpanes were cool to the touch from the night air. It was dark and quiet where I sat, and I soon felt my head nodding.

A noise woke me, bringing my head and back away from where I had leaned on the side of the window opening. I looked out through the gap between the draperies in time to see a woman's skirt and foot disappear around the turn toward the main stairs.

I listened for a moment, but no one else appeared to be stirring. I climbed out of my hiding place and dashed in my dancing slippers to the top of the stairs. Looking down, I glimpsed the hem of a skirt glide down the far hallway.

Rushing along the staircase and foyer, I skidded to a stop when I reached the far hall. No one was in sight. I stopped in front of the door that led to the study. Taking a deep breath to calm my racing heart, I opened the door. A quick check showed there was no one inside and there was no way out.

The next door led to a parlor with a connecting door to another parlor. I continued through the empty rooms, trying each locked, bolted door to the terrace in turn before reaching the door that brought me to the library.

The library's exit leading into the back garden was unlocked and unbolted. Could Snelling be meeting his buyer on the terrace at this moment? I opened the door, stepped outside, and tripped. I waved my arms and stumbled, landing heavily on my hands and knees. Groaning, I pulled myself up using the half wall that encircled part of the terrace.

Rubbing my knees, I swung around to see what was in my path. A body lay on the ground with its arms and legs sprawled. The moonlight was bright enough that I could make out Mick Snelling's features and the odd angle his head lay from his body.

I glanced around. No package. No blueprints. His attacker had beaten me to it. I was about to run back in and go upstairs to get Blackford when the door opened. Baron von Steubfeld blocked my path. His furious expression was nearly as intimidating as the pistol he aimed at me. A pistol I couldn't fail to see glittering in the moonlight.

I stared at the gun rather than his face as I said, "Baron von Steubfeld." I kept my shaking knees from carrying me back a step. There was no way I'd show fear to the top German spy in England, even if he planned to kill me. If? The pistol left me in no doubt as to his intensions.

"You killed him."

"No, I—" Surprise jerked my gaze up to look at the baron's face. "You think I killed him?"

"What have you done with the blueprints?" His voice ground out the unmistakable note of threat.

"Nothing. I found things just as you see them."

"Do you want the money I would pay him? Because I assure you, there are other ways of making you tell me where the drawings are." The moonlight showed the cruel smile beneath his mustache.

"She doesn't have them."

I made out the solid shadow of the Duke of Blackford behind him. The duke reached out his hand in front of von Steubfeld's face. The German grimaced and gave him his pistol. "How can you be sure? She might have killed him and taken the plans for herself."

"I am certain." The duke must have pocketed the gun, because it was no longer in his hand when he stepped around the baron and knelt by Snelling. "He's had his neck broken."

"Professionally done?" the baron asked.

"Yes."

"Then I apologize, Mrs. Monthalf. You are not a professional killer."

I pressed my lips together to hide my smile. This was not the time to admit I was a professional, but one who lacked knowledge of breaking necks. "Sumner?" I asked Blackford.

"Possibly, but he would have waited here guarding the ship plans until help arrived. And he's in London." The duke rose. "What about your valet?"

A deep sigh rumbled through von Steubfeld's chest. "Not him. I told him I would handle the transaction, after he botched the transfer last night."

"Why wouldn't Snelling deal with your valet?" Blackford had probably learned more from Sumner last night than he'd told me.

"He'd always dealt directly with me before. I suppose he didn't trust an unknown intermediary."

"Snelling had already been visited by Sir Henry Stanford with an offer for the blueprints. Perhaps he thought your valet worked for someone other than you," I suggested.

"Perhaps," the baron agreed. "And it cost Snelling his life. Meanwhile, my valet waits in my room to carry the drawings into the village. By morning he would have been well on his way to London to catch a boat across the North Sea."

"After the first handoff, during the ball, failed. Our people were the ones who blocked the first attempt, Baron." I was ready to give credit to the work the Archivist Society had done.

"You are to be congratulated, Miss Fenchurch."

I looked at the baron in surprise. "You were the one who sent the notes?"

"Yes. One of my agents is a porter. Very handy when I want to find out what is being moved around London. He was puzzled by the number of sea trunks moved from a dressmaker's to a house in Mayfair. I had you followed from the house to your bookshop. A few discreet questions gave me your name. When I began to ask around, I learned about your connection to the Archivist Society." The baron gave me a considering look. "No one else figured out your true mission or your identity. You are to be congratulated."

I nodded to him graciously. I wasn't ready to finish playing the well-brought-up lady. "Those notes. Would you have killed me?"

"If I couldn't find a better solution."

I shivered.

"I think it's time to wake our host and have him call the police," Blackford said, an edge to his voice.

"Does my interest in this man need to be made public?" the baron asked.

"Not if you give me your word as a gentleman that you don't know where the drawings are currently, don't have them in your possession, and won't try to retrieve them." The duke stared at the baron.

The baron held his gaze. "I neither have them nor know where they are. If they should fall in my lap, I will of course attempt to send them to Germany. That is how the game is played."

"It's not a game. A man is dead," I said.

"Unfortunately, Snelling is the only man who could have testified to Gattenger's innocence in his wife's death," the duke told me.

"Surely all this will be enough to free him from prison." I sounded slightly desperate to my own ears.

"All what, Georgina? We have a dead man miles from the Gattenger home with no apparent connection to either the husband or the wife. No, finding the drawings on Snelling might have been sufficient. The testimony of a live Snelling certainly would have helped. Finding a dead man without the plans does nothing to prove Gattenger didn't kill his wife or commit treason." The duke prowled the area around the body, no doubt looking for the blueprints.

The baron leaned against the door frame, watching him.

"Do you have any other operatives in the area, von Steubfeld?"

"No."

"Truly?"

"Truly." His grumble told me he now saw that as a mistake.

"How do we know he didn't kill Snelling instead of paying him, then hide the blueprints and come back here to move the body, only to find I arrived first?" I asked the duke.

"Snelling was a skilled thief. I needed him alive. And I've never minded paying him his fee," the baron said. "I will take an oath as a gentleman to that effect."

"Your word is sufficient," the duke said.

Baron von Steubfeld gave a sharp military bow in reply.

"He's telling you the truth," the duke added. "I showed the drawing Gattenger did of Snelling to some friends at Whitehall, who showed it to a witness in another case where the baron was suspected. He's used Snelling before."

"And so you are indirectly responsible for Clara Gattenger's death," I pointed out. "You sent Snelling to her house to steal from them and he killed her."

The baron crossed his arms over his chest. "I am not responsible for Snelling's foolish mistake. And I have diplomatic immunity as a member of the German embassy staff."

I glared at him, knowing he was right. There would be no charges filed against him, and nothing that would clear Gattenger's name. Clara's killer, Snelling, was dead. But who killed him? And where were the blueprints? This was going to be a very long night.

CHAPTER TWENTY-ONE

I rubbed my gloves along my chilled arms. "Do you want me to tell Lord and Lady Harwin they have a dead body in their garden?"

"Yes. Von Steubfeld and I will wait here for reinforcements." Blackford smiled. "That will assure both of us of our mutual honesty."

I went back in through the door I'd exited, knowing whoever had killed Snelling couldn't have come this way. I'd have seen him. And he'd have to be a hulking brute to snap a man's neck. At least the criminals I knew with that talent were.

Hurrying up the stairs, I hesitated for a moment, trying to remember what door I'd seen Lord Harwin enter. Mercifully, one of the footmen appeared from down the hall. "Are you coming from Sir Henry's room?"

"Yes," the footman said with a yawn.

"How is he?"

"Still unconscious. He's breathing. One of the maids is with him now." He took a step to move on, his eyelids drooping.

"Could you wake Lord Harwin? We have a body in the garden."

The footman stared at me for a moment, groaned, and then hurried over to a door and tapped on it. When that didn't bring a response, he tapped harder. A sleepy grumble could be heard.

The footman walked in and I followed as Lord Harwin sat up in bed. Seeing me, he quickly threw a robe over his striped pajamas. "What's going on?"

"There's a dead body in the garden," I said.

Lord Harwin gawked at me as if I'd grown a second head.

"Baron von Steubfeld and the Duke of Blackford are guarding it until the police are summoned."

"You'd think these people would have better manners than to kill each other off in my garden. I'll be right there." His lordship stuffed his feet into slippers and rose, belting his robe as he crossed the room.

I ran downstairs again, planning to go out to the two men. Instead, I began to move around, checking room by room, looking for anything out of place. Anything that might tell me where the drawings were.

There were too many hiding places. Chests, bookshelves, drawers in the servers. I'd have to turn on the lights and start searching room by room. Or get the duke or Lord Harwin to order it.

I went out onto the terrace and began to try the other doors into the house, watched by the duke and von Steubfeld. The doors to the ladies' parlor and the red parlor were still locked. I went the other direction past the two men and tried the first door on the other side. It opened easily. I stuck my head inside and didn't recognize the room.

"What is this?"

"The smoking room."

I'd check this as the most likely room in which to hide the plans as soon as Lord Harwin or the police took over watching the crime scene. The killer I'd followed hadn't had much time to snap Snelling's neck and get back into the house before I came out.

I walked back to Blackford and told him my suspicions. "If he hasn't run into the village instead," was his reply.

"Then someone will be missing from the house, and that will be easy to discover."

"Could it be Lady Bennett, Baron?"

He looked at me and laughed. "Good heavens, no. I don't trust her, but I'm sure she is only out for the pleasure of being seen at the best parties. And I only use her for—social occasions and gossip."

"Was she out for pleasure in breaking Clara Gattenger's heart by telling her another woman's secret?" I asked. "You did ask Lady Bennett to tell Mrs. Gattenger, didn't you?"

The baron frowned but did not reply.

Blackford said, "What is this?"

"The reason there was a fire in the Gattenger study the day Clara was killed. The baron told Lady Bennett of Gattenger's secret the same day Gattenger took the new warship plans out of the Admiralty. It turns out that both times their engagement was called off, Ken Gattenger had an affair. Lady Bennett immediately told Clara Gattenger what the baron told her. Clara insisted on facing the woman and demanding any love letters or trinkets her husband had given the woman. She took them home and burned them." I stared angrily at the baron.

"Von Steubfeld, is this true?" The duke employed his most commanding tone.

"Yes. I thought it would keep the Gattengers out of the study that evening, allowing Snelling to get in and take the blueprints. Regretfully, it didn't work." He shrugged.

I wanted to punch him for being so callous. "The baron told Lady Bennett that delivering bad news was her payment for dancing with the devil."

Blackford winced.

"What's more, Your Grace, I've been told Lady Bennett was trying to get her hands on the blueprints Snelling possessed." I glared at the baron.

"Lady Bennett was trying to get the ship blueprints for herself? That's impossible." The baron laughed. "Lady Bennett understands clothes and manners and decorating. She wouldn't know what a blueprint looked like."

"We're going to need to search every inch of this house to find the blueprints. You can refuse on diplomatic grounds, von Steubfeld, for your luggage and wardrobe to be searched, but I ask that you agree. It will make it difficult for anyone else to object," Blackford said.

"And therefore easier to find the person who cheated me." The baron smiled with a look that made me shiver. He was already planning revenge. "Very well. I agree."

Lord Harwin arrived accompanied by the footman I'd spoken to earlier. The weary footman was ordered to send someone into town to carry a message to the police station and to bring back the doctor. He shuffled off, head bowed. Then Harwin went inside to wake his staff and his wife.

The baron, Blackford, and I went into the house when a second footman came to stand watch over the body. I glanced back to see the young man gaze nervously over his shoulder and then look longingly at the house. The baron went upstairs, presumably to tell his valet the bad news. After a few minutes, sleepy-eyed members of the staff were fanning out throughout the main floor with their morning duties, lighting gas lamps as they plumped cushions and dusted and swept. The dining room was prepared for an early breakfast.

I guessed Lord Harwin had warned his servants that the police would soon arrive and some of the guests would either be disturbed out of their rest or would come downstairs out of curiosity.

"I think we should check the smoking room. It's the most likely place for someone to have reentered the house." I started in that direction.

"Why not the ladies' parlor? It's as close to the entrance where the body was found as the smoking parlor."

"Because, Your Grace, Lady Bennett could have known what the baron was up to and wanted to get there first. She could name her own price for those blueprints with half a dozen countries, including ours. And she would know, like I do, that the parlor door to the terrace was locked and bolted tonight by the butler when everyone went to bed. Lord Harwin had given specific instructions in front of everyone after Sir Henry was attacked in the garden. That door is still bolted, and I found the smoking parlor door unlocked."

"Your Grace," Lady Harwin called from the foot of the stairs.

He walked over to talk to her, and I went into the smoking room. The gaslights were now lit, and I could easily see there was no bolt on this door. The key was on a table a few feet from the door.

"Does my lady require anything?" The man's voice made me jump.

I swung around to find myself facing the butler. "Was this door locked last night?"

"I'm sure it was. I asked the gentlemen still in here when the rest of the guests had retired to lock this door."

"Who were these gentlemen?"

"Baron von Steubfeld and the Bishop of Wellston."

I immediately eliminated the Anglican bishop from espionage. The baron could have pretended to lock up, leaving it open for a meeting with Snelling. A meeting someone disrupted.

"Thank you." I gave a gracious nod and turned back to my study of the room.

His footsteps barely made a sound as he walked away.

There was a small chest against the side of the room. I carefully opened the dry leather clasps of the old trunk. Empty. There was a server with several drawers. The only thing I managed to do was wrinkle the linens stored there and shuffle the paper and ink bottles. I looked under chairs and tables. Nothing lurked between the furniture legs.

I was about to give up in disgust when I looked at the top of the server and a table that ran behind the sofa in the direct path from the terrace to the hallway. Various boxes of cigars were scattered around. Boxes large enough to hold the papers we sought.

One after another, I reached into the painted wooden boxes to make certain they contained only cigars. Finally, I put my hand in one and hit something that was too bulky to be cigars under a single layer of Havana's finest. I dumped the cigars on the tabletop and found blueprint paper underneath.

Laughing with relief, I unfolded the papers. While I couldn't understand them, I could make out the outline of a ship on the top sheet. I swung around, the papers in one hand, and froze where I stood.

Rosamond Peters stood before me, a pistol in her hand and

her bag tucked under her arm. Her gun was smaller than the baron's, but it looked just as lethal.

"Lady Peters. This isn't what this appears to be."

"On the contrary, it is. This appears to be the second time you've taken something that belongs to me."

My expression would have been comical in a cheerier situation. "You? Why would you want this?"

"Not for myself, you understand. For France."

At Lord Fleetwhite's dinner party, I had heard that no one knew who the French spy was. "You're the French spy. A woman. How clever. Of course none of those men would realize you were a spy."

"You didn't, either."

"Because I thought you were my friend." And then I remembered another incident. "The hatbox the thief wanted was yours. That's how you pass messages."

"That's one way." She smiled, but it was a colder, less friendly smile than I'd seen on her face before.

"Why did the thief take Lady Phyllida's hatbox instead of yours?"

"He was hired by my contact—"

"The jeweler Henry at Fortier's."

She smiled but didn't admit it. "—to take my hatbox, but he didn't know what I looked like. He grabbed the first box from Gautier's that he saw."

"You knew that Baron von Steubfeld planned the theft of the drawings? And you decided to take them instead while everyone was looking in another direction?"

"Everyone was busy making arrangements to come here, so there had to have been something valuable attracting all this attention. I came along to find out what it was." She walked toward me.

For once I obeyed my cowardly feet and took three steps back, frantically refolding the blueprints. Then I began to edge around the end table and the sofa.

"Please, Georgina. I don't want to shoot you. But I will to get those drawings back."

"Back? You were the one to put them in the cigar box?"

"Of course. I came down to retrieve them while the police searched my room. Unfortunately, you got here first."

"Then who broke Snelling's neck?"

"I did."

"You know how to do that? I'm impressed." I stopped, stunned to be in the presence of a woman who was deadlier than Emma. What I wouldn't give for Emma's knife at that moment. And the knowledge of how to use it.

She chose that moment to lunge toward me to grab the blueprints.

I jumped back, clutching them to my chest. "Did you strike down Sir Henry?"

"He told me he'd figured out my secret."

"Which one?" I took two more steps away from her, backing up toward the door onto the terrace. The door was unlocked. If I could open the door fast enough and get outside, it would buy me time. Open the door faster than a bullet?

"That I spy for France." She matched me, step for step.

"You won't shoot me, Lady Peters. There are too many people around."

"But none to see who fired the pistol. I shoot you, grab the drawings, drop the gun, and slip outside. I'll come in another way and join the group who comes running to see what has happened. I'll of course lament the loss of my friend Georgina."

I swung around a chair and backed along the far side of the

room toward the door standing open into the hallway. "There's a footman standing guard on Snelling's body on the terrace. He would hear the gunshot and see you leaving."

"Then I shall have to open the door and call to him that a madman is shooting at us and to help. You won't be in any position to disagree with me."

Her plan would work. The only thing I could do was try to reach the hallway before she fired. Once there, I'd certainly be in sight of someone. I kept backing up.

She raised her pistol.

I covered my chest with the blueprints, hoping Rosamond Peters didn't want a bullet hole damaging the warship drawings.

"Stop right there."

I'd never been so glad to hear Blackford's voice.

"You're unarmed, Duke." Lady Peters glanced from Blackford to me, calculating her chances, which had suddenly turned against her.

"But the man standing behind you isn't."

The gaslights wavered in the breeze from the open door to the garden. I looked past Rosamond to see Fogarty in the doorway.

She lowered her pistol. "Damn you, Georgina. How did you know to look here for the blueprints?"

"I followed you downstairs. When I found Snelling, you had disappeared, but I knew you hadn't gone far."

"I didn't think anyone would suspect me."

"I didn't. For the longest time I thought it was Lark Bennett."

She laughed, but the sound was brittle. "I showed my hand too soon."

"You said Lady Bennett wanted the blueprints in exchange for her silence."

"I lied to you, Georgina."

I hoped she was sorry. I was. I'd liked her.

Once Fogarty had taken the small pistol from her hand, she gave me a searching look. "You've not given away all my secrets, have you?"

"No. I wouldn't."

"Thank you."

Leave it to the duke to put things together at that moment. "Lady Peters is the one who had the affair with Ken Gattenger."

"Yes, Your Grace. She had an affair that Clara found out about the day she was murdered. They were his letters to Lady Peters that Clara burned in the fire that evening."

"Is that all of her secrets?" Blackford asked.

"Yes. Of course. Aren't spying and a sexual liaison enough for one woman?"

Rosamond Peters gave me a grateful look.

His mother may have killed a man, but there was no reason a young boy should pay for her sins with the loss of his name and title.

The police raced in and took Lady Peters into a hesitant custody. She said, "Duke, would you contact the French ambassador for me, please?"

He bowed as she was led away.

Only then could I allow myself a gasp. I smacked Blackford in the chest with the blueprints and left the room to go upstairs and sleep for what little was left of this night. I'd had my fill of aristocrats.

CHAPTER TWENTY-TWO

I awoke to sunlight streaming in my window. "What time is it?" I mumbled.

"One in the afternoon. You've slept through everything, including the local vicar and the Bishop of Wellston discussing whether you should have been awakened for Sunday services. The duke forbade it." Phyllida smiled. "But now the duke has sent me to wake you. He said you have an appointment this afternoon."

My eyes flew open and I sat straight upright in the bed. "I'll need Emma to help me dress. Ring the bell for her, will you?"

"She's in with the police, giving them the official line. You're stuck with me." Phyllida was fairly gloating.

"Well, help me, then." I pulled off my nightgown and yanked on a shift, rolled my stockings up my legs, and then grabbed my corset. "What is the official line?"

"You went to your old friend, the duke, to ask for his help in proving Clara's husband didn't kill her. The duke learned about the missing blueprints for the new ship the Admiralty has ordered. When you had Gattenger draw a picture of the burglar, Blackford passed it around Scotland Yard. Once he was identified as Mick Snelling, the duke had him followed. When the burglar came here, Lord Harwin came to your aid by inviting you to his house party."

"This story seems to leave out a lot," I said as Phyllida finished tightening my laces. Between us, we hooked my stockings to the ribbons dangling from my corset.

Her next words were lost as we pulled my petticoat over my head.

"What was that?"

"The two of you discovered Snelling approaching the house. By the time you caught up to him, Snelling was dead and the plans were gone."

I slipped on a blouse, and Phyllida hurried through fastening the buttons. "Are the police buying this?"

"Dukes can be very persuasive."

"How did he say we caught Lady Peters?"

"You found the blueprints while searching the downstairs, and she tried to kill you, confessing her crime. The French ambassador is in negotiations with Whitehall to have her sent back to France. He's citing diplomatic immunity."

I'd completely misjudged the French spy. "What about her son? He's staying with relatives currently, but will she be allowed to see him? She is his mother."

Phyllida shook her head. "I have no idea."

"What about Baron von Steubfeld?"

"What about him? No one is mentioning his name." Phyllida helped pull my skirt over my head.

"He hired Snelling to steal the plans."

"There's no proof of that, so the duke decided Snelling must have burgled the house, found the drawings, and saw his opportunity."

"Blackford has a lot to answer for." I slipped on my shoes and raced for the door.

"We have to put your hair up," Phyllida cried.

My hair didn't look like much when we finished pushing pins into it, but everything was staying in place. Phyllida grabbed a simple hat with a wide brim to protect me from the sun and pinned it on. The brim fortunately hid the worst of my hairdo. Then I grabbed my gloves and ran out of the room and down the hall to the stairs.

"Finally." Blackford's voice rose from the front hall. "Are you ready to go?"

I skidded to a stop and proceeded with decorum. "Of course, Your Grace," I said while smoothly descending the staircase. "How nice of you to escort me."

We climbed into Lord Harwin's carriage. Once we were settled and the horses were in motion, I asked, "What has happened to Lady Peters?"

"She was taken to London under police escort. The baron also left this morning, so the blueprints will return this afternoon under armed guard. No sense tempting fate. Lady Peters did explain about the stolen hatbox."

"What did she say?" And what would they do about Henry at Fortier's? He was also part of France's spy network.

"She had taken something for her contact in a hatbox. His shop was busy, so they'd made previous arrangements under these circumstances for her contact to hire someone to take the hatbox from her and bring it to the shop. The young man grabbed the wrong hatbox."

"He must have been shocked when Emma and I gave chase. He dropped the hatbox and tried to run when he was cornered, no doubt thinking he'd get away and continue to look for the woman who had the hatbox he was supposed to take. No one could have foreseen how many Gautier hatboxes were being carried that morning."

Blackford smiled. "I take it Emma had her knife with her?"

"Yes. Suggest to Whitehall they keep an eye on Fortier, the jeweler. She came in with a hatbox and looked unhappy to see us in his shop, Your Grace."

"I will."

I looked out the window at the sunny afternoon. The weather was ideal. "Did Lady Bennett leave?"

"She's taken over the nursing duties for Sir Henry. Apparently she's bossing the servants around unmercifully."

"And everyone still thinks I'm Georgina Monthalf?"

Blackford lifted my gloved hand and kissed the back of it. "Yes, my love." In a drier voice, he continued, "Although people are starting to wonder why I'm not visiting you at night. As a widow, it would be appropriate if we were discreet."

I held his gaze. "And what does His Grace think?"

He squeezed my hand before he let it go. "His Grace is conflicted. Do you want me to visit you in your room tonight?"

I did, but my heart would be ground to dust when he chose a suitable duchess. "I appreciate you not beginning something that will end badly when you marry Miss Amanda Weycross."

He jerked his head back. "Miss Amanda Weycross? Good God, woman, I wouldn't spend the rest of my life with that addle-brained female for all the crown jewels and Buckingham Palace."

"Lady Anne Stewart, then."

He raised an eyebrow. "Have you met her mother?"

"Briefly." At dinner and the ball the evening before. I planned never to make that mistake again.

"She'll turn into her mother. She's already a close approximation." He started laughing. "Georgia, are you jealous? Don't be. There isn't a woman in the British Isles to match you."

"But you have to produce an heir."

"That necessity is the curse of being a peer." He looked out the far side window of the carriage, giving me a clear view of the short, damp curls at the nape of his neck.

I studied that stiff neck, memorizing it for the times ahead. He'd soon be gone from my life, while I'd be back in my bookshop dreaming of becoming a duchess.

And he'd said there was no other woman in England to match me.

When he faced me and said, "We're here," it took me a moment to remember where "here" was. It took me longer to give up on the pleasant daydream of being the Duchess of Blackford.

I was about to face my parents' killer with a heavy heart from thinking of the man who would never be mine, while Blackford stepped out of the carriage looking completely unruffled and held out a hand to help me out.

I smoothed my afternoon dress with my palms, straightened my hat, and climbed down. I couldn't hide the pleasure his words gave me.

Lord Harwin's footman knocked on the front door while I looked at the house. Much smaller and older than the Harwins' palatial block, it had a faded air from the grimy stonework to the chipped paint on the window sashes. When the door opened, Harwin's footman announced us and handed over our calling cards. The butler held the door wide, and we walked in.

I glanced back to see the footman saunter back to the carriage, the driver sliding over in the seat to make room for him. No doubt they planned to take advantage of their freedom from work by sitting and gossiping.

"If you'll wait in the parlor, Sir Wallace will join you in a moment," the butler said as he shut the front door and opened one off the hall.

The room was done in washed-out gold and pale blue. Sunshine didn't seem to penetrate beyond the overgrown bushes outside the windows. The duke grabbed my hands, and I discovered I was wringing them.

"Sorry."

"Don't be, Georgina. I know how much this means to you, meeting an old friend of your father's from India."

Was he suggesting I pretend that was why I was here when I finally met him? It wouldn't work. He would recognize me as surely as I'd known him the moment I saw him.

Sir Wallace Vance entered the room and we went through a round of bows and curtsies. After we were seated, he asked, "To what do I owe this honor, Your Grace?"

"Actually, I came at the request of Mrs. Monthalf. She recognized one of your guests at the ball last night as a friend of her father's in India. She hopes to renew the acquaintance."

"I'm afraid you're too late. They've left already. Which one of my guests was it?"

"He's a well-dressed older gentleman with silver hair."

"That describes both my guests."

"Tall, has a faint accent—"

"Again. Both of them."

"He's in the antiquarian book business."

"Any guest who's ever been here is interested in antiquarian books. That's what we have in common." Sir Wallace shifted in his chair, clearly wanting to stand and end our interview, but reluctant to upset a wealthy, antiquarian-buying duke.

I couldn't say that the man I searched for had icy pale eyes and a cruel mouth. "He has the habit of carrying his newspaper neatly folded and tucked under one arm."

"We all do that if our hands are occupied."

"He does that even if his hands are free."

Sir Wallace squinted in concentration. "It must be Mr. Wolf. He has that habit."

"I was told your two guests were Count Farkas and Mr. van der Lik."

"Formally, he's Count Farkas. In England, he often goes by Mr. Wolf. He finds it simpler when doing business."

"Is that a translation of his name from his native tongue?" Blackford asked.

"Yes. Hungarian. He's a member of their nobility."

The same name I'd heard from my South African contact. I had a name and a nationality for the man who killed my parents. I could have cheered. Remembering that I mustn't destroy my persona, I asked, "Do you know where Mr. Wolf is headed?"

"To the continent. Where, exactly, he didn't tell me. There's a Gutenberg Bible he's pursuing." Sir Wallace shrugged. "He's been seeking it for years. I hope he gets it. What a trophy."

"I'd hoped to renew his acquaintance, but I guess that's not to be. If you hear from him, please tell him I was hoping to speak to him."

"Where should he get in touch with you?"

I glanced at the duke and smiled. "Have him write to me at Blackford House."

* * *

UNFORTUNATELY, THE DUKE had already agreed to stay until the morning, which meant Phyllida, Emma, and I had to. Our house party was joined for dinner that night by the Marquis of Tewes and his guests. Dinner was pleasant enough, seated between a younger son, who was far too interested in the wines being served, and a married, middle-aged earl whose passion was outdoor sports. I didn't believe England held as many birds as he claimed to have shot. At least the food was good and no one took credit for shooting any of the courses.

I looked down the long, crystal- and white-linen-covered table at Blackford. He was seated between Lady Harwin and Lady Ormond. Two middle-aged women wearing jewels and dour expressions. The picture of his wife in twenty years. Neither woman looked capable of joyous laughter, frightening exploits, or wild passion.

I'd never be a duchess.

Blackford didn't appear to be enjoying their company. I couldn't hide a small smile of satisfaction.

Lady Bennett, sitting nearby, said, "What are you smiling about?"

I went for the blandest explanation. "I'm enjoying the food, the conversation, everything about this dinner. The Harwins are excellent hosts."

"Too bad you're leaving in the morning. My sister and her husband, the Viscount Chattelsfield, will be here in the afternoon for tea. You could have reminisced about Singapore with them."

I smiled as if that were a wonderful idea. Thank goodness I'd be back in London by then. "What a shame. Perhaps I'll be introduced to them another time." But not if I could help it.

I was leaving in the morning for stifling London and my own comfortable, middle-class life, my friends, and my bookshop. I could hardly wait. But I'd leave a little piece of my heart behind.

When the ladies retired to the parlor after dinner, I found myself the subject of Lady Ormond's inquisition. "How is your ankle, Mrs. Monthalf?"

"Fine, thank you. I've quite recovered."

"That was a foolish thing to do, to race out into the street. Whatever caused you to do that?"

She wore a sly smile as if she hoped the duke and I had quarreled. "I thought I saw an old friend of my father's. I wanted to let him know I was in the area."

"So did you get in contact with this—old friend?"

"No. I saw him at the ball last night, and then went with Ranleigh, I mean Blackford, to the home where he was staying. Unfortunately, the gentleman had been called away in the morning, and I missed him." I glanced around the room. No one looked in our direction, but no one else was speaking. Apparently their curiosity about Georgina Monthalf hadn't been satisfied.

I planned to retire Georgina tomorrow. I wondered if any of them would wonder what had happened to her.

"How unfortunate. And after your clever search of Lady Harwin's main floor looking for stolen documents."

I stared at her, wondering how much she had guessed. "Thank you."

"The Duke of Blackford must like clever women. Of course, he liked Lady Peters, and I'm now told she was a spy."

"I liked Lady Peters. I'm sorry she killed a man and endangered England's naval superiority."

"I feel so sorry for her son. Losing both his parents so young," a woman's voice said.

"I know his father's sister. She, her husband, and their children love that little boy. They've been raising him as much as his mother has," another upper-class woman's voice said.

"Sounds like Lady Peters was engaged in men's work to me. Aren't you afraid being clever will make you too masculine to attract a duke?" Lady Ormond's smile was pure venom.

"Cleverness isn't masculine. I can think of several married ladies who are clever." I turned to Lady Harwin. "I've had a wonderful time in your lovely home. I'm so sorry events ruined your delightful party."

"Not at all." Lady Harwin gave me a cheery grin. "I've never known such excitement. I can't wait to tell my friends about what happened. They'll all want to come and visit the scene of murder and espionage. Our terrace will be the envy of all."

"Oh, Celeste, you'd be too ashamed," Lady Ormond said.

"Nonsense, Mildred. It was almost like a play. The events happened here, but we didn't know the dead man. He was a burglar, wasn't he?"

"Yes, he was," I answered when no one else would.

"Well, there, you see? Nothing to do with us. Events just came and happened here." She smiled gleefully around the room. "Such excitement. And the good and loyal subjects of the crown triumphed. Thank you, Mrs. Monthalf, for bringing us such a diversion."

I needed to disabuse her of that idea immediately. "I'm afraid I didn't bring you anything. Lady Peters and the burglar brought the excitement here. I just went on a scavenger hunt and found the missing plans. Nothing you couldn't have done."

"But you were the one who saved England. You, a gentlewoman. Makes me proud to know you."

"But no more likely to become a duchess," Lady Ormond sniffed.

"A duchess? Of course not. But perhaps the wife of a baronet. Or one of these modern industrialists you read about. I'd imagine they'd want a wife with spunk," Lady Harwin said.

The aristocrats present had considered me for duchess material and found me lacking. I wondered what they'd say if they knew how we'd deceived them. The person I couldn't deceive was myself. I knew I could never be a duchess. But, oh, how I wanted to be.

CHAPTER TWENTY-THREE

WE returned to London the next day and dropped Phyllida off to oversee the packing up of our borrowed town house. Then we dropped Emma off at Fenchurch's Books, and Blackford and I traveled on to Newgate Prison to talk to Ken Gattenger.

He had already been taken to the visitors' room by the time we marched down the hallways, our steps ringing in the stone passageways. He stared at us but didn't speak until we sat across from him. "Well?"

"The blueprints have been recovered and are back in the Admiralty records room. The records room clerk on the German payroll has been apprehended. Despite my doubts, Sir Henry Stanford appears to have had no hand in the theft or the death of your wife," Blackford said.

"Thank goodness the drawings are safe. And you heard there was nothing wrong with my calculations? You know my new warship design is everything I promised it would be? You do realize that means I never needed to take those drawings out that night and Clara wouldn't have died." Tears flowed down his cheeks.

Blackford cleared his throat and looked away.

I reached out and took his hand. "The man who killed Clara is dead. He was killed for the blueprints, and the person who took your drawings has been captured."

"Is that supposed to make me feel better?"

I had no answer for that. I said, "Your solicitor is working on having the treason and murder charges dropped. You never responded in writing to the letter from the German embassy, did you?"

"No. Only verbally. And I never agreed. Not really. I ended up turning them down almost immediately."

"Good. Then your solicitor should succeed. Once he does, you'll be able to walk out of here a free man."

Gattenger shook his head. "Free. And alone. I'm going to leave London, perhaps leave England. I can't stay here. Not after what has happened. Would you have the servants close up the house and give them good references? None of this is their fault."

"What about your ship designs?" Blackford thundered.

"The Admiralty has everything I've done. I don't care about them anymore. Perhaps I'll go to Paris and join the Expressionists. I know I'll never draw another ship."

"Think what a loss this would be to your country."

Gattenger looked at the duke and shrugged his shoulders. "It doesn't matter to me now. Nothing does."

"Where were you the night before Clara died?"

He hadn't expected my question. His gaze shifted between the duke and me. "I was at home."

I glared at him. "Don't lie to me. Where were you? We know you weren't home in the evening."

"It doesn't matter now."

"If it doesn't matter, why don't you tell us?"

He ran his hands through his fair hair. "I went to see Lord Watson. The present Lord Watson."

"Who?"

"Mrs. Gattenger's cousin. The man who inherited her father's title," Blackford told me.

"His title. His house. His money," Gattenger said. "I knew Clara would be in danger if the man who'd threatened me the night before decided to attack me at home. So I went to Lord Watson and begged him to take Clara in for a little while to keep her safe."

"Did you tell him why?" the duke asked.

"No. Only that I'd made a stupid mistake and I'd been threatened. I wasn't afraid for me, but I wanted Clara where she'd be safe. Lord Watson employs a butler and a footman. A larger staff for a larger house where she'd be protected."

"What did he say?"

"He's recently married, and he told me he feared I was saddling him with his cousin so I could be free to do as I liked. I told him nothing could be further from the truth."

"So he said no?" I asked.

"He said he'd think about it."

Lord Watson hadn't invited Clara back to her childhood home. I'd never met the man and already I didn't like him. "Did you tell Clara this?"

"How could I tell her Lord Watson, her cousin, wouldn't take her in for her own safety? If only he had."

"His testimony may be enough to have your charges dropped. I'll tell your solicitor and he'll soon have you a free man," Blackford said.

"Watson's never liked me. Finding out I told him the truth will come as a shock to him." Gattenger stared at us with a look of pure devastation. "Clara's gone. There's nothing left for me."

BLACKFORD STEWED THE entire ride across London to my shop. I didn't say a word. I understood Gattenger's pain. He'd have to find his own way, alone, into his future.

Just as I would eventually have to face a future without Blackford. A future without love.

Once we arrived at the bookshop, Blackford handed me down to the street. I dashed inside to find Frances waiting on a customer while Grace, Emma, Jacob, and Sumner carried on a hushed conversation between two rows of bookshelves.

I took a deep breath of warm, slightly musty air and felt at home. My bookshop was still in one piece. Dickens ran over to greet me, swiped at my hem with the claws extended from his paw, and stomped out the front door of the shop. I watched him, fascinated. I had never seen a cat stomp before.

I had also never seen a duke hold a door open for a cat.

"I'm glad to see you're all right," I said, hurrying over to the four. I knew Blackford would follow.

"Thanks to Sumner. The baron's valet tried to kill me last night after I saw him arguing with one of the Admiralty clerks. The clerk was beaten up worse than I was," Jacob said. One eye was blackened and he had a bandage on that side of his head. I could see the bottom of another bandage sticking out below his shirt cuff.

Fortunately, Sumner showed no ill effects from the encounter, because Emma now stood a modest few feet from him, looking him over. The protective expression on her face told me I didn't want to think about what Emma would do if Sumner had been hurt.

He was staring back at her and grinning. "Sir William Darby spoke to Sir Broderick yesterday afternoon. He said you looked a treat in a pale blue dress. Any chance the rest of us will get to see you in it?"

Emma raised her eyebrows but didn't respond.

"You've heard about what transpired with Lady Peters, von Steubfeld, and Snelling, and no one thought to report what happened here?" the duke asked in an outraged voice.

Sumner stopped grinning and stepped forward, his rigid posture left over from his army service. "We sent a telegram to Cheltenham Spa this morning, only to receive a reply saying the telegram was undeliverable since you were on a train to London. We were discussing the best way to reach you when you walked in, Your Grace."

"So putting you in the Admiralty records room paid off, Jacob? The clerk who's been helping von Steubfeld was arrested?" I asked.

"Yes. The baron paid the young man well enough to tip him off, but not well enough to keep his mouth shut when beaten up and facing a long prison sentence," Jacob said. "It turned out the clerk had been instructed to carry on a conversation on the weaknesses of Gattenger's ship design within hearing of Sir Henry, knowing Sir Henry was most likely to press Gattenger on the issue. When Gattenger requested a full set of blueprints to take home an hour later, the clerk told the baron, putting the plan into action."

"Baron von Steubfeld must have immediately hired Snelling for that night, having used his services before, and then visited Lady Bennett to tell her to pass along the rumor about Gattenger